Staffordshire Library and Information Services
Please return or renew by the last date shown

BREWOOD	11. MAY	
7/k		22. JUN 16
30. AUG	01. NOV 13.	15. NOV 16
		07. 01. 17.
11. NOV	12. DEC	04. MAR 17.
10. MAR 12		28. NOV 17.
	16. MAY 14.	19.
05. APR 12	07. OCT 14.	25 MAY 12
08. MAY 12	28.	04. 08. 18
17. MAY 12	30. JUN 15.	
03. JUL 12		
	25. AUG 15	
02. OCT 12	23. JAN 16.	
09. APR		

If not required by other readers, this item may may be
renewed in person, by post or telephone, online or by email.
To renew, either the book or ticket are required

24 Hour Renewal Line
0845 33 00 740

Staffordshire
County Council

www.staffordshire.gov.uk

FLY IN AMBER

He had the motive, the opportunity ...
and no alibi.

Briony Eastwood is looking forward to a glamorous Christmas, catering for movie star Roz de Taffort and her family. It turns out that Roz has a not-so-secret drinking problem, however, and a toy-boy trainer on the premises. When Briony finds Roz's dead body at the bottom of the cellar steps, suspicion immediately points to cuckolded husband, Carey. But Roz's death is only the beginning . . .

"...Hitchcock homage from Armstrong."
Kirkus

FLY IN AMBER

Vivien Armstrong

Severn House Large Print Books
London & New York

This first large print edition published in Great Britain 2001 by
SEVERN HOUSE LARGE PRINT BOOKS LTD of
9-15, High Street, Sutton, Surrey, SM1 1DF.
First world regular print edition published 2000 by
Severn House Publishers, London and New York.
This first large print edition published in the USA 2002 by
SEVERN HOUSE PUBLISHERS INC., of
595 Madison Avenue, New York, NY 10022

British Library Cataloguing in Publication Data

Armstrong, Vivien
   Fly in amber - Large print ed.
   1.   Television personalities - England - Fiction
   2.   Women cooks - England - Fiction
   3.   Detective and mystery stories
   4.   Large type books
   I.   Title
   823.9'14 [F]

ISBN 0-7278-7104-8

Printed and bound in Great Britain by
MPG Books Ltd, Bodmin, Cornwall.

One

Last night I dreamed Charlie came back.

This is a recurring nightmare which any analyst would find disturbing particularly as he often appears cunningly disguised. Last night, for instance, this big friendly dog broke into my unconscious and wagged its tail, looking for all the world like one of those appealing mutts featured in TV pet-rescue programmes. It was only when I bent down to pat the beast and it ran off with my purse that I knew my husband had come back to haunt me yet again. In my dream bells started ringing, jangling like the Victorian servants' bells I sometimes come across at work. I jolted awake, bathed in sweat. The ringing continued insistently. Archie started yapping and my stupid brain finally sorted itself out. It was the telephone in the living room.

I groaned, dragged myself out of bed and picked up. It was Diana Winterton from the agency. Wedging the phone to my ear, I filled the percolator and slumped at the kitchen table, counting my blessings.

5

Twenty-nine years old, fanciable and leading a full if nomadic life as an agency cook-cum-housekeeper. The studio flat in Chelsea I occupy between jobs is functional if somewhat sparse and I make enough to run a car and take high-season holidays in the Caribbean and the Alps. I poured the coffee.

"You still there, Briony?"

"I was in bed."

"Not unwell I hope. I've got a nice little job lined up for you." She sounded suspiciously sparkly for nine thirty on a Monday morning.

"Not more geriatrics!"

"Absolutely not. I promise you—"

"Where?" I barked, never at my best after one of Charlie's visitations.

"Sussex. Lovely country house, mostly weekend guests but wife and child generally in residence."

"Aga?"

"But of course!"

I stirred my coffee, feeling better already. "How long?"

"About three months. Current woman's on maternity leave till after Christmas. There's plenty of help on a daily basis and the kid's at school in the village. I'm also trying to fix up a new au pair."

"No French ones, I beg you. They always smoke in the kitchen and you know how I feel about that."

"You *know* I try to do my best for you, Briony." Diana was now clearly on the defensive and rushed in with a glowing forecast of high wages, minimal hours and fringe benefits. When she readily agreed to my taking along Archie, my beloved but horrible Jack Russell terrier, I just *knew* there was something terribly fishy about this job. Still...

"Hang on, I'll get my book."

It was all Charlie's fault, this working life I'm driven to. It had never occurred to anyone that I might actually need a career and with just a debby cordon-bleu course on my CV, that left only agency work or the dreaded directors' dining rooms to choose from. As it happens I like cooking and the work's well paid. Not everyone – especially a girl with no ties – is willing to trail round the country from job to job like a Flying Dutchman. That analyst, if ever I get round to finding him, would say I am still searching for Charlie but he would be wrong. I'm running away from Charlie. Trying to shove his slap-happy grin from my mind, forget the bloody man ever existed.

Mother spotted his deficiencies the first time she clapped a beady eye on my freshly minted spouse. We married in Scotland in October having met at Fleur McAllister's house party in August. We had a big boozy send off, mostly Charlie's horsey crowd. Mother didn't come to the wedding.

"Charlie's an accountant," I told her, nervously pushing him forward into the drawing room of her Tite Street flat. She smiled. A smile I had seen many times before. More of a grimace really. Afterwards she always referred to him as Our Fraudulent Converter which was all lies. A con man, perhaps. An inspired shuffler of tax returns, certainly. But Charlie's real vice was the race track. Or the casino. Or, if pushed, the progress of two flies up the wall.

"Sorry, Diana, what did you say? I was dreaming."

"The address is Kington House, Northchurch. It's a village four miles from Heathfield, handy for Tunbridge Wells and the coast. The owner's a TV personality. You'll never believe this. Carey Barnes!"

"Never heard of him."

"Of course you have. Don't be tiresome, Briony. He's on the box practically every night."

"Not another actor?"

"You've never heard of him? Really?"

"Indulge me. I had a rough night. My head's not in gear." I let Diana rabbit on about Barnes like a love-sick groupie and took a slug of caffeine, kicking out at Archie who had, in his evil way, started gnawing the chair leg. As my brain warmed to the wake-up call of the raw Italian blend, Carey Barnes swam into focus – I had seen him now I came to think about it. Several times in fact. Once emerging from a shoe repairer's just round the corner from my place, though, even at the time, it had taken a while to fix a name to the TV image filed away with all the other junk that infiltrates one's memory bank. But I patiently waited for Diana to have her say, letting the coffee sharpen the edges.

"Gorgeous eyes," she murmured. "Does wonderful in-depth interviews – mostly political but since he married Rosalind de Taffort he's on the inside track with the theatrical crowd. You *must* have seen him!"

"I thought Roz de Taffort was dead. Some sort of car crash."

"Semi-retired."

"Christ, Diana! You're not sending me to some sort of hospital job are you? You know I can't stand illness."

"I'll fill you in later. Come in after lunch and we'll have a complete run through. Must dash – I've got someone waiting," she said, cutting me off with indecent haste. But every job has its knobs and I mentally calculated the effect on my ski budget that a stint chez Barnes would have. My mother would have heard of Carey Barnes all right. She had been a mine of information when it came to hotshots on the celebrity circuit.

She's dead too, of course. It would wring your heart out the way my family's been blown away lately.

When the solicitor read Mother's will he had the grace to flush when it came to the acid quotes about Charlie. Old Phipps pressed on, eager to get the thing over.

"Mrs French left most of her disposable assets to the Sunset Home for Retired Horses." He coughed, hurrying on. "'As I know' – and these are her exact words of appreciation," he murmured, "'how devoted to equine charities my dear son-in-law has proved to be.'"

The flat and its contents were specifically willed "to my only child, Briony, so that she may at least have a roof over her head." It was all tied up very effectively. Charlie could not touch a penny of Mother's money and to be fair he seemed unperturbed, still relishing the abrupt exit of his unlamented *belle mere*. It was a heart attack in the council offices during the course of a bitter exchange about the renewal of her resident's parking permit that did it.

"Bloody hell, Bri, you must hand it to the old girl for going out in style. Maximum impact. Headlines in the local rag. A queue of goggle-eyed motorists as witnesses," Charlie whispered at the graveside, his hand on my shoulder giving it a squeeze.

"Fancy having to close the permit place

for the rest of the morning," I croaked. "All those people who'd been waiting for ages sent away. Practically a riot. No wonder the girl on the counter had hysterics – thought it was all her fault, poor thing. She didn't know Mother." I wiped away a tear and Charlie stifled a chuckle with his handkerchief as loose earth pattered on to the lowered coffin. The undertakers' men politely looked away. That was the way with Charlie: even in a churchyard he could never resist a laugh.

As it happens, Mother needn't have gone to all that trouble to cut Charlie out. He disappeared soon after during a one-man fishing competition. We were on holiday off the west coast of Ireland. It was a bet: to bring back a really big fish to the pub that night. There we were, crowded round the bar, tipsy with whiskey and blarney, celebrating in advance, waiting for Charlie to burst in to claim his winnings, me privately certain Charlie would have bought some huge sea monster from the boyos down at the quay before setting out. But the hours slid by. A squall blew up and Charlie's boat was found two days later further up the coast. Empty. Holed. A few dead fish still sloshing about in the locker. They never found his body.

After weeks trawling through the debts, I knew I had to find myself some paid employment. I registered with Winterton's, an up-market domestic agency for gentry caught on the hop with "the unreliable servant class one has to deal with these days". I insisted I would only accept short-term contracts. At my age who would want to find themseleves buried below stairs in any permanent job? Anyway, emergency callouts pay better and I had convinced myself from the start that the only way I could endure life on my own would be to keep on the move.

Charlie's bookmaker finally drew a line under his account, feeling sorry for me I suppose. I got to know Reilly quite well after Charlie disappeared – in fact Reilly had been the one to tempt us into going to Ireland for that fatal holiday. Perhaps he felt guilty. "Charlie spent a good deal with us over the years. I reckon, on balance, we came out on top," Reilly admitted, "though don't you let on to any other punters, Bridie!" He sometimes called me Bridget as well. I gave up trying to make him get it right. Briony is, after all, a silly name. Who'd choose to be called after a pernicious weed? Maybe it was one of Mother's little witticisms – like that business about all her cash going to the old nags' home. That rankled with Joe Reilly, never a man to let animal rights spoil the bottom line. But don't try to tell me bookmakers have hearts of stone.

I shut Archie in the kitchen with a couple of Bonios and took my coffee to the bathroom and ran a shower, gulping the last of the black brew as I blow-dried my hair. By the time I'd buttoned my Levis and crammed my none too elfin feet into the gorgeous Emma Hope boots I'd bought after that last unhappy stint with the aged Fox-Thompsons, the prospect of three months at a TV star's country mansion didn't sound so bad. These people were never at home; chances were Barnes' house was one of those show places kept for entertaining the luvvies at weekends. It could be fun. It might even dispel the nightmares.

Who would have guessed that ever since that night eighteen months ago Charlie would still be insinuating himself into my waking and sleeping dreams, his laugh echoing in my head like he was some sort of sick joke? Trouble was I'd missed the punchline. Sometimes I never got the point of his jokes. I'd begun to hate Charlie Eastwood, the love of my life, who threw it all away on a stupid bet.

Until his body turns up I can't, deep down, believe the guy is really dead. Charlie haunts me day and night. Why won't he just let me get on with my life?

Two

After taking Archie for a couple of circuits of Burton's Court, an oasis of green where local subscribers are reluctantly permitted to run their dogs, I went to meet Jonathan Lusty, the estate agent who manages the letting of my late mother's flat.

Jonathan, straight from central casting when it comes to sharp-suited young men who oil the wheels of the London property market, runs his business from an office in a side street off the Royal Hospital Road. When it became clear that Mother's flat was my only immediate means of raising cash, I approached Lusty's agency with a view to selling.

"Take the money and run, babby," had been old Reilly's advice. But Jonathan persuaded me to think again.

"The rental market's booming, Mrs Eastwood," he said, his smile attractively underpinning his argument. "Why don't you give it a whirl? I've got dozens of people on my books who'd jump at the chance of a furnished place in Tite Street."

"And wreck it no doubt." I snorted, discordant background music ringing in my ears of bilked landlords suing in court to regain possession of trashed apartments.

"No way! My clients are exclusively company lets – a lot of European businessmen and American bankers. An excellent investment. Trust me."

I had looked into his serious blue eyes and Reilly's hard-nosed advice went straight out of the window.

"You could manage *everything*? It's my only asset, Mr Lusty. I have to find a job and it may be outside London. Abroad even."

"Jonathan, please. Here let me show you a few figures."

I was a pushover, naturally. At that low point in my life I was ready to lean on just about any rickety old fence which offered some support. And to give Jonny Lusty his due, his management of the Tite Street flat was first class. My original tenants, a Belgian couple, had departed the previous week and Jonny was keen for us to see over the place and make good a few deficiencies before the next people moved in.

We met outside, the sun gleaming through the leaves of the plane trees in the golden glow of early October, the air still warm from a kindly Indian summer. He kissed my cheek, grinning away like a Cheshire cat, really glad to see me it would seem. Wow.

Since signing up with Lusty's, Jonathan and I had had a few dates. Nothing heavy, but comforting to my bruised ego since Charlie disappeared. The fact that Charlie's body has never washed up has left me in a sort of no-man's-land. I didn't believe he would pop up again, of course I didn't, but something flickered at the back of my mind despite the police insistence that people who drowned off that treacherous Irish coastline were gone for good, never to be seen again. Bodies could be trapped by the strong currents, sloshing between busy shipping lines, snagged on the rocks of the seabed like washing on the line. Was it surprising bloated corpses were unrecognisable even if they did float ashore? I shivered, thrusting the nightmare back in its box, gratefully grabbing Jonny's smooth sleeve like a lifebelt while he unlocked the door.

"Hey! You've missed me," he crowed.

"Not half! That last job was with a pair of old farts in Cheltenham. Talk about geriatric."

"All work and no play, sweetie. We both deserve a mini-break. How does Paris grab you? It's your lucky day. I'm free this very weekend!"

He squeezed my hand, the tang of his aftershave catching in my throat.

"Nice, but no time. I've got a new job starting up on Saturday. Sussex. Country-house stint till after Christmas."

We moved inside, the wide hall opening up to an oak staircase, the house smelling pleasantly of pot-pourri and beeswax.

"More wrinklies?"

"Absolutely not! A TV bloke's family. Barnes. Carey Barnes. Some sort of political commentator."

Jonathan whistled. "You don't say."

"You've heard of him?"

"Sure. In fact, strictly *entre nous*, he's a client of mine. Rents a flat above my office, but it's very hush hush. Since his brush with the Libyans over that bombing he's para- noid about security."

"Above the agency? Hardly Fort Knox, is it?"

"Well, it's only a pied-à-terre and a scruffy hole like that attracts no attention. He keeps his car in a lock-up behind the Physic Garden and can access his place through a back entrance so he's well suited."

"Does his wife stay?"

"Never. Told me she's something of a recluse. Prefers the country. Used to be an actress or something."

I nodded, mulling over the coincidence of this tenuous link with the Barnes' set-up.

Jonathan unlocked the first-floor entrance to Mother's flat and we passed into the vestibule. Sunshine flooded through the open doors off the tiny hallway and my mood lightened. I was glad I hadn't taken Reilly's advice. It was a nice place and having it was like a crock of gold under the mattress. It gave me the only security in this rackety lifestyle I forced myself to endure.

"I checked the inventory myself," he said. "Everything's OK. Bit of wear and tear – but the de Landeaus were ideal tenants. I knocked a bit off the deposit for the hell of it – it'll cushion any repairs."

"They've gone back to Brussels?"

"On to New York apparently. But his replacement in the London branch is keen to take over the flat so, if you agree?"

"Of course. I leave it to you."

I wandered round, tweaking the curtains, seeing the familiar battle ground clearly for the first time since Mother's funeral, the high windows offering a glimpse of the solid mansion block opposite. Perhaps I was mellowing. Gradually, it seemed, the bad vibes of the place were greening over, like moss creeping over jagged rocks.

Jonny was fiddling about in the kitchen, crouched in front of the washing machine, hair flopping, looking like a boffin contemplating a tricky experiment.

"Bloody thing's been on the blink all month. I had to get the repair man in twice. How about replacing it, Briony? The rental warrants it and, frankly, a dodgy machine's more trouble than it's worth."

I shrugged. "Fine by me. What about the paintwork? Could do with a freshen up."

"Really?"

"Women like a nice clean kitchen. It's the first thing that strikes me when I start a new job."

Jonny laughed, picturing me in my Mrs Beeton mode I guess. He jotted down some notes and made a call to the decorator on his mobile. He grinned, punching the air, cocky as hell.

"Well, that's fixed. Fred can be in and out in four days. Starting tomorrow. He's giving the bathroom a quick lick too while he's in."

"Right. I'll pop down to Peter Jones and ask them to deliver a new washing machine. Can Fred plumb it in while he's here?"

"No problem. He'll cart away the old one in his van and take it to the tip. How about lunch?"

I glanced at my watch, passing a hand through my hair, hoping my growing affection for this guy was not leading me down another pointless byway. That was my main trouble. Charlie had left me invisibly lame when it came to relationships. My trust in men had taken a tumble since my laughing cavalier of a husband disappeared and an estate agent with a smooth line in patter was, as my mother's sardonic reminder seemed to echo round the empty rooms, a

19

Charlie clone if ever there was one. Still. Lunch?

"Why not?"

We locked up and headed up the street to Foxtrot's, hand in hand like any other Sloany couple out for a bit of light relief from the sheer brutality of making a living. Afterwards I stopped at his office to sign a few papers and share a coffee with his Girl Friday, an amiable woman with a glass eye. While I was catching up on Freda's on/off romance with an express-delivery van driver and Jonathan was checking the post, she took a call and turned aside, flushing painfully as Jonny made soundless kissing mimes, assuming it was the boyfriend, Terry.

She masked the receiver and whispered, "It's Mr Barnes. He wants the locks changed."

He stiffened. "Why?"

"Someone's found out about his flat. He thinks an intruder may have been inside. He's spitting mad. Wants to talk to you."

Jonathan grimaced and hurried into his private office, pulling me inside and shutting the door before picking up the extension.

"Lusty here. I gather you have a problem, Mr Barnes."

I leaned against the filing cabinets watching Jonny field the bouncers which were clearly being lobbed his way down the phone. It wasn't difficult to make sense of the one-sided conversation: Freda had got the message loud and clear.

"But nobody, *nobody*," Jonathan patiently insisted, "knows about the tenancy. And no one has access to your keys except myself ... Yes, I do understand your anxiety, Mr Barnes, but being so well known you could have been spotted leaving a taxi or even been followed ... Oh, I see. Well, absolutely ... Just leave it with me. Freda will deal with it straight away and you can pick up the new keys tomorrow if that suits you." Barnes rang off, presumably mollified.

"Christ Almighty! That man's a walking nutter."

"You keep spare keys here?"

"Too right, I do! The whole fucking building could burn down before I could get inside to check the smoke alarms!"

"This has happened before? New locks I mean?"

"Sure. Only last summer when he was in Tuscany. The chap's off his trolley." He lunged at the door and shouted through to the front office. "See to it will you Freda? Pronto? Tell Keymaestro's it's an emergency. I'll speak to the locksmith myself when he gets here. And Freda, I'm just popping out for a tick but I'll be here all afternoon if anyone rings."

21

He took a bunch of labelled keys from a row of hooks mounted inside a hole in the wall concealed by a boring Canaletto print.

"What do you think's on his mind?" I ventured.

"Says he's been receiving hate mail addressed directly to the flat upstairs."

I laughed. "Surely someone as controversial as he is would be flattered. Hate mail's as good as a fan letter in media circles."

"He was sure no one knew about this hidey-hole of his. He's terrified this particular guided missile's got his number on it. He's got a bee in his bonnet – thinks someone's out to do some real damage. Obviously, I only got half the story – he can't be that worried about a couple of threatening letters." Jonathan took me in his arms, hugging me like I really mattered.

"Listen, don't take this job at his country place, Briony. You'd be walking into a target area."

I thought at first he was pulling my leg. But Lusty's a rotten liar. He was perfectly serious.

"You're being ridiculous."

"Have it your way, but don't say I didn't warn you. Come on. Let's have a dekko at the flat while we've got the chance. Let's see what this crafty bugger's really hiding."

Three

I planned to drive down to Sussex on Saturday afternoon ready to start work officially on Monday. With live-in jobs like mine it is useful to have one full day to get sorted. No two jobs are alike and country-house stints usually peak at weekends. It would give me twenty-four hours to form a line of attack. Diana had warned me that working for the Barneses would involve some tactful manoeuvres and Diana was not one to send up warning signals for nothing.

"Carey Barnes is in charge but his wife is not entirely out of the picture – you'll have to play it by ear, Briony."

We had known each other long enough to lay our cards on the table and Diana knew she could trust my discretion. But, hells' bells, the woman couldn't just push me in blindfold, could she?

"What is it with Roz de Taffort? Is she sick or not?"

Diana sighed, shuffling the printed sheets on her blotter. My agency boss is a decent soul, doing a tricky job. Fiftyish, stylish and very very efficient. She has to be. Some of our customers are less than honest about their circumstances and it would be easy to put an inexperienced au pair or nanny into a nest of vipers. Checking references is Diana's forte and over the years Winterton's domestic agency had maintained an unblemished reputation.

She laid her specs on the desk and said, "Roz de Taffort is a beautiful woman. Tragically, her acting career came to a sudden halt three years ago. A car accident. She was driving her daughter back from a party and—"

"The kid who goes to school in the village?"

"No. Miranda. Nineteen years old now, the child of a former relationship. I'm not sure of the details. I understand Miranda has recently arrived back home after a teenage walkabout of a couple of years – some sort of pre-university break, you know the sort of thing. Carey Barnes' child is about six. Another daughter, but no problem to you – an au pair normally supervises but I'm still interviewing girls for that."

"So who's the boss when Carey Barnes isn't around? Who am I answerable to, Diana?"

"Roz." She sighed. "Problem is she drinks. And since the accident her health is variable."

"Oh no! Now we're getting to it. She's bonkers, isn't she?"

"Absolutely not! Carey Barnes hasn't got a mad wife locked in the attic, Briony! But she did suffer massive head injuries in the crash, was in a coma for days. She made a wonderful recovery but her memory is poor and her moods erratic. She can't work any more apart from voice overs and opening supermarkets but she still has scads of fans. Learning scripts is quite out of the question and the one time she made a comeback in a theatrical rehash of her TV hit *Sunset Raj* she had to leave after three weeks – kept drying up on stage."

"*Sunset Raj*. I remember that show. Went out every Sunday night for weeks. One of Ma's favourites. Roz de Taffort played the glamorous wife of my teenage heart-throb, Merrill Chanters."

"Hooray. You're finally in tune."

"Don't knock it, Diana. I'm no telly addict at the best of times and *Sunset Raj* was more of a Grannies' Pick of the Week you must admit."

Diana shrugged, replacing her glasses to check the file in front of her. "I should find a replacement for the au pair in a day or two. In the meantime, Carey Barnes has wheeled in a retired nanny who looked after the little girl until she went to nursery school. A Miss Phyllis Cannock. Not one of mine but a necessary fill-in. But I'd better warn you that she doesn't hit it off with the mistress of the house. Mr Barnes mentioned that the woman was a family retainer of the de Taffort tribe, brought up Miranda from a baby and has a great deal of experience, but Roz dismissed her in the course of some trifling contretemps and has only agreed to Cannock's reinstatement as a temporary measure after the au pair ran off."

"Yours?"

"I'm afraid so," Diana admitted. "A Croatian girl, Wanda. Been working at the Barnes household for nearly two years without a breath of trouble and then the silly girl packed her bags and vanished without so much as a cheerio."

"Another row with Roz?"

"Possibly. Actually, I'm rather worried about Wanda. I interviewed her myself and by all reports my confidence in her was entirely sound. A nice quiet girl. Well educated, but from a poor family. Told me she needed to send money home for a sick member of the family. Who knows what ghastly experiences she had before she came to England? Wanda was all set to pass her English-language certificate at the college in Brighton and that certificate would have been worth a mint when she returned home. What a waste!"

"Young?"

"Twenty but looked younger."

"Perhaps she got homesick."

"I checked. She hasn't gone back to Croatia. Her parents aren't bothered so I presume they're still getting the money she used to send home. Went to London to taste the good life before her visa expired I expect. To give her her due, Roz de Taffort is as anxious as I am myself. Reported her missing. But girls of that age ... the police have enough on their hands."

We chatted on for another half hour and I thought I had everything under control. How wrong I was.

Jonathan Lusty and I had a final date on the Friday night before I packed up. I had been spending quite a bit of time at the Tite Street flat while Fred freshened up the decorations and I got the kitchen cupboards up to scratch.

Archie sniffed his way round that apartment like a bloodhound, searching out the fading traces of my mother's presence I suppose. Poor little tyke probably missed her. Looking back, I wonder why she acquired the dog in the first place, never having expressed *any* desire for an animal and obdurately refusing all my own childish pleadings over the years for a pet of even hamster proportions. My astonishment at the unheralded arrival of the pup in her beautifully appointed drawing room had been shrugged off with a smile. Even her friends were shocked. She refused to explain.

"I saw poor Archie in Harrods. Isn't he *adorable?*" she bleated, daring me to disagree. Adorable he was not. Archie, either from original sin or careful training, had one undeniable drawback: he hated men. He particularly hated men in trainers and would launch himself at the ankles of any unfortunate who came within range. He loathed Charlie, of course. I went for Mother about all this several times, warning her that the dog was a menace and she was likely to end up in court when he bit a child.

"But Archie *loves* children!" she retorted. And it was true.

"Listen, Briony, Archie quite rightly distrusts men in trainers. Muggers and car thieves every one. Honestly, my child, he's got a sixth sense for villains. You should be glad I'm so well taken care of now I'm alone."

I groaned. Mental blackmail had not been one of her traits up till then. Archie was part of "A Plan".

"But, Mother, perfectly respectable middle-aged joggers wear trainers. And newspaper boys. Really, darling, you're taking an awful risk. What about the ladies in Burton Court?"

"The ladies in Burton Court wouldn't be seen dead in those ghastly plimsolls."

I gave up. After Mother died Charlie and I tried to find a new home for Archie. But none of her friends would volunteer. After Charlie's disappearance I even drove Archie to Battersea Dogs' Home but couldn't bring myself to take him inside. So Archie stayed. We rub along. Archie tolerates me and I drag him to as many jobs as the agency will allow.

When I'm on holiday and for odd stints Archie has a willing foster home with the only man the beastly animal takes to. Charlie's bookmaker, Joe Reilly. Reilly has a way with Archie and stands no nonsense. Whenever I'm stuck, Reilly keeps Archie at the betting shop and one of the girls on the counter has won him over with crisps and peanuts. Reluctantly, I have to admit, Archie is my mother's final grip on me from beyond the grave. Archie vets my men-friends, guards my car and delights any children of the household when I'm at a job. Archie is also a fantastic ratter though his performance at the Fox-Thompsons was far from welcome, their crumbling outbuildings proving a pied piper's haven, and laying his trophies at the old folks' feet had naturally caused ructions. Archie hated the Fox-Thompsons.

On that last Friday before I started work

at the Barnes' place, I put in a full day at Tite Street clearing up after the builders. Fred remained to plumb in the washing machine and to save any bloodshed I turned Archie in at the bookie's for a go at the punters. Reilly had racing at Lingfield that day but was happy to tote Archie along and I guess he respected Reilly's boot because I never had a word of complaint about any doggy misbehaviour at the track.

"I'll be back late, Bridget, me love—"

"Briony!"

"Briney it is! Your ma must have loved the sea. Meet me in the Queen – say about nine o'clock." The Queen is Reilly's local, a place with an odd clientele but offering real ale and discreet lighting. The atmosphere is strangely "underworld" but maybe that's its attraction because it's always packed out.

Jonny and I were settled in a dark corner of the saloon bar just after eight thirty and were well into our second round when I spotted a Carey Barnes look-alike slip in and join a scruff at the bar. I nudged Jonathan and he confirmed my suspicion. His eyes narrowed, squinting to get a clearer look. "Yes, it's Barnes all right. Want an introduction?" he said with a sardonic grin, not Jonny's usual self at all.

I felt awkward, nagged by guilty misgivings about our illicit search of Barnes' flat, but Jonathan has his own priorities and who was I to play Miss Prim? In fact we had wasted our time, the flat being as anonymous as Barnes' poison-pen letters. Not a clue to his personality was stamped on the place and as it was, at best, an emergency overnight stop for a man with an offbeat schedule, that in itself was not surprising. There were no books, nothing in the fridge except a half-empty bottle of Sauvignon and a mouldy carton of milk, and no dirty laundry. Its only expensive features were a massive TV set and state of the art computer and fax. All eminently nickable – no wonder the man was worried about the locks. Satisfied that there had clearly been no break-in and no evidence of any sort of tampering I had eventually managed to pull Jonathan back to his office downstairs. But he wasn't convinced. Something had him rattled, something he wasn't sharing with me. Sighting his client in the saloon bar of a pub with a reputation for shady goings-on didn't help.

I took a furtive look at the target of Jonny's rancour. Barnes stood with his back to the bar, deep in conversation with his companion. My prospective employer was a thickset man in a dark overcoat, a tweed fishing hat jammed well down over his eyes as if the poor devil couldn't quite decide whether he was having a dress down day or not. He was deeply tanned, but not in the flashy way of media types trying to look sexy, this was the real McCoy earned, at a guess, on dangerous forays to Bosnia and Algeria and the leathery look probably stopped short where the bullet-proof vest cut out the glare.

"Hey, Reilly!" I shouted, spotting my godfather-figure coming through the door, Archie tucked firmly under his arm all muzzled up.

I pulled Reilly to our table, introducing Jonathan who went off to order another round. I watched him nod curtly to Barnes who seemed just as keen to keep things low key.

"Archie been causing trouble?" I whispered, eyeing the little brute now wedged under the table between Reilly's boots.

"Nay. The muzzle's a precaution merely. Better safe than sorry. With all these nasties in here the poor beastie could not be blamed for taking offence and who knows what a taste of blood would do to the little man?"

Jonathan was exchanging a few words with Barnes and his friend at the bar, his face inscrutable. The crowd shifted about to let him back to our table with a tray of drinks and some peanuts, Reilly's little black eyes fixed on the TV personality and his pal. Jonny set down the drinks, his manner stiff, the usual bonhomie overcast. We were due to eat out and go on to a club later for a bit of a boogie but his mood augered badly.

"You know that bloke at the bar?" Reilly said.

"A client."

"Trouble with the rent?"

"What?"

"The enforcer. Fancy McGill."

"Oh, you mean the guy in the dirty mac? No, never met him before. I thought you meant the TV man, Barnes." Jonathan shuffled his feet causing Archie to snarl and strain on his tight rein.

Reilly leaned across the table, speaking so quietly I almost didn't catch his words. "I'll introduce you some time, boyo. Useful man to know, McGill."

"A debt collector?" I wondered if McGill had ever had Charlie Eastwood on his hit list.

"You name it, Bonnie, my girl. Credit-card defaulters mostly. Started off in the Met. Got chucked out for assaulting a prisoner. Useful at persuasion and works alone, which suits me. McGill never gives up – memory sharp as a razor."

"*You* use him?" I muttered, now thoroughly rattled.

"Sometimes. For account customers who try it on. But for searches too. Missing punters. Any sort of undercover job I want to keep private."

Archie started bucking under my chair,

testing my ability not to cave in and buy some crisps.

Jonny rose, his not inconsiderable height making Reilly look like a gnarled old garden gnome crouched over his beer. "We'd better go," he said. "Nice to meet you, Joe."

I scrabbled under the table to collar Archie and from the corner of my eye watched Carey Barnes disappear into the gents. I shoved a carrier bag between Reilly's feet, leaned across and squeezed his hand. "Hey pardner, here's a bit of home cookin'," I said. Reilly has a love affair with any old plummy fruit cake and every now and then I bake a Dundee for him to take back to the betting shop. "Thanks for looking after Archie today, Joe. You're a pal."

Joe half rose as Barnes' sidekick, McGill, joined us, nobbling him for what I can only guess was a bit of private business. Jonny and I made our escape.

It had started to rain. We shoved Archie into the back of the car and dumped him at my flat. The poor animal made straight for his basket and was out cold almost before we had checked out; a day at the races more than his bandy little legs could deal with.

Jonathan's mood lightened and I didn't rock the boat by referring back to the sighting of his shifty client in the Queen. The pub wasn't a drug-pushers' rendezvous or neither Reilly or I would have gone within a mile of it – for different reasons Charlie's bookmaker and I share an abhorrance of users. Perfectly normal couples like Jonny and me, not to mention a few brave tourists, enjoy the raffish atmosphere. But the place attracts a funny crowd: a few hookers, some theatrical hangers-on and regulars, including some determined old soldiers from the Royal Hospital for whom the Queen proves a generous watering hole especially if they're wearing their scarlet.

But why would somewhere like that attract a celebrity such as Carey Barnes? A place where he could easily be recognised, badgered, confronted by irate viewers determined to buttonhole a political commentator with a dangerous bias. And in the company of "an enforcer" as Reilly put it? I shivered, wondering if Jonathan Lusty had been right and I should have turned down this bloody job at the Barnes' place.

Four

I spent half the night at Jonny Lusty's loft-style pad in Battersea before waking to the noise of what sounded like a storm at sea, not helped by the unnerving effect that closing my eyes had on the bed which seemed to make it sway like a hammock. I churned about, vowing never to touch another drop, but jerked up at the sound of splintering wood and the undeniable crash of a fallen tree.

Sleep was impossible. I slid out of bed and stood shivering at the window, watching the roof of a shed in the allotment gardens below sheer off and shatter against one of the other huts, the whole scene spasmodically lit by flashes of lightning and accompanied by a cacophony loud enough to wake the dead.

Jonny snored on, oblivious, our night out leaving him happily unconscious and me wide awake with a thumping great hangover. I crept into the bathroom and five minutes later was out in the street. With little chance in the small hours of a cruising taxi sailing over the horizon I decided to jog back to my own place and, luckily, the fresh air cleared my head. The vroom and whoosh of the storm created an atmosphere of Wagnerian drama in a city now almost deserted, the usual late-night ravers keeping their heads down until the tempest blew itself out.

I let myself into the flat and threw my wet clothes in a heap on the floor. Archie, half-witted with fear, went crazy welcoming me back and eventually crawled on to the bed as I attempted to snatch some sleep in what remained of the darkness. The little runt farted with satisfaction, digging a nest for himself in my duvet, not such a brave soldier after all.

Next day the results of the hurricane were all too clear: broken tiles littered the pavements, workmen hard at it cutting up fallen timber and securing scaffolding on the building sites. In a city normally safe from meteorological disasters, the havoc struck a fearsome note as if some ancient gods were waking to a vengeful power.

By the time I had skirted diversions and made slow progress to Sussex the worst of the storm had long passed and I got down to Northchurch just after lunch. The house stood well beyond the village but was clearly signposted, presumably to facilitate the arrival of Barnes' townie guests. Two men were struggling to fix a tarpaulin to the roof of a gatehouse, another victim of the night's mayhem. Archie started up a racket from the back seat as I wound down the window and called out to a bloke on a ladder, a hunk in tight jeans, well lashed up against the weather in an authentic and expensive Barbour, an upmarket estate worker of some sort.

"Barnes' place?" I shouted, trying to be sociable.

He glowered, holding tight to his end of the tarpaulin, clearly not in the mood for pleasantries.

"Park by the stables – a tree's blocking the drive at the front."

I smiled and drove on, hurling insults at Archie, who was playing Rottweiler and dancing about on my recipe books stacked on the parcel shelf.

The house came into view at the end of a long curving gravel drive, a typical Edwardian manor house, tile-hung with a rippling roofline, lots of mullioned windows and tall chimneys. The garden frontage was dominated by a large lake with a naff oriental teahouse on an island joined to the lawn by a mimsy bridge straight off a willow-pattern plate. I sighed. I had been to this sort of place before – all draughty corridors and a far-flung kitchen annexe. I crossed my fingers, trusting that the de Taffort family fortune, which Diana had assured me was considerable, had been lashed out on new plumbing and mod cons.

Parking in the stable yard as Sexy Pants had instructed I left my luggage in the boot while Archie and I did a little recce. The gardens were superb even at this fag-end of the year, a walled vegetable garden and hothouses taking my breath away with their abundance of produce. Dwarf fruit trees lined the paths and a glimpse of peaches and a vine in the glasshouse warmed my craven little chefette's heart. It was the closest I had come to a French potager and the thought of plundering those rows of luscious fresh veggies and herbs made me dribble with anticipation.

I curbed Archie's determination to mark out the territory in his usual style and dragged him through to view the chicken run behind the compost heaps which impressed him enough to perform with alacrity. Showing off, I guess.

I knocked loudly at the back door, heavy rock music shaking the very portals, and a smiling girl in a mini skirt and furry sweater opened up, her heavy-duty washing-up gloves giving a distinct impression of serious business. She wasn't tall but was very, very slim and beautifully proportioned in a way which I can only describe as "Pocket Venus". The one surprising note was a glittering diamond stud through her bottom lip.

"Hi! I'm Miranda," she bawled against the noise. "You must be Briony Eastwood, please God. I was hoping to finish cleaning the Aga before you arrived, to make a good impression – to start with anyway." The girl opened the door on to a stone-flagged scullery and washhouse lined with wellingtons, buckets and an assortment of fishing gear. She turned off the boogie box and we could actually hear ourselves speak.

"Excuse the mess. Doris doesn't come on Saturdays and the storm has caused a few problems, rain getting in the downstairs loo and a window blown out, but we didn't want you to turn tail and run. We *need* you, Briony!" she wailed, grinning in the knowledge of charm learned at her mother's knee.

"I've brought my dog. OK? He's pretty harmless." We moved into the main kitchen which was everything I could desire: a large deal table, a butcher's block with a battery of superb knives and choppers, lots of daylight flooding from the east windows and an immaculate tiled floor spread about with colourful rag rugs. We shut Archie in the scullery while we looked around.

Miranda gave me the cook's tour, opening cupboards, revealing, as the *coup de grâce*, the marvels of an immense American fridge freezer.

"It's new. Only arrived last week. I've been in the States and just nagged and nagged till Ma caved in and chucked out the old one."

"Wow!"

"I knew you'd love it. Isn't it *great*?"

Miranda had acquired an all-American college-girl style, clear-eyed and with the sort of confidence I had always longed for. We were just establishing a real rapport, busy hauling my stuff from the car into the kitchen, when a small girl bounced into the room, chunky in that nicely rounded way of six or seven year olds, and without a doubt Roz de Taffort's child. The same heart-shaped face and silvery blonde hair, straight and silky as the fringe on a lampshade. After my recent stint with the wrinkly Fox-Thompsons the sheer attractiveness of these two sisters was a bonus.

"Briony, this is Pebbles."

"Pebbles?"

"The Flinstones' kid," the child muttered. "I do have a proper name but it's much worse so I'm not going to tell you."

"Say how-do-you-do properly," Miranda said firmly, "and then we'll find mummy and tell her Briony's arrived."

Pebbles shook back the fall of bright hair and grinned, two missing front teeth lending her smile a certain gappy charm.

"You've lost your teeth already," I said, burbling on about tooth fairies and the

41

going rate for baby gnashers.

"Yeah! A pound each."

"Heavens, that's gone up since I got mine."

"Poor Miranda didn't get anything at all, did you, Mirry? Gone, all in one go and she didn't get a sausage. What a swizz! And do you know what mummy said? She said—"

"Just shut up!" The older girl's face darkened, anger suddenly dousing the big sister act. "I had a car accident," she rattled out, the words chilly with repetition. "I hit the dashboard – wasn't wearing a seatbelt you see – and lost my front teeth."

"N-nobody could possibly guess," I stammered, trying to forestall Pebbles' obvious eagerness to relay the grisly details.

"Oh, shove off, Pebbles!" Miranda threw her rubber gloves on to the draining board and rushed out, her footsteps echoing on the parquet as she clattered through the hall and slammed the front door.

Pebbles gazed at me with unblinking aplomb. "Take no notice of my sister. She gets these moods. Touchy. Nanny says it's her jeans."

"Her genes?" The sang-froid of this little girl was formidable.

"I think Nanny meant her tight jeans give Mirry tummy ache and that's what makes her cross."

"Ah, yes. That must be it."

I tried to change the subject but, undeflected, she rattled on, ghoulish as only kids can be. "Mummy explained it all to me when Miranda came back in the summer. They were both in this terrific crash, you see, and mummy got awfully sick. Miranda bashed her mouth and had to have loads of visits to the dentist. Ugh! But now she's got nice new ones, all screwed in, not dunked in a glass at night like Nanny's."

Fortunately, at that moment Archie began to bark, scrabbling away at the scullery door, tired of being left out. He erupted into the kitchen like a firecracker and Pebbles went into raptures, hugging the smelly little beast in a headlock which he was polite enough to endure. That's the funny thing about Archie. Absolutely vile with men and sweet as a nut with kids. I guess it's his only virtue.

After a little romp round the kitchen we tied his lead to an iron hook in the scullery wall and Pebbles led me upstairs to meet her mama.

Five

Meeting Roz de Taffort was a bit of a letdown. Pebbles burst into what I can only describe as a boudoir and shook her mother awake. I stood awkwardly in the doorway waiting for the explosion but the woman sprawled out on the chaise longue emerged from her nap like Venus rising from the waves, not a hair out of place and a beatific smile on her pale lips. Nevertheless, a glimpse of those sapphire eyes, now swimming and unfocused, confirmed my worst fears. The lady of the house was boozed up to the eyeballs.

Pebbles rattled on, bumping about on the couch, chirpy as a cricket and unconsciously giving the grown-ups the necessary minutes to adjust. Roz extended an elegant hand, smiling graciously, and we introduced ourselves. One had to hand it to her: her ability to behave like a duchess despite being so obviously hungover deserved an ovation. Before we could get on to details of my housekeeping duties another woman hurried into the room, a stout party in a

44

tweed skirt, her grey curls set as if in concrete. This could only be Phyllis Cannock, the recycled nanny. Roz's manner cooled.

"Ah," she said, "Phyllis. Briony Eastwood, our new cook, has just arrived. Would you do the honours for me? I think the gatehouse is prepared."

Roz turned to me, smiling wanly, shuffling her feet like an anxious patient in a waiting room. "We'll talk later, sweetie. After tea perhaps...?" Her voice trailed off and she gave Pebbles a gentle shove. The older woman crossed the room, took the child firmly by the hand and began to usher me out. It was very neatly done and Nanny Cannock could clearly have run rings round any military commander when it came to tactical manoeuvres.

"Katie's mummy is waiting downstairs, poppet. Run along now." She turned to Roz as the little girl flew off. "Pebbles is staying the night in the village, Mrs Barnes. The vet and his wife, you know." Roz closed her eyes, her lips barely parting in mute response. The woman bundled us out and closed the door. "I must apologise for the apparent disorganisation here. No one told me to expect you this afternoon, Mrs Eastwood. I gather Miranda introduced herself and then rushed away leaving you in Pebbles' hands." Miss Cannock tut-tutted, vigorously shaking her head, the coiffure moving not a jot. Perhaps it was a wig.

"Please don't be anxious on my account. Pebbles has been very entertaining and I was warned by the agency that Mrs Barnes has bouts of ill health. I'm used to finding my own way about."

The nanny glanced at me with an appraising look, leading me through to a part of the house which I vaguely felt must be above the kitchens.

"Mrs Barnes mentioned the gatehouse," I prompted.

"The former housekeeper's cottage. Yes. That was the plan but storm damage has made it temporarily uninhabitable. I've taken it upon myself to place you in the au pair's room, if that suits you? It is not as private as the gatehouse, I admit but," and here she took a breath through clenched teeth which caused an audible whistle, "I very much doubt that you would require the degree of privacy that Jennie Thomas demanded."

I said nothing, having experience of the snake pit which spats between the staff could open up.

In fact, the au pair's accommodation was charming and I immediately decided that when Diana managed to replace the missing au pair I would refuse to budge.

"Perhaps I can offer you tea when you have washed your hands? The back stairs connect this part of the house directly to the kitchen. My own rooms are in the nursery suite, of course – but you'll find me quite easily, I'm just a step along this landing, I'll leave the door ajar. You look a nice sensible girl, Briony Eastwood."

This parting accolade was the sort of euphemism my mother used to trot out and the inference was well understood between Miss Cannock and myself. "A nice sensible girl" was another way of saying, "The class of person I am familiar with. The sort who knows which fork to use and when to keep her mouth shut." Oh yes, I had learned things at my mother's knee too.

Having tea with Phyllis Cannock was tedious but instructive. In the absence of any direction from Roz de Taffort, the retired nanny had taken a firm grip on the household and as Pebbles was at school for most of the day, her self-appointed duties had taken on fresh impetus. Nevertheless, I could understand Roz's determination to pension her off again as soon as a new au pair could be found to ferry Pebbles back and forth and fill in as a sort of backstop behind the baize door.

"When did the au pair leave?" I asked, all innocence.

"About five weeks ago, I believe. That's the trouble with these foreign girls – no sense of loyalty. Just swept off overnight

47

without so much as a by your leave!" Miss Cannock fussed with the teacups, plying me with a very hard rock bun. I began to worry about Archie staked out in the scullery, but first things first.

"Miranda would prefer to take over the entire care of Pebbles herself and her mother is putty in her hands. Weak as water that one, always was. But Mr Barnes insists, quite rightly, that one cannot rely on Miranda."

"I thought she would be away at university by now."

"That was the intention. And Miranda is a clever girl, no doubt about that." Miss Cannock's pursed lips indicated that being "clever" was a dubious attribute best discouraged. "But when Miranda finally arrived back in the summer, she decided her mother needed her at home."

"Very noble."

Miss Cannock bridled. "Not in the least. Miranda is, without exception, the most egotistical child I have ever come across. Take my word, there is an ulterior motive."

"She's been in America she tells me."

"Oh, all over! Australia. Chile. Los Angeles. Not even a postcard in all that time, would you believe? And yet she bounces back here, bold as brass, pretending nothing's happened. Mr Barnes isn't taken in, of course, but the rest of us are all expected to treat that little madam like the Queen of the May! Quite what she was doing in California is anyone's guess. But genes will out." I choked back a giggle and hastened to compliment Miss Cannock on her rock cakes. In an effort to steer her off this dangerous seam of gossip I told her about Archie.

"I don't care for dogs," she said, her manner unequivocal. "But if Mr Barnes has agreed..."

As if on cue, Pebbles and her friend Katie burst into the room, their eyes incandescent.

"Briony! Can we take Archie into the woods? Katie's *ace* with dogs. Honestly!"

"Excuse me, please. Manners! I didn't hear anyone knock, did I?" The Nanny Incarnate tried out her puzzled expression, the bushy eyebrows raised like arched centipedes.

"Yes, of course you may," I said, scrambling up. "I'll come down. But you mustn't let him off the lead. Promise?"

"And on no account go near the lake," Miss Cannock admonished, determined to have the last word. I thanked her for tea and hurried off in the wake of the excitable girls, more than anxious to escape the vision of Nanny Cannock in the mesmerising role of Ancient Mariner.

About eight o'clock I made myself supper

on a tray and took it back to my rooms, my official duties not due to begin until Monday. Archie trotted behind and immediately settled in his corner, snoring like a steam kettle, clearly bushed by the energetic attentions of Pebbles and Katie. Hearing a car drive up, I glanced out to see Carey Barnes parking his MG in the stable yard below my window. The house was deathly quiet, no rock and roll from Miranda and no squeals and laughter from Pebbles who was sleeping out. Their absence left a gloomy void and I only hoped that things would perk up next day when, Nanny Cannock breathlessly confided, there was to be a special Sunday luncheon party, a catered affair, and several of Roz's old theatrical chums were invited. That should brighten things up.

The rooms I had been allocated were far from basic and at a guess had been constructed from a warren of attics and servants' bedrooms. The missing girl, Wanda, must have had urgent reasons to skip, cosy billets like Kington House not being thick on the ground, especially for Eastern Europeans who were still a novelty in the au-pair line.

Wanda's flatlet was low-ceilinged and, guessing from a lingering fruity fragrance, part of it had probably been an apple store. The double bed was draped with a pricy coverlet, and matching mugs and china were stacked on the shelf, not at all the household throw-outs with which the domestic quarters were normally furnished. And I should know! There was a telephone, a TV and a radio on a chest of drawers, a small coffee table and pretty curtains. The kitchenette sported a mini cooker, fridge and pine table, and the bathroom a power shower. It was, in fact, just as comfortable as my studio flat in London and if I could shunt Archie between here and the kitchen via the back stairs, chances were the Barnes family need hardly know of his existence.

I emptied my suitcases on to the bed and hung up my winter clothes in the closet, wondering if I should ring Jonny Lusty to say hello. I decided against. We had an easy relationship unburdened by clinging demands and I hesitated to give him too much encouragement. After all there was Charlie to consider. Until I had finally exorcised that particular ghost, making promises was just mouthing empty words.

I struggled with the drawer of the bedside table to store my books and the tin of crackers kept for midnight nibbles. The thing wasn't jammed exactly but obstructed in some way causing the drawer to jerk on the runners. I pulled it right out and turned it over, running my fingers along the underside of the smooth woodwork. Nothing. Being bloody-minded I got down on my knees and shone my pencil torch inside, the laser beam pricking out the shadows. Right up in the corner, firmly stuck to the underside of the cupboard space, was a manilla envelope sealed in plastic. Eventually I managed to prise it out with a nail file and sat on the bed with the package in my hands wondering if Wanda, in her hasty exit, had forgotten to take her love letters. I tore off the plastic cover and the envelope spilled open, the contents rolling all over the place, under the bed, under the cupboard. Archie raised his head, ever hopeful, but subsided again as I raised a warning finger. I counted my haul. No doubt about it. Briony Eastwood wasn't born yesterday. Here, hidden inside Wanda's bedside table, were about eight hundred pounds worth of Ecstacy tablets. Enough to set up a rave.

Diana had been totally bamboozled by this Croatian girl. This bundle of joy was not for private consumption: our little Wanda was a dealer. But what had caused such panic that she had run off overnight without her valuable bag of goodies?

I turfed Archie out of his bed and re-taped the E's underneath it. Wait and see. I'd just sit tight and see if anyone tried to claim them.

Six

Nanny Cannock and I breakfasted together on Sunday morning, Miranda sleeping in and Roz, I was told, never surfacing until coffee time. Archie had taken himself off on a private garden tour.

"Mr Barnes likes to make his own breakfast when he's home," Phyllis said, liberally buttering her toast. "Lunch is their thing and unless there are house guests which is rare, you need not bother with the dining room till midday. Pebbles has a full breakfast before school, of course, but doesn't need a lunch box. I drive her there myself and do any little errands Mrs Barnes requires. Wednesday is your day off, isn't it, dear?"

I nodded. "What happens then?"

"Well, Jennie generally left a casserole which only needed to go in the oven or sometimes a cold buffet on the sideboard."

"She's been working here some time?"

"Oh, yes. Years. Quite a good cook, too, but I doubt she will return after the baby."

I stiffened. "My employment here is only

temporary, Miss Cannock. I always go abroad at the end of January."

"Quite so." Phyllis patted her hair and poured herself a second cup of tea. "On Jennie's day off Mrs Barnes got a woman in from the village if necessary but Wanda was, so I'm told, adequate in the kitchen."

"Did you know Wanda?"

"Not at all. I was summoned here at a moment's notice when it became clear the girl had gone for good. I'm retired, you know. I share a little cottage in Rye with my sister Edna. She's a widow and sharing expenses suits us both."

"Could you tell me if—"

Phyllis Cannock gulped her tea and rose to go, fending off more questions with a firm gesture. "I can't sit here chatting, Briony. I'm due at nine o'clock communion and then I'm spending the day with my friend. I'll be back before Pebbles gets home at four. You just relax, my dear; enjoy a quiet day. The caterers will be here at ten and they'll take entire charge. Derryk and Graham or Gray and Derry as they like to call themselves. Excellent young men. They even do the flowers, so there's not a thing for you to bother your head about."

Phyllis put her crocks in the dishwasher, shrugged into a beige raincoat, checked her umbrella and keys and made a rush for the door. Mary Poppins she was not and a

54

malicious old trout to boot, but Nanny Cannock – in the absence of any other informative source – was disappearing over the horizon like a galleon in full sail and my plaintive enquiries were now as likely to be answered if I'd put a message in a bottle. When her car had trundled off down the drive I cleared the table and set about a thorough stock-take of the kitchen equipment and larder before the caterers moved in. I drew up a preliminary shopping list and started counting the utensils. All very much in order except there was no food processor. Bugger. I ransacked the kitchen units and even the scullery without success. I couldn't believe that an establishment like this functioned without one. Perhaps the pregnant Jennie had pinched it as a parting gift? But I maligned her. Searching for a clean teatowel I came across a bundle of bills clipped together with a repair ticket for the Barnes' Moulinex from an electrical shop in Tunbridge Wells. I'd phone in the morning and see what was what. I was just examining the invoices when Carey Barnes breezed in, making me jump and making me feel as if I'd been caught out reading his private mail which, if Jonny Lusty had been luckier in his search of Barnes' London flat, I probably would have been. Guilt: it does terrible things to one's blood pressure.

"You must be Briony," he said, all very

jolly, his hand extended. I dropped the bills back in the drawer and stumbled through a mini CV which was far from my usual style with employers who, in the normal way, exhibited such craven gratitude at my arrival that nervous justification on my side was never on the cards. Trouble was, this man had a certain charisma which put me quite off balance, his intelligence and battered good looks more alluring than I had expected. The shifty bloke in the Queen with his dubious drinking partner, Fancy McGill, seemed something of a doppelganger to this man in the brown cords and tartan shirt.

"They've told you about the caterers coming today?" he asked, getting to grips with the toaster and kettle.

"Can I do that for you?" I stuttered.

"Absolutely not. It's your day off. Tell you what though, Briony, shall I quickly show you the wine cellar while it's quiet? You'll need to know the ropes."

He produced a key on a ring with a brassy toggle and led me to a locked door beside the pantry. I stepped up beside him, very much the new girl on her best behaviour. He jammed open the door with a two pound cast-iron weight from old corn-measuring scales and switched on the light. A steep stone staircase with no balustrade led down, turning at an angle near the bottom to skirt a metal sink and glass-fronted fridge on a narrow half-landing. At a glance the fridge seemed stocked entirely with party packs of ice cubes. I crept down behind him, hugging the wall, the place cold as a tomb, the only natural light filtering through a barred air vent with a broken pane. He showed me through another door which led to an adjoining basement area, this part was set up as a games room with a table-tennis table, some armchairs, a dartboard and its own shower room and toilet. It was a dreary play area and, at a guess, hardly used.

"I keep it shut up down here because of Pebbles. The door from the kitchen is self-locking and it would be terrible if she got shut in. Kids are so inquisitive, aren't they?"

I nodded, mumbling something fatuous about "better safe than sorry", my mind clicking like a manic metronome. He was lying, of course. Carey Barnes kept his wine under lock and key because his wife would be dipping in the cellar like it was a swimming pool given half a chance. Poor devil. Providing minders for a dipso when his work took him away sometimes for weeks at a time must be a nightmare.

He selected a dozen bottles and stacked them in a wicker basket, chatting away as we toured the cellar as if we had known each other for ever. Actually, I know only the basics when it comes to wine and was relieved when he apologetically explained that this was out of bounds for culinary purposes.

"Order what you like from the village stores, Briony. Put it on the bill. You cook with wine, I imagine? My wife runs her own account with the wine merchants in Tunbridge Wells so please don't feel obliged to place extra items on the kitchen account for her."

It was very nicely put and we regarded each other with clear understanding. The underlying message was: Don't get involved with my wife's habit, miss, she is quite capable of organising her own destruction.

"Perhaps you would like to join our little luncheon party for tea later? They're an interesting crowd and Miranda's invited one of her chums, not all old has-beens like myself." He stood close, his breath fanning my face. I felt quite wobbly.

"Er, no, thank you, Mr Barnes. If you'll excuse me I'm still unpacking."

"Oh, call me Carey, do. We're not grand down here I assure you."

He waved me ahead of him, back up the steps, the whiff of his aftershave sharpening the dank smell of the double basement. I could never believe that apology for a games room would appeal to a lively child like Pebbles even on the wettest day.

Back in the kitchen Carey carefully re-locked the door and pocketed the key. The kettle on the Aga had almost boiled dry and he restarted his breakfast from scratch, munching an apple as he waited for the toast. He watched me finish my shopping list and I felt my face redden. Archie barking at the back door let me off the hook and, grabbing my mac and his lead from the hook, I made my excuses and fled.

We strolled over the fancy wooden bridge to have a look at the teahouse, the decking littered with brown leaves stripped from the trees in the storm giving the place an abandoned air. Inside, a bench provided a perch out of the wind, the bare branches of a denuded willow whipping fiercely against the shutters. Archie bundled about looking for vermin and I sat alone like a winter queen.

From this vantage point the house looked less formidable, the autumn sunlight lending a rosy glow to the brickwork. The lake rippled with an invisible undertow, the expanse of water presumably created from a partly dammed stream which flowed into the lake at the south end between a tangle of reeds and disappeared underground in a mini whirlpool. Several coot quarrelled loudly at the margin of the water lending a melancholy topnote to the scene. The prospect of several lonely weeks quartered here filled me with chill foreboding. I shivered, bunching my collar to my throat, wishing now I had stayed in London for an extra night at Jonny's loft.

This conjecture was cut short by the flurry of the caterers' van speeding round the circular drive to disappear through the stable yard to the kitchen entrance. It was a sparkling little vehicle painted bright blue, *Silver Service* spelt out with an italic flourish.

I decided to give Derry and Gray a clear run and felt in my pocket for money and car keys. Archie and I would explore the wine bars in Brighton, a day at the seaside would blow the blues away. I tucked the millstone under my arm and drove away at a fair lick, noting with amusement as I reached the road that Sexy Pants' efforts to secure the tarpaulin to the gatehouse roof had been in vain. The thing had broken free at one end, flapping over the top windows like a flag of surrender. I would look forward to meeting that guy again. He couldn't be ratty all the time, could he? But perhaps the pert little Miranda de Taffort had already marked him down for herself?

I got back just after four, the afternoon already dusky, and parked in the yard which was still jammed with a variety of vehicles including a Rolls. The caterers' van had gone and Nanny Cannock's little runabout was yet to return, which was a surprise. I breezed into the kitchen which was all lit up like a cruise ship and found two little girls seated at the table playing snakes and ladders, and a pleasant-looking woman with red hair and freckles thumbing through the Barnes' copy of *Country Life*. She looked up and grinned.

"Hello. You must be Briony. I'm Katie's mum. Teresa George. Nice to meet you."

The girls fell upon Archie with delight, producing a squeaky plastic rabbit which he obligingly toyed with though I know for a fact he prefers the real thing. I hung up my coat behind the door and chatted away, curious to know what had happened to Nanny Cannock.

She shrugged. "God knows. But now you're here I'll push off if that's OK?"

"Oh, if you can spare a moment, Teresa, can I pick your brains?" I rummaged in the drawer and produced the repair ticket for the mixer. "Do you know an electrical shop in Tunbridge Wells called Fosters? I *really* need the mixer and if it's ready I'll pop over in the morning and pick it up. I don't want to waste time touring the streets."

"Yes, sure. It's just behind the Pantiles, anyone will direct you. Fosters has its own car park at the back of the shop. They're very quick – I'm sure they'll do a rush job if you say it's urgent. Why don't you pop in for a coffee on your way back? We're at the crossroads in the village – big notice says Veterinary Surgery – you can't miss it."

"Thanks a lot. That would be great. Would you like some tea before you go? It was nice of you to entertain Pebbles for the weekend." I eyed a trolley laid up presumably by Derry or Gray with teacups, a plate of savouries and a luscious lemon sponge.

Just then Carey Barnes burst in looking frazzled and greeted Teresa, then collared me with a sigh of relief. Roars of laughter reverberated from the dining room, the luncheon guests obviously having one hell of a good time.

"Ah, Briony. Where's Phyllis Cannock?"

"No idea, Mr Barnes. She's not back."

"Oh shit. She's never late." He crossed the kitchen to lock the cellar door, frowning like a man who had mislaid the staff rules book.

"Look here, Briony, I hate to ask you this but could you be an absolute angel and make a couple of pots of tea? I can't find Miranda – she's invited her American boyfriend, Gizmo, to stay on for a few days. Maybe she's sorting out his room ... Unless I get these people out of the dining room and a bit sobered up they'll be here till midnight. I've got work to do," he added fiercely, sketching an abstracted farewell to Teresa as she discreetly bundled Katie out of the door. Archie was hiding under the table in the grip of Pebbles who, pressing her finger to her lips, willed me to stay mum.

"No problem," I said, urging Carey back to his guests. "Where would you like tea?"

"There's a fire in the library. I'll try and get their bums off the seats and you can wheel the trolley through straight away, if you would?"

He strode off, clearly bent on moving the lunch party one stage nearer the exit.

I made tea and checked the trolley for napkins and teaspoons. No doubt about it, Derry and Gray gave a five-star catering service. I wished now I'd hung about and picked up a few pointers.

I wheeled the trolley along to the library which at a guess doubled as Carey's work room being far from the usual manor-house smoking room lined with unread leather tomes. Rows of paperbacks and government publications were stacked in untidy piles on the bookshelves, a fax machine winked in the corner. Nevertheless it retained a certain charm, oak panelled, the darkening sky a foil to pools of yellow lamplight. A log fire blazed merrily in the hearth and open French doors led out to a conservatory silhouetted with palms where several tall church candles in metal stands burned on a garden table partly obscured by a rattan sofa enveloped in a pall of smoke.

I hurried to investigate, thinking to blow out the candles and close off the conservatory with the library curtains. As I bustled in a man's head reared up and he practically shot his invisible companion off his knees in his haste to rise. The unmistakable aroma of top-quality cannabis clogged the air, lending the jungly atmosphere of the conservatory a decadent luxury.

"Oh, sorry," I muttered, backing off.

Miranda untangled herself from her bloke and, glowing in her amber catsuit like a well-fed tiger cub, stretched scrawny arms to reach for black patent thigh boots. The man stubbed out their joint in a plant pot and tucked in his shirt.

"Hey, Briony, don't go! Come and meet my guy."

He stretched out his hand, a real meathead, all bulging neck muscles and big feet.

"Good afternoon, Miss—?"

"How do you do," I countered, wonderfully professional. "Mr Barnes mentioned that Miranda had invited you to stay over."

Miranda giggled. "Oh, this isn't *Gizmo*. This beautiful hunk is Kyle Chapman, Ma's personal trainer. If you're very good, Briony Eastwood, Kyle will give you one of his special massage treatments."

She extinguished the candles and grabbed Kyle's hand, pulling him through to the library to take up her hostessy role behind

64

the tea trolley just as the well-oiled luncheon guests straggled into the room. I quickly
closed the French doors and drew the curtains. As I passed, Kyle winked – some sort
of complicity between the hired help in his
mind, at a guess – and took up what was, I
presume, his official stance, supporting Roz
de Taffort. She beamed up at the chap with
an air of calm possession. By contrast,
Carey, I later concluded, had looked decidedly jaded, the strain of keeping his wife
entertained in the country being a costly
and exhaustive process.

Seven

Sleeping in Wanda's flatlet has become a bit
of a problem. Even Archie was restless,
whimpering in his sleep like a love-sick
ferret. The room has bad vibes whether
from long-dead servant girls or from the
rumbling of the outdated central heating is
hard to say.

To add to my troubles Charlie has decided
to join me, haunting my dreams in his worst
guise to date: the bloated corpse, a mani-
festation I have been spared so far. But the

final flourish was something entirely new and utterly spine chilling. Barely conscious, I was distinctly aware of stifled sobbing from somewhere close, a child's wretchedness borne of pain and misery.

I shot up, bathed in sweat, straining to listen for a repeat of the poor kid's lamentations. Pebbles? Her room was in the nursery suite with Nanny C and she wouldn't be ignored, not if her cries had managed to percolated my, admittedly restless, night. But maybe Pebbles was alone. If so, where *was* Phyllis Cannock? When I retired to my room after the cannabis fiasco the nanny had still not returned from her day out. I had popped Pebbles in with her mother's friends for tea in the library where she had been greeted with shouts of affection. Perhaps Miranda had put her to bed in Phyllis's absence and the little girl *was* on her own, far from the rest of the family. Roz slept at the front of the house and presumably Miranda was tucked up with her boyfriend. It was a big house and a child waking from a nightmare would be too frightened to start looking for her mother in the dark. And if Phyllis had never returned was it possible she had lit out without warning like the missing au pair? Were there things going on in this house? A sub plot to which I was excluded?

I switched on the light and opened the

door on to the landing. Not a flicker. The weeping child seemed to have cried herself to sleep. Maybe it was a dream, my own feverish imagination fuelled by Charlie in his bloody winding sheet. I made a cup of camomile tea and glanced at the clock. Three thirty and the world outside quiet as the grave, not a breath of wind, not even the creaking of storm-damaged trees to counterfeit the mysterious sobbing. Charlie's manifestations I was used to, but this childish keening was a new twist. Moving around so much and sleeping in strange beds for most of the year, getting the collywobbles was not my scene. It was time for a holiday. Roll on New Year and the cleansing chill of the pistes. I put out the light, determined to salvage some sleep from what remained of the night.

My duties did not include an early morning tea run and breakfast in the kitchen for me and Pebbles seemed adequate. Acting as body slave for Miranda was definitely not in my brief. I pulled back the bedroom curtains and was relieved to see Phyllis Cannock's rusting Ford parked in the yard. One problem solved. The MG had gone, presumably the work Carey had been worried about had demanded that he leave early. A four-wheel drive vehicle, appropriately mud spattered, was slewed across the stable yard and, as a final tally, I could only conclude that Roz's car was in the garage if she still drove at all which, judging from Nanny Cannock's bitter asides, was questionable.

Archie was raring to go as usual and took the back stairs like the Cresta run. The kitchen was warm and reasonably tidy and, after recovering the tea trolley from the library and surveying the chaos of the dining-room table, it looked as if the priority was restoring some semblance of order after the weekend's partying. Doris, the cleaner, was due at nine. She could make a start.

Pebbles bounced down soon after eight closely followed by a distinctly rattled Nanny Cannock.

"Good morning, Miss Cannock," I chirruped, steering Pebbles to the table before she started searching the room. "Archie's out," I told her. "Let's get breakfast over, shall we? What time's the school run, Miss Cannock?"

"Half past but I am a little worried about my car."

"You broke down last night?"

"A double puncture, both offside tyres – I foolishly hit a kerbstone and lurched into the hedge. Miles from anywhere too! I had to telephone the recovery service from the nearest cottage and, do you know, they wouldn't let me inside – made the call themselves and then shut the door on me.

Folk these days are so suspicious! Do I *look* like a mugger? Then I had to tramp back to the car and wait for the patrolman and being Sunday there was a bit of a wait. So I sat in the car with the heater on and some music on the radio just to keep up my spirits and then, of course—"

"The battery went flat," I put in, determined to cut off the inevitable punchline.

"What a calamity. I didn't arrive back until after nine o'clock and Pebbles was already asleep."

"I think she may have been worried about you though. I thought I heard her in the night? A bad dream?" I whispered.

Nanny Cannock bridled, two bright spots staining her cheeks. "Certainly not! You're mistaken, Briony." I seemed to have caught the old girl on a raw place. Maybe she had been out cold, as drunk as Roz after her mystery tour? Perhaps she and the lady of the house had more in common than anyone suspected – I still didn't know why Phyllis had been given the push before the au pair was engaged. I grinned at the little girl who made a very telling little moue, a child familiar with the ups and downs of the adults in this strange set-up.

"What's wrong with the car this morning then?" I persisted. "You drove it back all right."

"Actually, I got a tow. It broke down again

69

in the lane and Mark happened to be check-ing on some foxes and came to my aid. I'll have to get a mechanic out here from the village."

My heart sank. "You would like me to run Pebbles to school."

"Oh, would you? Miranda hasn't wakened and I hesitate to ask Katie's mummy to do the school run though she is a very obliging woman and a *much* safer driver than that wretched girl."

"OK, but I really can't spare the time. If the car's not fixed by this afternoon I'm afraid you'll have to get a taxi to collect Pebbles."

Early on in this funny career I've got, Diana had warned me about being helpful. "Stick ruthlessly to your job description, Briony, my dear. Believe me, people will take advantage once you start running errands."

But, to be fair, the poor old trout looked whacked out with her little adventure and bearing in mind that her child-minding act was already cut to the bone, I felt she would hardly willingly chip away at the few duties still remaining.

Archie scrabbled at the door and I let him in. He shook himself vigorously, spraying muddy raindrops in all directions.

"Can't think what Doris is going to make of all this extra work," Phyllis remarked, which was pretty rich in view of my barely expressed offer to drive her charge to school.

Pebbles choked down her cereal and under Nanny's hawk eye consumed some scrambled egg before being allowed to fall upon her new pet.

Rushing to rinse the glasses before setting off, I took my eyes off their romping just at the wrong moment. The back door swung open and Sexy Pants burst in with a basket of fresh vegetables. Archie flew at his ankle and hung on, snarling like a tiger, the man bawling obscenities and kicking out in all directions. Pebbles screamed and Nanny Cannock rose to her feet, ashen faced. Quick as a flash I moved to empty the bowl of washing-up water over the little runt but the gardener beat me to it, smashing a straight right to the dog's head. Archie let out a yowl and fell on his side, panting, like a pair of bellows, out for the count.

"You've killed him," Pebbles shrieked, turning her fists on the man, a veritable virago.

I pulled her off and shoved Archie under the table where he lay shivering and looking cross-eyed.

"Let's go," I said, bundling Pebbles into her dufflecoat. "We'll take Archie with us. He's quite all right, really he is. You can show us your school."

71

I snapped on the lead and Pebbles dragged the dog outside, her tearful outburst doused by the little tyke's swift recovery.

I turned back to the shocked pair staring at me from the safety of the far side of the kitchen table.

"Look, I'm desperately sorry, Mr – er—"

"Mark," he said, grim as ever.

"It's your trainers. The wretched dog's got a thing about them. He didn't break the skin, did he?"

"Thick socks," he muttered. Phyllis started twittering on about "dangerous dogs" but to my relief the bloke came up trumps, shutting her up with a curt gesture.

"No damage done, Miss Cannock. Feisty beasts, terriers. Good ratters. It was my fault barging in like that. I should have knocked."

I drove out of the yard like a bat out of hell, Pebbles strapped in the back seat and Archie trapped behind the metal dog grille I keep for emergencies. By the time I had dropped her off, the beastly dog had resumed his usual cocky demeanor but, no doubt about it, his respect for Mark had been firmly established by that sock on the jaw. I'd have to watch him in future.

I caught sight of Teresa outside the school with Katie, and the two little girls held hands and raced off across the playground without so much as a goodbye kiss.

"Look, Teresa, may I take a raincheck on

that offer of coffee this morning? It's my first day at work and I'm behind already."

"Of course. Tell you what, we've got a couple of friends staying this weekend. Why don't you join us for supper on Saturday night? We eat late and you should be able to get away by nine. What do you say?"

"Sounds wonderful."

"Where's the Gorgon?" she said as we walked back.

"Her car's on the blink so she says. Mind you she's got a fishy look about her, don't you think? Been with the family too long I expect. Thinks she can get away with murder."

"Carey marked her card ages ago when he employed Wanda."

"I thought Roz was the one who sacked her."

"There was no proof, but—"

I cut in, my mind flashing back to my horrible restless night. "She didn't ill-treat Pebbles, did she?"

"Gosh, no, nothing like that. A classic situation and old as the hills. It was all hushed up, of course. Miss Cannock was accused of pinching the silver."

Eight

I did a quick recce of Tunbridge Wells before collecting the repaired food processor and buying some food. A nice town, not too obviously touristy but at first glance the sort of place to attract retired colonels. Later I had good reason to revise this flip opinion but on first impression the ambience seemed entirely without menace.

Arriving back at ten I hoped to inveigle myself into a private interview with Roz de Taffort when I took up her coffee. There were certain questions to be answered, not to mention the matter of choosing menus and my access to the list of any expected guests. But finding a strange man standing rather helplessly in the kitchen bearing a butler's tray loaded with the remains of breakfast, stopped me in my tracks. Archie growled, but backed off smartly when I booted him under the table, fearing more knock-out right hooks perhaps. But this young man was no gardener. About thirty years old at a guess but very smooth with it.

"Hi. I'm Miranda's friend. Gizmo." He

placed the tray on the table and moved forward, his honeyed drawl straight out of *Gone With the Wind.*

We shook hands and I turned to put away the shopping. Gizmo was far from the type I'd imagine to appeal to Miranda, his tasselled loafers and neat haircut placed him more in the Mormon mould and the exact opposite of Kyle. But why should I care? Miranda at nineteen was hardly old enough to specialize, and presumably the new boyfriend was regarded by the family as "a good influence".

"Miranda's getting dressed," he said. "Doris kindly laid a cloth for us in the TV room – I was dying to see your British breakfast show. Wow!"

I nodded, wondering if, on my first day, I had already got myself into the cleaner's bad books, leaving poor Doris to pander to the house guests. I need not have worried, the amiable soul who trundled into the room dragging a bag of assorted bedlinen for the washer was not one of life's moaners. We hit it off straight away and were well into a dry run of the normal Monday-morning routine in the Barnes household when a delivery boy knocked at the back door. I grabbed Archie and signed for a beautiful basket of orchids addressed to Roz. From one of her Sunday visitors at a guess.

Miranda strolled in and claimed Gizmo

with a proprietorial smoothing of his suede jacket, eyeing Doris and myself cagily. "Come on, Gizmo, let's roll. No lunch today, Briony, Kyle will be taking Mother to the tennis club and we shan't be back till six, eh lover boy?"

He saluted us with an apologetic gesture and allowed himself to be bundled out, the squeal of the Range Rover's tyres on the cobbles of the yard making me look out. Yes, Miranda was driving, wouldn't you know?

I filled the coffee pot and laid a tray for Roz, managing also to tote the basket of orchids and reach her bedroom door without incident. Luckily it was ajar. I coughed and Roz called out, her actor's voice alluring in that breathless stagey manner normal people find a little camp.

"Come in, darling. Coffee! How delicious."

She had obviously just emerged from the bath and, wrapped in a huge towelling robe, her hair damp and clinging to those wonderful cheekbones, she did indeed look every inch a star. I clumsily dumped the orchids on a side table and the card fell on the floor. I slipped it under the saucer and poured her first cup of coffee. Roz sat on the chaise longue, patting the empty seat beside her, all smiles.

"Now, tell me all about yourself, sweetie. With all those boring people hanging round on Sunday we never got a chance to get acquainted, did we?"

I took out my notebook and perched beside her, feeling a bit as though I'd landed a walk-on part in one of those avant-garde productions in which the cast have to invent their own dialogue.

"Briony," I reminded her. "Briony Eastwood. The agency said you need a cook/housekeeper until the New Year. While your regular woman's on leave..." I added, not entirely sure whether Roz or Carey Barnes had made the arrangement.

"Yes, of course." She sipped her coffee, the famous blue gaze unclouded, a good time for me to jump in with both feet I felt.

"If you have a moment, Mrs Barnes, might we discuss menus?"

She nodded, reaching for the florist's card and taking it from the envelope with a little cry of pleasure. I'd have to be quick – this lady's attention span was barely enough to sustain a two-minute take on camera, boredom settling in like a mist between us as I rattled out my suggestions. After a bit she waved me aside, smiling courteously but the curtain had definitely come down.

"I leave all that to you, sweetie. Something light for luncheon if Miranda and I are in – souffles or fish, you know the sort of thing. Miranda is a poor eater, needs coaxing, so delicious little portions are best. Unless my husband is home my daughter and I eat in the TV room about eight, after I've read Pebbles' bedtime story."

"Meat?"

"Oh, yes, but no beef for Pebbles. And Carey insists on organic vegetables wherever possible. Do your best, darling. But I suggest you save the comfort food for weekends – puddings and so on. He loves a clubman's menu, you know, but otherwise..." Her voice thinned and I decided to leave my other queries for another time, no point in flogging a dead horse.

Slightly piqued, I pocketed my notes and left her to it, marching back to the kitchen, suddenly sure that the Barnes' contract was not going to be the walkover I'd envisaged.

Doris had flicked the dining room back into order and cleared the fires. We sat down together in the kitchen at the pine table with our mugs of tea and got to grips with backstairs' gossip.

"Where's Miss Cannock?" I asked.

"Think she went to the village with the bloke from the garridge. He took 'er car off on the break-down lorry and I 'aven't seen hide nor hair of 'er since."

"But she'll be back for lunch?"

"Prob'ly. But likes to bring in her own little fancy bits. Potted shrimps, cartons of nettle soup from the health shop, uses the gas ring in the nursery upstairs. Jennie used to fuss round her, make bits of fish and that. Eats in her room most days." She laughed, her big belly shaking. "No great loss, eh? I finish up here at one. Got my Trevor's dinner to think about."

She tossed a biscuit under the table for Archie who had already cosied up to Doris, marking her down as a soft touch.

"What did you think of Wanda, Doris?"

She stirred her tea, suddenly serious.

"Nice girl that. Really sweet. Pebbles loved her to bits and her English come on smashin' – spoke real posh in the end. Used to save her wages to send money to her old mum at home, would you know! Could have knocked me down with a fevver when she 'opped it overnight like that."

"Did she have a boyfriend?"

"Nah! Well, not one I ever heard tell of. But she *did* have one nice friend, a girl called Lili, works for the vicar in the village. Another foreign girl, Russian or sommat, not sure what. They used to go discoing together weekends. Loved dancing, Wanda did. Lili had the lend of Mrs Barrett's mini so it was ever so convenient."

"Didn't Lili know why she went?"

"No, I'm sure she didn't. The police was asking questions in the village but I heard in the post office Lili got a postcard from Wanda sent from London last month. In their lingo, Mrs Fisher said. She asked the vicar outright if it was from the missing girl and he said yes, but no forwarding address so we was none the wiser. Wanda's keeping her 'ead down if you ask me. Playing for extra time on her visa whatnot. Or there was a bit of a row."

"A quarrel with Roz?"

"Can't pin that on the woman, though I wouldn't put it past her when she's had a few. A nasty side to Mrs Barnes if you're unlucky. No, I think it was Miranda what upset her."

"Really? Why?"

Doris shrugged, deep in thought. "Just my little fancy. Once Miranda got back from America, Wanda changed. Turned very quiet, secretive like. Went off her food an' all, which was a turn up for the book. You should have seen the amount that poor girl could put away when she first come over. Made you wonder if she'd ever seen a square meal before!"

"What makes you think Miranda caused the trouble?"

"I put it all down to jealousy meself. Wanda 'ad been looking after Pebbles for a long time and the kiddie naturally thought the world of her. Miranda come back and tried all ways to edge Wanda out and corner her sister for herself. Bought the little mite silly presents, made no end of a fuss as if she couldn't abide Pebbles liking Wanda best."

"Perhaps Miranda craved affection?"

"Never took no notice of the kiddie *before* she went off, did she? Quite the opposite. Once the new baby arrived six years ago Miranda's nose got put right out of joint, but being the only bird in the nest up till then, and being only a kid herself at the time I suppose it was hard seeing Pebbles gettin' so spoilt. And after that terrible accident Miranda never seemed to *want* no love from nobody, even from her own mother. Showed off something chronic!"

"Smashing up your face at sixteen years of age is traumatic enough. Watching a pretty three-year-old take your place as the centre of attention wouldn't help."

"Mrs Barnes was in no fit state to deal with any tantrums. But don't get me wrong, Miranda was never a vicious teenager like some, not jealous in any cruel way with Pebbles. And make no mistake about it, Briony, she saved her mother's life when that car hit the tree then fell into the river. Dragged the poor woman out and towed her to the bank. Mrs Barnes would have drowned if that brave child hadn't acted like a little heroine. Should have got a medal, she should. And must have been in terrible pain herself for months after. A broken jaw and lost most of her front teeth." Doris grimaced, shaking her head in despair. "A terrible, terrible thing."

I rose to clear the mugs away and we chatted on about tidying the guest rooms. As Pebbles would be home for tea I decided to make some cakes and put together a fresh salmon mousse as a starter for tonight's supper.

After Roz and Kyle had driven off together and Doris's bike had disappeared down the drive, I went upstairs to have a quiet smoke, Archie hopping behind in that jerky way Jack Russells have. It came as a terrible shock to come head on with Phyllis Cannock in my doorway, the old woman looking fussed, bearing my jar of coffee aloft like a password.

"Oh, Briony dear. Caught in the act! I thought you were out and without my little runabout shopping is impossible. Just nipped into your kitchenette to raid your larder. You don't mind, do you?"

"Of course not. Keep it for the present. I prefer tea myself."

"How kind. I *do* like a little coffee after lunch. It's all dash and go once Pebbles is home from school. I thought I'd walk into Northchurch and fetch my car from the garage later – the walk will do me good and Mr Mather said it might be ready at three."

She hurried off, still twittering, and I closed my door. "Borrowing" some coffee from my room hardly seemed her style, especially when there were oodles of supplies to hand in the kitchen downstairs.

I lay on Wanda's bed pondering my options. On Wednesday, I would leave early and spend my day off in London. I needed some advice from Diana. I also wanted to find out a bit more about Phyllis Cannock's dismissal from the Barnes' employ and I felt sure Diana knew more than she was letting on. Stealing silver was all eyewash. What really bothered me was the sound of that child sobbing in the next room, or nearby at the very least. It could only have been Pebbles and if the nanny had lost her temper and I had done nothing to help, I felt criminal for not stepping in.

But Pebbles seemed totally composed, a very together little person, hardly the picture of abuse. And if Cannock did not ring true as a thief, fitting her up as a child tormentor seemed even more bizarre. Well, Diana *might* know something...

I jolted up, my mouth dry. Jesus! In all this conjecture, I'd forgotten my own guilty secret: the illicit Ecstacy tabs taped under Archie's bed! Getting nabbed hoarding drugs would do my career no good at all. There was nothing for it, I'd have to take Wanda's cache back to my own flat in Chelsea. It would be safer there. No need for explanations, no direct involvement. After all, who would believe that I'd found the stuff in Wanda's room?

I could also show Diana and see how that little bombshell affected her opinion of the sainted au pair. So much for agency character guarantees! No doubt about it, appearances could be deceptive. Everyone who knew Wanda insisted she was spotless as a virgin and anyone looking at Phyllis Cannock saw an elderly spinster with years of loneliness behind her and genteel poverty ahead. But maybe both impressions were wrong. Perhaps Cannock had hidden the drugs in Wanda's room for someone else. Perhaps it wasn't a spoonful of coffee she had been searching for?

Nine

Miranda told me Gizmo was staying all week. The American was certainly a buffer zone between Miranda and Roz whose relations were no more and no less than the rocky road trod by most mothers and teenage girls. Gizmo had a sweetening effect on the whole household and I reassessed my first poor impression of Roz's elder daughter. Miranda was, in fact, a nice kid who, at a guess, had had a rough ride of it.

Even Phyllis Cannock was entirely charmed, allowing Gizmo to take over Pebbles' school run in the mornings while her wretched boneshaker continued to be under repair. I sped round the house like a whirling dervish those first couple of days, determined to get my act together before taking a day off. But it was vital to slip back to London soon and, so as to cause no aggro, I loaded up the fridge with goodies which Miranda assured me she would be happy to heat up.

Apart from Gizmo, our only other regular visitor was Kyle Chapman who was practically under full contract to Roz and certainly earned every cent. He bullied her gently to get out of the house, dragging her off to the gym and other healthy pursuits, and generally succeeded in keeping her off the booze at least until happy hour. Kyle slid in and out of the house at will and I suspect had his own key. At any event he seemed determined to keep out of my orbit and when he joined the others for lunch, kept his gaze closely on his plate as I served at table. Roz's insistence that Miranda ate like a bird was a load of old cobblers – or perhaps the boys' company tickled her appetite – because she certainly polished off the meals I prepared and dived into the cakes and pastries laid out for tea in the library each afternoon.

I drove off before seven on Wednesday morning and as I dumped my gear inside the door of my flat I felt as if I'd been away for weeks. Archie fussed about, sniffing round like a truffle hound, making sure no other beastie had fouled his patch. I took him straight off for a run in the park, gratefully breathing in the traffic fumes like all the perfumes of Arabia.

Battersea Park is my favourite park by far, bounded as it is at one end by the fairytale Albert Bridge and, as a complete contrast, by the brutal outline of the power station at the other. A real hotchpotch of a place with a lake, geese, mini zoo and the most outlandish addition to date, a pagoda tended by Buddhist monks in their saffron robes.

Archie and I jogged past the bandstand, watching the toddlers feeding the ducks and enjoying the panorama of the river craft gliding by. By the time I got back home I felt restored, the edginess of the past few days dissipated by the fake country landscape of a city pleasure ground. This contrary comfort must indicate something about me that has some deep psychological significance if only I could decide what it was. Ah well, it at least goes to show that a walk in the park is cheaper than a shot of Prozac.

Archie settled in his bed after that and I made a couple of phone calls while the coffee was brewing. Jonny Lusty assured me the new tenants had moved into Tite Street and were well pleased, and we arranged to meet for an early supper after work.

"Leonardo's?"

"Sure. But I'll have to get back tonight," I insisted, "I don't want to take my eye off the ball too soon."

"Roz de Taffort playing Drama Queen?"

"No. She's so vague I practically run the show single-handed. But Carey's coming down on Thursday night to make a long weekend of it and it's not an easy place to run."

"Give it up then, Bri. Come and play house with me. I could do with a few square meals."

I put him right on that score and grinned to myself as I tripped round the flat sorting out some extra woollies. Since the storm the weather had settled into a cold snap, the skies leaden, nothing like the kindness of usual October days and nights.

Diana greeted me with a raised eyebrow, waiting for a flurry of complaints. I reassured her and gave a run-down of my first few days at Kington House before voicing my concerns about the nanny situation.

"Where's this new au pair you promised me?"

"Hold on! What's the rush? I'm still sorting out a few possibles. But most of the girls prefer living in town. More fun all round."

"Wanda Whatsit seemed to find living in the country fairly amusing."

I slammed the packet of Es on her desk and watched Diana turn saucer-eyed as the stash of illicit drugs I had recovered from one of her most innocent employees was revealed. She didn't argue. Diana knows me better.

"What are you going to do, Briony?"

"Nothing. Getting involved with the law is never a good idea. Anyway Wanda's not really missing, you know. Her friend in the village got a postcard."

"I still don't like the idea of one of my girls running loose in London, getting herself on a missing-person's file, not to mention outstaying her visa. Can't you get this friend of hers to discreetly cough up her address? Then I'll track Wanda down and get the silly girl on the first plane out before she gets herself into more trouble."

"I'll try if you like but it's a slim hope – Lili told her people Wanda didn't give an address."

Diana's laugh was brittle as cracked ice. "These foreign girls stick together like glue and the Eastern Europeans are absolutely terrified of the police. If Wanda knew the authorities had her in their sights she'd just dig in. A friendly approach from you would do the trick. Tell Lili Wanda's not in any trouble – yet! Tell her we'll sort out any debts and get her safely home. Roaming round London, a naive girl like Wanda could end up on the streets."

Diana lobbed the Ecstacy tabs to me like a vicious round of passing the parcel, and briskly shuffled a sheaf of CVs on her desk. "I'll contact Carey Barnes at home on Friday and suggest a couple of possibles from this lot – he'll probably want to interview them himself. Anyway, what's wrong with this old bird who's filling in? Sounds perfect to me."

I outlined my anxieties about Pebbles, giving Diana a dramatic re-run of the crying in the nursery which had woken me in the night.

"Oh, tosh! I don't believe it. Cruelty to a six-year-old's practically impossible to sweep under the carpet."

"The nanny's been snooping about in my room. And the reason she was sacked was, just for the record, pinching the silver."

"Well, she's not one of mine," Diana swiftly put in. "Briony, do you really think the child's being mistreated? Sometimes these old-fashioned nannies are over strict but kids these days can turn on the waterworks to order. You should hear some of the stories my girls tell me about the ghastly little toddlers out there!"

"You haven't heard anything bad about this Nanny Cannock then? Carey didn't say anything when he booked Wanda?"

Diana stared at the Barnes' file before her, biting her lip. "Nothing specific. Tell you what though, I'll mention it when I speak to him. Ask him if he's worried about the little girl."

"Don't bring me into it! If I've got to work there for another three months I don't want to get a knife in my back for telling tales." But Diana is an expert at oblique questions. A breezy general enquiry would fool even a professional TV interrogator like Barnes. She promised to give me a call if anything turned up and I, in turn, promised to shake down Wanda's friend Lili and ring her back.

I left the agency feeling quite queasy, the undercurrents of what had seemed a normal job giving me the squits. Something off-course was called for. I flagged down a taxi and took myself to Joe Reilly's betting shop where a crop of new jokes was always on offer. I only just caught him. He was on his way out for a pint and a sandwich at the Queen.

The place was as dimly lit as ever, a row of regulars hogging the bar stools and back-ground music supplied by the wheeze and clatter of a pinball machine being given a pummelling by two yobs in baseball caps.

"Well, babby, what's the trouble?" Professionally calculating the stamina of odds-on favourites had sharpened Reilly's perceptions no end.

"This job at the Barnes' place," I mumbled. "There's something funny going on and I can't put my finger on it." I gave Joe a brief rehash of my nebulous fears and waited for his shout of derision. But he sipped his beer, eyeing me like I was a filly that might not, in fact, be spooking at shadows.

"Have you heard anything, Joe?"

"Wouldn't pass it on to anyone else but Fancy McGill had a big payout off the Tote at Epsom Saturday and we ended up celebrating his win at the bar. I nudged him on a bit. Asked him what he was doing with that TV celebrity I'd seen him with in here. Got quite gabby for a man who makes his living on the dark side. He don't know about you working for Barnes as well, of course, or that you and me are mates into the bargain. And so I kept the whisky flowing and let old Fancy ramble on."

"And?"

"You know why he's working for Barnes?"

"Back-up pictures for some sleazy TV scoop?"

"Well off the mark, Bridey! No, Fancy wasn't hired for that sort of dirt. Much closer to home and if you're living under the same roof as that slimy bastard I don't want my girly to walk in blindfold. You watch your step."

"Carey's employing McGill for *himself?*"

Joe nodded, deadly serious.

"And for the one thing I can't abide. McGill showed me a bundle of poison-pen letters Barnes's been getting for the last three weeks."

"At the TV centre?"

"And his flat."

I whistled, not wishing to spoil Joe's story but his supposed "news" was something Jonny Lusty had already let slip. "And McGill's trying to trace the sender on the QT?"

"Barnes don't want the police involved, do he? Mud sticks. So Fancy reckons this stuff in the letters is right on the button. Stands to reason, if a few bits of paper put the wind up a pro like Barnes so easy – your so-called Mr Clean, who blows the whistle on all them thieving MPs, is being lined up for blackmail. Bloke who's putting the bite on, 'as found out about his party games and means to cash in. Barnes ain't got that sort of money himself and he can't ask his wife who is the one with all the dosh. He told McGill a divorce is the last thing he can afford. If it wasn't such a shitty business I could feel quite sorry for the poor sod."

"Barnes has been cheating on his wife?"

Joe sighed, looking at me as if I was some sort of cretin.

"You mean he's gay?" I floundered about, skewered by Joe's contempt, and tried

92

another tack.

"Do you think McGill's on to the sender of these threats?"

"Can't say. But in Fancy's line of business a bullet in the back of the head's the only likely payoff for a blackmailer."

I tried to laugh, but it came out like a nervous twitter.

"You've been reading too much Dick Francis, Joe!"

"McGill showed me the bloody evidence, girl. Barnes likes little girls. Your boss is one of them fucking paedophiles!"

Ten

I didn't believe it, of course I didn't. Well, at first I did. But Fancy McGill's "evidence" was merely a bundle of anonymous accusations and who could blame a TV personality like Barnes for preferring to keep it quiet? Poison-pen letters were never true, were they? Just the malicious ramblings of someone with a grudge. Elevating the sender into extortionist was just the whisky talking, McGill trying to impress his bookmaker with the gravity of the job. It occurred to me Barnes wasn't so much exercised by the contents of the horrible letters as the fact that they had been delivered to his flat above Lusty's estate agency, the tenancy of which it was important to him to keep secret. With the sort of investigative journalism Carey Barnes made infamous, perhaps having a place where no one could get at you was vital.

These musings carried me through my date with Jonathan but I said nothing about my conversation with Joe Reilly because any mention of Barnes' name was guaranteed to put my current squeeze in a nasty mood. Anyway, it was only scandal. Wasn't it?

When he took me home, the night was still young and I asked him in for coffee just to be sociable. One thing led to another, of course, and the upshot was I wasn't on the road back to Northchurch till six in the morning. Still, it had been worth it. I'd had my first decent night's sleep for days and arrived back at Kington House raring to go.

Mark was already at work in the hot-houses, the lights blazing for some reason. I decided to make my peace with the guy later and persuade him to give up some of his delicacies for the kitchen over the weekend. In my experience head gardeners were a touchy lot, keen to show off but only on their terms, dog in the manger the rest of the time.

The routine at Kington had quickly fallen into place, a stage of any contract which makes my job so much easier. Doris was a godsend: reliable, hardworking and unfailingly cheerful. I kept a close eye on Pebbles but detected no underlying anxieties and, once her car was repaired, Phyllis Cannock expanded like a full-blown rose, her awful nursery clichés ringing round the house with predictable banality. My relations with the woman had become distinctly frigid and now that Miranda and Gizmo were home, I persuaded Roz to allow Pebbles to have tea with them all in the library every afternoon. Cannock hated this diminution of her status and Roz made it patently obvious that the nanny's presence was not welcome. Pebbles loved being with the grown-ups of course and Cannock's complaints about the child's table manners being spoilt by Gizmo's all-American informality fell on deaf ears.

Carey was not expected until after dinner on Thursday night but I prepared some cold duck and a side plate of salad and baby vegetables in case he felt peckish. After Reilly's appalling assertions about the man the prospect of coming face to face with him over breakfast next morning filled me with apprehension but I shoved the wretched business to the back of my mind, reassuring myself with the knowledge that when Jonny and I had searched Barnes' London flat there hadn't been so much as a dirty video tucked away. Mind you there was always the Internet ... But if, by any chance, he *had* been compiling some undercover research for a programme on child abuse, the only place he would keep such material would be at his pied-à-terre safe from the prying eyes of other journalists at his office or his wife and young daughters at home. Even so, I could not pretend that Reilly's bombshell did not affect my view of the man. At the very least I would be watching his attitude towards Pebbles.

I prepared a gourmet feast for Saturday night, Gizmo's Last Supper as it were and an occasion to impress my boss with the quality service he was getting for his money. Next day the entire family was invited out for lunch followed by a trip on a cabin cruiser moored at Brighton marina, and even Phyllis Cannock was taking herself off, which left me a free Sunday I had not been expecting.

Before the brood left the dining room that evening I laid coffee cups and liqueurs in the library and checked the fire. It all looked very *Country Life* and I was feeling thoroughly pleased with myself. Dinner had gone well, the game ragout earning a charming compliment from Roz who, for once, seemed entirely sober. On her good days one could understand the enduring appeal of an actress who had never been much more than a glamorous icon but whose looks and husky delivery could make the most God awful screenplay sing.

Passing the downstairs loo on my way back to the kitchen, I was distracted by the muted sound of retching. I stood by the door. No mistake. Someone was being violently sick in there. The lavatory flushed and I heard water cascading in to the hand-bowl for several minutes as if Lady Macbeth herself was washing her hands. I moved away, turning aside as the door opened, curious to know whose stomach had been churned by my Michelin-starred blowout.

Miranda emerged, white faced, wiping her mouth with her hand, sweat glistening on her forehead. She pushed past me, blood-shot eyes full of distrust, her breath fresh with minty toothpaste, and ran back to the dining room. Suddenly, the penny dropped. The girl's extreme slenderness despite the hearty appetite? Why hadn't I twigged it before? Miranda was bulimic. The only way the silly fool thought she could maintain her model figure was by throwing up after every binge.

Did Roz know? Unlikely. Roz de Taffort was too taken up with her own appearance to notice any eating disorder in her daughter. And if she were told, was Roz psychologically strong enough to be of any support to the poor kid? Miranda was slowly starving herself to death and she had no one to turn to. A mother who was obsessed with her own looks and a stepfather – if what Fancy McGill had told Joe Reilly of his own suspicions regarding the truth of the allegations in the poison-pen letters were correct – who was possibly obsessed with Mirandas pretty little half-sister? It was not a healthy set-up by any standards.

I waited till they settled in the library and got the go-ahead to hop off for my own evening out with my new-found friends, Teresa George and her husband, the vet. I shut Archie in my room and wished I had a key to the lock but, if Nanny Cannock resumed her perambulations, disturbing Archie's dreams would cause enough racket to put off a professional burglar let alone a grey-haired kleptomaniac. At least the Es were safely out of harm's reach in London.

The Georges' home proved to be a rambling timber-framed cottage with outbuildings plus a modern surgery and car park added on at one end. The rooms were blazing with light and the curtains open, giving the Northchurch dog walkers plenty to gawp at. Teresa George was just my sort of woman, not over-fussed about tidiness or germs – dust and dog hairs lying everywhere.

Teresa wore baggy harem pants and a Mexican shirt, all fancy embroidery and little tassels, a sort of United Nations outfit, not the usual hostess gown one finds in the home counties. Holding a glass of wine in one hand and a ciggie in the other, she swept me straight into the sitting room before I'd even got a chance to toss my coat on to the pile on the settle in the hall. Two dogs of undefined breed lumbered up, dribbling over my precious boots and gently barging me in the crotch. Teresa introduced me all round, her husband last of all, a giant of a man with ham-like fists, just the bloke to have around in a cattle stampede, an unlikely enough event in rural Sussex, but then Northchurch was full of surprises.

They had kindly waited supper for me, Teresa explaining my working-girl status, and we sat down almost immediately. If Teresa was a lousy housekeeper she was certainly a brilliant cook and it was great to have someone waiting on me for a change.

After an initial skirmish with my fellow guests who were eager to know if the fabulous Rosalind de Taffort was *really* as beautiful as her pictures, we dug in. Once the first course was cleared and we were each fully occupied dissecting Teresa's stuffed poussins, talk became more intimate.

The elderly man sitting on my right had been introduced as Bernard Froud, an antiques dealer from Heathersfield, a nearby village.

"How interesting," I said, admiring his beautifully manicured fingers deftly deboning the chicken. "Furniture?"

"Not any more. I've been running things down for the last year or two, semi-retirement, you know. I mostly specialise in expensive bric-a-brac these days. A bit of insurance assessment on the side, valuations for clients. All helps pay the bills and I still cover auctions, sometimes bidding for clients. It's nice to see a bit of the country away from the stockbroker belt."

"Looking for bargains?"

"Sadly such things come to light very seldom, Briony. People are convinced every boot sale item's worth a mint since that *Antiques Roadshow* became popular viewing."

"Lovely to move around though. That's what I like about my job – don an apron and see the world!"

He laughed, a decent full-blooded guffaw, not the genteel response I'm used to hearing when serving at table. I gave the man my full attention, taking in the fine linen peeping from his jacket cuff, the white hair, thinning at the temples, carefully distributed.

"Country auctions are my weakness," he

said. "Drive miles to view a house sale. Full of generations of junk for the most part, but what telling junk! Breaks your heart to see an old place taken apart like that, the buyers pawing everything like hyenas. Me included," he ruefully added. "Last really big job I did was, funnily enough, the de Taffort estate sale in North Wales. Several years ago now. Wonderful old manor house."

"You mean Roz's family home?"

He nodded. "Rosalind's brother died of leukaemia and the old couple passed away within six months of each other. Tragic. Your current lady of the house was at the height of her career, no way interested in taking over."

"There was no other heir?"

"No one. And after tax I imagine the estate was hardly paying its way. Best all round to sell up, absentee landlords are a disaster. For myself I was only interested in the porcelain but I was bidding on behalf of another dealer, a friend of mine who has a shop in the Lanes, Brighton you know, and a pitch at Bermondsey Market at dawn – a terrible trap for Japanese tourists," he added with a chuckle.

"So you had a good look at the de Taffort inheritance?"

"Oh, yes. We're a nosy bunch and the old touts like myself all know each other, meet

101

up on view days like an old boys' reunion."

"Roz de Taffort need hardly have pursued her career then, even if she hadn't had the accident?"

He sobered. "An exceedingly wealthy young woman in her own right and the last of a handsome line. Rosalind kept back most of the family silver as you are no doubt aware. A real cleaning headache for you, my dear, with no butler to ease the strain."

"There is silver but I've only seen it once. Roz keeps it locked away, says she prefers a china service and I'm the last to argue."

Bernard sipped his wine, searching my expression as if for an assay mark. "I have a particular interest I must admit. I'd like to drool over the de Taffort silver again. A set of eighteenth-century salvers were particularly fine I seem to remember."

He was fishing. Maybe thinking I had some influence with my employers, could put in a word for him perhaps?

"Why not suggest a re-valuation?" I asked. "I'm sure insurance claims are under-assessed ninety per cent of the time and break-ins in this area must be a terrific problem."

"The de Taffort salvers went missing two or three years ago as it happens. I was fortunate to be able to help recover them."

In moments of excitement my voice deserts me and "Really?" came out in a squeak.

"The friend I mentioned phoned me about some stuff he'd been offered in the half-light at Bermondsey one morning. The place does most of its business before breakfast, of course, dealers mostly, but the word has gone out that there are treats to be found, stolen items going for a song. Very unlikely, of course," he said smoothly.

I sat bug-eyed waiting for the old chap to elaborate, feeling guilty about the woman on my left who had been totally abandoned since I became mesmerised by Bernard Froud.

"You were saying – about the de Taffort salvers. They'd been stolen?"

"Not exactly. No report had been made so the stuff was not on any police handout, but my friend knew I had examined the collection at the de Taffort sale and he didn't want to put his hand in the fire and be accused of handling stolen goods."

"But you recognised it?"

"Unmistakable. Anyway, the salvers bore the de Taffort crest. I took them off to show Rosalind and explained my friend's dilemma. She bought them back, double the price, and insisted I took a generous commission to boot."

"And the one who sold them to your friend? An elderly person? I've heard rumours..."

"Oh, no – absolutely off target there,

Briony. The fence was no more than a girl –
acting on someone else's behalf, of course.
A cat's paw. My pal Tommy remembers her
well, a scrawny little piece with an ortho-
dontic brace like a horse's bit. She could
hardly speak for the amount of metal in her
mouth."

The woman on my other side tapped my
arm, interrupting politely to ask me to settle
a bet with Teresa: my secret of a really
infallable souffle. I was forced to abandon
Bernard, stuttering about oven tempera-
tures, my mind whirling with the awful
injustice of poor old Phyllis Cannock's
indictment. Had no one even told her that
the missing silver had been recovered? Had
no one ever apologised for tossing her out
under suspicion of theft, allowing the slan-
derous accusations to fester unchallenged
all these years?

The rest of the evening sped by, my
thoughts in turmoil. As I stood on the doorstep making my farewells, Teresa pulled
me aside and whispered, "A word of advice
to Pebbles' nanny if you wouldn't mind.
Katie's class have been struck by nits." She
giggled. "The photographer's assistant
combed all the little girls' hair for their
group picture using the same comb. Head
lice are desperately catching but the school
don't want to make a scandal of it. Makes
you laugh really. As if nits are socially

restricted to council-house children only. Try and get the Gorgon to be sensible about it, would you, Briony? Keep an eye out without panicking the child. You know how horrible kids can be with each other. I heard Katie tearfully asking Ted if she'd have to wear a flea collar like the cat!"

Eleven

Archie has perfected his favourite sport: ratcatching. If he were a golfer his handicap would be phenomenal. A spin-off from this was the hysteria caused when he laid a corpse at Phyllis's feet at the breakfast table on Tuesday morning. I threw him outside but, undeterred, he followed it up by dumping a dead frog on the doormat. Pebbles, beside herself with glee, is naturally delighted at the beastly dog's prowess.

"Don't you have any farm cats to keep down the vermin?" I muttered. "You can't expect a place like this to escape rats, Phyllis, not with chickens scattering corn everywhere."

"Jennie Thomas used to keep a tabby but

it never caught so much as a fieldmouse."

"Well, I'm desperately sorry. Archie's a holy terror with his hunting. Rabbits especially. I'll try to keep an eye on him, shut him in the scullery at mealtimes."

She still looked rather white, eyeing me with scant forgiveness as she dabbed at her lips with her napkin. "Come along, Pebbles dear. Go and clean your teeth. We don't want to be late for school, do we?"

Doris appeared just then, tossing her mac on top of the washing machine as I was carrying the dead rat by the tail to put in the dustbin out of Archie's reach. She roared with laughter, tickled pink by Pebbles' unstoppable re-telling of poor Nanny's awful screeching at the breakfast table. But it's no joke. Imagine the hoo-ha if he had presented his prize to Roz?

Since the weekend the household has thinned – Miranda sloping off with Gizmo for a few days in London, and Carey flying to Prague on an assignment. I have become quite a fan of his, switching on the late-night news in the hope of catching one of his investigations.

Carey Barnes comes across very well, his manner authoritative but with undeniable sex appeal, the perfect foil to the smudgy politicians he is generally grilling. Heaven knows what sort of salary he commands, a bloody sight more than an agency cook for sure. Even so, according to Joe Reilly's informant, my current boss is not so flush that he dares jeopardise his marriage, even if the contents of the poison-pen letters are totally without foundation. From my own observations, he seems a very caring and protective husband, even willing to indulge Roz's need for masculine attention to the extent of paying a gigolo like Kyle Chapman to keep her company. Perhaps the Barnes' love affair was not so very red-blooded after all, or maybe, over the years, his passion had been channelled into his career: the wife in the country, however beautiful and starry, becoming something of a bore.

At coffee time, the only chink of light in the twilight of Roz's day when I am likely to get any sensible answers, I slyly winkled out a little information. The amazing thing was that she was entirely unaware of the existence of Carey's flat above Lusty's estate agency, her response so transparent that I am certain she has nothing to hide.

"Does Miranda stay with Mr Barnes in London?" I asked. "If I should need to telephone her urgently?"

"Oh, no. Carey always stays at his club. It's more convenient as his hours are so erratic and if I need to speak to him I can always get him on his mobile phone. Wonderful invention – no pussyfooting with switchboard girls! Miranda's with Gizmo. I'll write down his number if you like. Such a charming young man, isn't he? Does Miranda the world of good. He's trying to get her a job in fashion with a friend of his in the rag trade. I've asked her to chase up the agency about a new au pair while she's in town, Cannock really gives me the pip these days."

"Miss Cannock was Miranda's nanny I gather."

"Well, yes. Passed on from my cousin Sonia but Cannock was more on the ball twenty years ago and I was working, of course. She looked after Miranda from a baby – I hardly got a look in. That's what's so nice being home all the time with Pebbles."

"But Miranda doesn't seem to like Miss Cannock these days, does she?" I ventured.

Roz laughed, tossing her hair in a practised twirl worthy of a shampoo commercial. I've noticed that with people like Rosalind de Taffort. Every waking moment's a performance – as if they're never really off stage at all. It must be very exhausting. She jotted down an address and telephone number and passed it over.

"Raphael?" I queried.

"You didn't really think his name was Gizmo, did you? Hilton Raphael III. Killing, isn't it?"

I left the room and closed the door, hearing Roz switch on the TV while waiting for Kyle to clock on. I glanced at the scrap of paper in my hand. Chranston Mews. Funny that. Gizmo's pad was only a stone's throw from my mother's flat in Tite Street. Small world.

On Wednesday I decided to skip a return trip to Chelsea and catch up on that little investigation Diana had dumped on me. Kyle was driving Roz and her friends over to Henley for lunch and would be out all day, leaving only Nanny Cannock on duty. Since the antique dealer's revelations at Teresa's supper party on Saturday night I had made a real effort to be nicer to Phyllis. She *might* have nicked the blasted silver and bullied Miranda into fencing it for her in Bermondsey Market but pinning the blame on the hapless nanny just didn't ring true. On what grounds had she come under suspicion in the first place? Then again, why would Miranda steal from her own mother? It wasn't as if the child was kept short of pocket money, thoroughly indulged most likely, especially after that horrendous accident.

I began to concoct possible scenarios.

Cannock had been brought back as nursery nurse to look after Pebbles as a baby and until the missing silver débâcle had presumably been well treated. But why would anyone assume an old family retainer would steal from them? A lack of alternative suspects presumably. Even so ... And once Roz guessed from old Froud's information who *had* been toting the stuff round Bermondsey Market, why wasn't poor old Phyllis openly exonerated? A callous move to protect Miranda? Even now, the go-between, Bernard Froud, had no inkling who the nameless skinny kid in the dental brace had been so Roz could have decided to let sleeping dogs lie. Maybe she wasn't as clueless as she pretended. Maybe Roz guessed the reason Miranda needed a lot of money all of a sudden, had discovered the girl's continuing dependence on painkillers. Had the child become hooked after months of medication? It would not be beyond the realms of possibility that she had pinched the silver to finance a drug habit. The girl's damaged ego after the accident and my own conclusions about a possible personality defect lurking there behind the bulimia, didn't exactly erase any doubts. Poor kid. A teenager unable to smile for weeks on end, her mother out of it owing to her own injuries and, to top it all, jealousy of a baby sister fostering an appalling lack of self-confidence.

If Roz never confided in Carey about her worries and the discovery that Miranda had been involved in the theft and simply let it ride, the official scenario would read: (i) Cannock stole the silver in a menopausal state of anxiety about her future retirement and (ii) Roz bought it back through a local dealer without the embarrassment of police involvement. If Joe Reilly was assessing the odds I'd bet he would back Roz to go the full distance: that she had never even confronted Miranda with the fact that her criminal skirmish had been revealed by an unlucky mischance and, if so, Carey also would be left in the dark. Trouble was, the elderly nanny got to carry the can and by a freaky conversation with Bernard I was the only person apart from Roz to twig Miranda's little sideline. No wonder the girl wanted rid of Phyllis Cannock. In her shoes the guilt would make me break out in a sweat every time I set eyes on the old biddy.

Since hearing Miranda vomiting in the downstairs cloakroom on Saturday night I had been mulling over certain things which had bothered me – food vanishing from the fridge, a bottle of very expensive mouthwash hidden behind the curtain in the scullery washhouse, Miranda's regular disappearances after meals and her insistence that the bedroom light remain on all night despite Phyllis Cannock's scathing rebukes about such childish behaviour. I had pumped Teresa about it, a fount of all knowledge in things medical, naturally without letting slip the reason for my curiosity.

"Ah well, bulimia's a fashionable thing

with teenagers but it's a pernicious habit to get into and can ruin one's teeth. Do you know, these silly girls – and it's nearly always girls, of course – can throw up after a binge as much as two and a half hours later? It's impossible to keep track of a kid with a problem like that. I pray such stupidity will have run its course before Katie gets to be figure-conscious."

I walked Archie down to the village after lunch and sought out the rectory. The vicar was out attending to parish duties his secretary told me but perhaps he could telephone me later? I muttered my excuses but shuffled about on the doorstep like a sinner wrestling with inner demons and the woman insisted I came inside. She showed me into his study, a perfect shambles of a room with papers and books strewn everywhere. I declined a seat, crushing Archie into a stranglehold in my arms, wishing now I'd let Diana do her own dirty work.

The vicar's wife bustled in, a horse-faced woman in a pleated skirt and Alice hairband, a Sloany style I imagine she adopted after boarding school and had retained comfortably ever after. She stood in the doorway, waving a hand towards the sofa.

"I'm Patricia Barrett. Take a pew. Gilly says you wanted a private word with David."

"Er, no – not exactly. My name's Briony

Eastwood. I'm the temporary housekeeper at Kington House." I shifted some books off the sofa and sat down as I was told, Archie still clamped to my chest.

"Have the Barnes' girls *both* gone?"

"The regular cook's on maternity leave, but it was the au pair I wanted to ask Mr Barrett about. Wanda. Your girl, Lili, was a special friend I understand."

"Well, yes and no," she answered, her eyes riveted on Archie's ominously bared teeth.

I produced one of Diana's business cards and passed it over. "Mrs Winterton at the agency is worried about Wanda's disappearance. She suggested I ask around, find out a little about Wanda's behaviour while she was living in the village. You see, Mrs Winterton prides herself on the reliability of her staff and feels responsible for Wanda leaving the Barnes in the lurch like that. I wondered if the vicar could throw some light on it? Some local gossip, to put it bluntly."

"Ah. Well, I don't really think David could help you there. We see very little of Lili's friends, though when Wanda popped in on the days they went to college I thought she seemed a thoroughly nice young woman. Less flighty than our Lili, who came to us through a Christian charity and, between ourselves, Mrs Eastwood, is rather dazzled by the bright lights of Brighton."

I nodded, saying nothing, and in the

silence one could almost hear Patricia Barrett's mind going clickety-click as her eyes darted between Archie and the business card in her hand.

"Would you like to speak to Lili?" she said at last. "She's in the kitchen. Ironing."

"If it's not disturbing you."

"Come then," she said briskly. "Follow me!" I leapt up and Archie fell to the floor in a flurry of fat legs and we marched along behind, me feeling for all the world like a first former being put on detention by the head girl. There must be a special finishing school for vicars' wives, "Cheery but Wary" being the school motto. Still, Mrs Barrett did have enough tact to leave us alone and Archie dropped his Rottweiler act and set out to charm the pants off the Barrett's au pair.

Lili proved to be a real eyeful, a yellow miniskirt skimming long tanned legs, her wide smile and bouncy boobs clearly a winning factor in the popularity stakes. The Northchurch vicarage must seem a tight fit after the "bright lights of Brighton" as Patricia Barrett put it.

Later, as I closed the garden gate carefully, I had to admit that Wanda was proving more of an enigma than ever. Lili's thumbnail sketch of her friend produced a mental photofit which was more like a hologram, two images superimposed, changing with the light. One picture showed Wanda as fun-loving, mad about pop music and clothes: in short, a girl discovering western culture in the raw and loving every minute. The other, a serious person whose only real confidante was a religious nut called Leonie who frequented the disco bars along the coast and whose burning crusade was to save the souls of the kids bopping their nights away at raves.

"Could you take me there, Lili? Introduce me to Leonie?"

She giggled as she clocked my outfit, her teeth as white and as perfect as Miranda's horrendously expensive dental replacements.

"I don't *always* wear this working gear," I retorted. "I need to talk to this Leonie person. Don't you worry about Wanda, Lili? Aren't you afraid for your friend out there in the cold all alone?"

A shutter came down. She shrugged, turning back to her ironing.

"You people don't know what it's like for us," she said. "We have to take what we can."

"But won't you help me? Help find Wanda?"

Lili sighed, resting the hot iron in its cradle, her eyes hooded. She turned to me. "OK. Leave your number." I thrust my own business card in her hand. It was swiftly pocketed just as Patricia Barrett bustled in, all smiles, and deftly showed me the door. A clean exit. A manoeuvre vicars' wives are really good at. It was the best I could hope for.

Twelve

Miranda stayed in London until almost the end of the month and when she did return Gizmo was still firmly in tow. And they hadn't been wasting their time either: the pair of them had cooked up a real bombshell.

"We're having a Hallowe'en party, Briony," she said, grinning away like crazy, thrilled at the prospect of running her own show at last. "It was Gizmo's idea. Don't worry, you won't have to do a thing – we've already booked mummy's caterers."

"Gray and Derry?"

"All fixed. Ma thinks it's a wonderful idea. It's to be a *big* party for *everyone*, starting at six with a bonfire in the garden and a barbeque for Pebbles' chums and their parents. Mark can keep an eye on the fireworks. Apple bobbing, trick or treat, pumpkin heads – the lot! And when the kiddiwinks trot off home about eight, the *real* party begins. Non-stop horror movies in the library, charades, a clairvoyant booked to do Tarot readings and masses of party games! And dressing up, of course. I've already invited Teresa George, her tribe are coming as the Addams family. Won't it be fantastic? You'll join in too, won't you, Briony? Bring your broomstick. You won't have to worry about a single thing – the caterers will be here all day Friday rigging up the decorations – cobwebs and black candles and things. And the food's going to be absolutely *ghoulish!*"

Finally she stopped to draw breath, her eyes shining, and, despite my own misgivings about anything under Miranda's control, she did seem to have planned it down to the last detail. And there was always Gizmo. A steadying influence.

"Derry and Gray are very efficient," I conceded. "But what does Mr Barnes think about all this? Does he know what to expect? He's due home Friday night and the party will already be swinging by then. You won't burn the house down will you, Miranda?" I quipped, only half in fun.

She grabbed my arm, laughing like a hyena, unaware that Phyllis Cannock had entered the kitchen, her face like thunder, the hairstyle most definitely askew. It *was* a wig.

117

Miranda spun round, her mood suddenly dark as if the electricity had been switched off.

"Your mother has just told me," Phyllis said, fairly sparking with rage.

"About our Hallowe'en party?"

"You know very well what I'm talking about, miss. That girl you brought back from London – the one you've installed in the gatehouse. The new au pair. Your mother mentioned it in passing as if giving me just days to pack my bags and be off was of no consequence. 'You can leave on Sunday, Cannock.' Just like that! Treating me like this week's refuse collection. It's all your doing, Miranda, egged on by that wicked mother of yours. A pair of harpies, both of you."

I tried to intervene, holding out my hand to the distraught woman, but she silenced me with a freezing glance before stomping out of the room, the heavy tread of her brogues on the back stairs echoing in our dumbstruck silence. Gizmo breezed in, guileless as a pet rabbit, unaware of the showdown he had only just escaped.

"Whew!" Miranda tried to laugh it off but I stood my ground, waiting for her explanation. "It's true, Briony. Ma just couldn't wait any longer for your agency woman to come up with Wanda's replacement. Gizmo found this girl working for an office cleaning company he's involved with. She's perfect. Italian, I think."

"And she's had experience of child minding? Surely Mr Barnes would wish to interview her before she's let loose on Pebbles?"

"Don't be stuffy, Briony. Maria's perfectly lovely. She can get to know Pebbles before the party. The sooner old Cannock clears out the better." The girl's natural ebullience bubbled up at the thought of the Hallowe'en junket and she was back on track, dragging Gizmo out into the garden, her excited plans for the tricking out of the little oriental teahouse piping away in the distance like the twitter of starlings.

I made myself a pot of tea and was sitting dejectedly mulling over this sudden turn of events as Doris trundled in with the vacuum cleaner, Archie tacked on her heels, hoping to share her elevenses. I filled her mug and broke the news.

"Well, I never! Never liked the old woman but fair do's. They could have given her more notice. Five days! But people like them never think the poor bloody workers got feelings. Just lately Miranda's got no thought for people if you ask me. And Pebbles – she ain't exactly been considered, 'as she?"

"Miranda just didn't think. I expect Gizmo had something to do with it. They

119

seem to have settled everything between them while they were in London. *Fait accompli.*"

"You seen this new foreign girl?"

"Not yet. She's been put in the gatehouse temporarily. Until Phyllis leaves I suppose. No point in having a child minder sleeping out, is there? And *I* don't intend to swap. No point. I'm only here till January. This Maria can have my room when I go."

I took Roz's coffee up with a heavy heart, determined nevertheless to prize some sense out of the woman about the Hallowe'en arrangements. Were any guests staying overnight for a start? And was I expected to play sous-chef to Derry and Gray?

Roz was in one of her Lady of the Manor moods, penning notes at her little writing desk, her adorable little gold specs perched on her adorable little nose as if it were some sort of role and the accessories props provided by the wardrobe mistress.

"It's Miranda's first grown-up party, Briony. I'm leaving it entirely to her whom she invites and so on. Gizmo's a perfect darling. I'm sure he will see everything goes swimmingly."

I flounced off back to the kitchen and decided to drive off straight after lunch and get some solid information from Derry and Gray. From my brief encounter with those guys I was entirely confident they would have everything sewn up. Still, it's a sad state of affairs when the housekeeper has to go cap in hand to the caterers to acquire some basic information about household management.

To give them their due, Gizmo and Miranda made a marvellous job of getting things together. At six on the dot a crowd of children from the village plus a bevy of mums and dads descended on Kington House. The kids had got clued up on the blackmail aspect of trick or treat, buttonholing every adult in sight. Mark guarded the bonfire and had fenced off the approach to the lake with a line of chicken wire, handing out sparklers like Father Christmas though still managing to stay as surly as ever. He had refused to dress up but with his saturnine expression I must admit it was hardly necessary. I decided to ask Doris what his beef was – a nice-looking man like that going to waste.

Derry and Gray had brought in a trainee to deal with the barbeque and the "first sitting", as Miranda termed it, threw themselves at the grill with the appetites of starving peasants.

The night was cold and the stars bright, a full moon lending an authentic silvery glimmer to a scene flickering with garden flares and candles in hollowed-out pumpkins.

Watching the little girls leaping about in their witchy hats and Hallowe'en get-up the unfocussed melancholy which had enfolded me since Cannock's freak-out melted away. The poor old thing had sensibly decided to lie low, keeping out of sight all day. Come to think of it, I hadn't seen her since tea. But Miranda and Gizmo had certainly laid on a wonderful show. It was really going to be a night to remember.

Much later the fun and games became less innocent, with Kyle leading a loud contingent of tennis-club hearties in a boisterous game of strip leapfrog round the bonfire in which every tumble meant the forfeit of a garment, even the winners, clearly the ones most able to hold their booze, finishing up clad in little but their smalls. Carey looked on at this bacchanalia with cynical amusement, the devil's horns Miranda had insisted he wore sitting comfortably like a crown.

I stood at the edge of the party feeling like Cinderella, wondering when I could decently duck out, Gray and Derry staying on, as they insisted, to the bitter end. One thing was definitely spoiling the fun for me: I had lost Archie. In an effort to lock him up after the children had departed and Pebbles had trailed off with Teresa to spend the night with Katie, the horrible beast gave me the slip, determined not to miss out on any delicious titbits discarded in the bushes.

I had hunted everywhere, searching out his favourite haunts, circling the walled garden calling the little brute with increasing irritation. With all these people about, cars coming and going, fireworks exploding, the dog might have taken fright, run off and got himself truly lost. I decided to go back inside and check Archie hadn't been accidentally shut up in one of the rooms.

A game of Sardines was in full swing, screams top-noting dramatic renderings of ghost noises, the adult end of the party, if anything, more infantile than the children's hour. The phone shrilled in the library but no one seemed to notice. I went in to answer it, wondering what I might interrupt but the room was empty, the TV churning out an old Christopher Lee video, some werewolf nonsense set in New York. The call was from Carey's cameraman, an urgent recall to duty and would I locate the master of the house pronto?

"Easier said than done," I muttered but as it happened my luck was in. Carey was pottering about in the kitchen after carrying up extra supplies from the cellar. I told him about the guy waiting at the end of the telephone in the library and he put four bottles of champagne on the table and rushed off, his black cape billowing behind him like Faustus.

I leaned against the sink trying to think

where Archie might have got to. He had never vanished for more than an hour before and it was already after midnight. Carey was back in a moment, throwing the cape and devil's horns on the draining board, looking like a man given unexpected parole.

"I've got to go to work, Briony. Don't tell them I've gone – I don't want to break up the party."

"Some hope! But what shall I say if Roz asks?"

"I'll be back at the weekend, Sunday anyway. There's been a leak at Sellafield nuclear plant and two men have been contaminated with radioactivity. Part of the building's already sealed off – I must get down there straight away, it ties in with something I've been investigating. Roz'll understand. I'll ring her in the morning. Here, take this wine up for me, will you? Gizmo'll deal with it. They're in the dining room playing charades or Blind Man's Buff or some such tosh."

The dining room was heaving, the crowd pressed shoulder to shoulder, assembled to hear Gizmo's detailed instructions about a round of Murder. Miranda sparkled from head to foot in a gold lurex leotard, Roz and Kyle clamped together in matching domino outfits and masks, Roz teetering on spindly domino motif stilettos, her eyes dilated. Oh yes, it was a real humdinger of a party. I wished now I had accepted Miranda's invitation to bring a friend. Jonny Lusty would have loved every minute.

I slipped upstairs to fetch my Barbour and a torch and went back outside determined to locate bloody Archie before I turned in. Two hours later I trailed back to the house too bushed to care *where* the little bugger was. The party had reached its final stage: smoochy music, people crashed out all over the place, many already gone home and even Gray and Derry signed off. I slumped at the kitchen table in my coat sipping flat champagne from a half-finished bottle dumped in the sink. Faintly, from the outer reaches of the big house, muted shrieks marked the dying throes of "one helluva night" and I slipped off my boots, shoved the torch in my pocket and laid my head on my arms on the table, utterly bombed out.

Suddenly I jerked up, scared stiff, as if I'd fallen asleep at the wheel. Yeah, it was Archie all right, his thin yelps sounding exhausted, a half-hearted whine barely recognisable. Scrabbling at the cellar door confirmed the whimpers and I was across the room in a flash. Carey's key was still in the keyhole but the door was firmly locked. The little beast had somehow slipped in unnoticed and been incarcerated. For how long? Hours probably.

I unlocked the door, the cusses dying in my throat. The cellar was half-lit, a single bare bulb glowing over the wine racks, but the two bodies sprawled at the bottom of the stone steps were all too clear. The man was moaning, quite loudly in fact, the other, a woman, lay inert, half buried under his weight, only one stockinged foot visible. I stumbled into the semi-darkness and grabbed Archie, then trod on something slimy and horrible which slithered under my bare foot like a piece of rotting meat. I screamed and Archie practically leapt out of my arms, all but sending me crashing down the un-railed steps to fall on top of the two spread-eagled below. I shoved Archie behind me into the kitchen, took the keys, and crept down the stairs, the awful chill of the place raising the hairs on the nape of my neck. The man waved his hand in a weak gesture and despite the fancy dress get-up and mask I recognised Kyle Chapman.

"Think I've broken my leg," he rasped. "Someone slammed the door on us for a stupid joke I suppose. Then the bloody dog got tangled underfoot and Roz broke her heel. We reeled about at the top for a sec then both of us went down like a ton of bricks. A weight, a dumbell or something, God knows – got dislodged in all this fancy footwork and came crashing down on top of us. Knocked out poor old Roz stone cold.

Is she all right? I must have passed out. The pain ... we were playing Murder. We were going to bunk up in the games room and—"

"Shush. Don't talk. I'll get someone in two ticks. Just roll over, could you, Kyle? So I can have a look at Roz."

He winced as I levered him off to shine my torch at Roz. She lay like a crumpled butterfly, her silly domino outfit fantastic in that dungeonesque setting, her hair splayed out on the bottom step, her white face averted. I raised her head, pressing my lips close to hers, hoping for a breath, fingering her throat for a pulse. Nothing. As I drew my hand away and let her head rest back on the floor, I realized that my fingers were steeped in blood, a dark pool of it spilled like wine on the flagstones. My torch clattered on the floor and I fell back, trembling all over.

Kyle gripped my shoulder. "She's going to be all right, isn't she, Briony?"

It was a moment before I could stop shaking enough to answer.

"No, Kyle, I'm afraid not. Roz is dead."

Thirteen

After I had raised the alarm I went back down to the cellar to sit with Kyle, hearing running footsteps above and Gizmo's frantic pleading as he tried to restrain Miranda. Her screams echoed through the house like a soul in torment but he succeeded in keeping her in check and Kyle and I waited it out alone with Roz's broken body.

When the paramedics had finally manoeuvred Kyle into the ambulance I stayed sitting on the cold steps unable to drag myself away, unwilling to abandon the poor wretched woman lying in a pool of her own blood in that dank hellhole, alone, waiting for the police surgeon and the photographer to pick her over like carrion. They humoured me, letting me squat to one side as if it were a vigil. It seemed the least I could do.

When at last the body had gone, a kindly policewoman took my arm, insisting I rejoin the land of the living, to "have a nice cup of tea". It was only as I was climbing the stairs that I recognised the thing on which I had slid as I took that first step down. It had fallen over the side and lay on the cellar floor, impaled like an obscene art object, the sort of exhibit people queue to see at the Serpentine Gallery. I pointed it out to the constable with a trembling finger and she shone her torch, barely interested in the ramblings of a woman in shock. It was a dead rat. Seriously dead, long deceased, its innards squelching with putrefaction. But the ghastly focus of my horror was not the thing itself but the spike driven half into its belly. It was the snapped-off heel from Roz's stiletto, one of the glitzy ones with the domino motif I had admired earlier.

I retched, vomiting into the void beside the cellar steps, my stomach churned at the realisation that Roz had stood on that dead rat, too, and almost certainly the thing had caused her to wobble, break her shoe, and sent them both crashing down the stairs. My mind erased Archie's involvement, unwilling to admit even a half recognition that I had indirectly contributed to Roz's death.

I walked through the kitchen, crowded with the police team, and the WPC accompanied me to my room, insisting on making free with my kitchenette, rustling up tea and biscuits like the pro she was. It flickered through my mind that this girl must often be called upon to perform such small kindnesses, cushioning the shock of bereaved parents, rape victims and all the other sad cases which made up her day's work. Archie leapt up on the bed beside me, licking my face, subdued as if he had been subjected to a beating which, if Kyle had guessed the importance of the Archie factor, might well have been the case.

When I refocussed on the PC she pulled a chair to the bedside, fixing me with her bright eye.

"My name's Ann Brewster by the way. Before I go, do you happen to know where we could contact Mr Barnes? No one seems to know."

"Sellafield."

"The atomic plant?"

"He got called away on a job. Some sort of fallout. Get someone to call the Press Office there."

She patted my hand and rose, replacing the chair at the table like a polite hospital visitor.

"Inspector Hayes will want to speak to you soon, Mrs Eastwood – as you were the one to find the body. Mr Chapman is sedated at present." She smiled, a nice-looking girl about my age at a guess. Someone I felt sure who would climb to the top of the ladder, a person with the ability to handle the uncertainties of a job as unpredictable as my own.

I drifted off to sleep after that, sandbagged

with exhaustion but woke before it was light, surfacing as the diminishing sound of a child's weeping drifted into silence. I lay there stiff with terror, knowing full well that my mind was playing tricks. Pebbles was not even in the house. The weeping which had roused me was a figment of my imagination. If I believed myself to have the slightest psychic sensitivity which I know I do not, the heart-breaking distress of that weeping could be explained away: some sort of premonition of Pebbles' anguish, a foretaste of the child's reaction to the terrible news that her mother had died in the night, been extinguished without warning by an unlucky juxtaposition of events. I closed my eyes, shutting out the burgeoning nightmare, acknowledging with grim finality that taking on this job with the Barnes family was fast becoming the worse decision of my life.

I switched on the bedside light and Archie sat up, eyeing me with a terrier's canny speculation. I glanced at my watch. Five thirty. Saturday. Oh, what the hell! I'd ring Jonny Lusty anyway. Get him to come down for the weekend, hold my hand. He took it well, asking for no details beyond the bare facts, promising to be in Northchurch by mid-morning, just as soon as he'd tied up some appointments.

Jonny has his limitations, and after Charlie

no one viewed them with more clarity than I, but, pushed into a corner, there are only two people I know who would drop everything and come running. And Joe Reilly was not the man I needed in my present predicament. A pair of strong arms about me would do – Jonny wouldn't need to *solve* anything, I wasn't expecting miracles. But the bloke was a romp and a half for a start and, in his line of business, smooth enough to infiltrate the present terrible situation at Kington House without frightening the horses.

I changed into my tracksuit and took Archie downstairs for an early run. The place was still locked up and I had to untangle the alarms before escaping. It was still barely light and the silhouette of a police car parked on the drive gave me a nasty turn. I put Archie on a lead and walked up to the constable who had scrambled out at my approach.

"I'm the housekeeper. All right if I take the dog for a walk?"

He nodded, moving in to pat Archie who, having no regard for the law, made a dangerous lunge at his hand. I pulled him off with a swift apology and stepped out towards the main road, determined to put some space between me and the horrific place. The grass was littered with paper plates, idiotic-looking pumpkin heads and spent fireworks. The bonfire still smouldered and no attempt had been made to clear the barbeque grid where a pair of crows were already picking at the fatty deposits and charred chop bones, the scene made bizarre by an abandoned witch's hat jammed onto the handle of Mark's garden fork spiked into the mud. A breeze lifted the cardboard rim of the hat in a mock salute scattering the crows like a bird scarer. No lights glimmered in the gatehouse – perhaps the new au pair had already decided to give this job a miss and hot-footed it back to London. Lucky Maria. I set off at a fair lick and Archie and I cleared four miles before breakfast.

When I got back the house was already astir and after shutting the dog in my room I knocked at Phyllis Cannock's door, concerned at the effect of the night's appalling events on an elderly woman already in shock at having been given notice only days before. There was no reply. I knocked again, unwilling to let it go at that. Being bloody-minded I tried the handle, quietly calling out to her, suddenly afraid that poor old Phyllis had found it all too much and topped herself.

I smelt it straight away. Smoke. Charred woodwork. I ran inside, putting on the light and opening the door to the nursery kitchen the merest crack. Luckily, the fire seemed to have burnt itself out, the walls blackened. I went in just to make sure. I checked Phyllis's bedroom, dreading what I would find. But she had gone and it took only a moment to conclude that she had made a very effective dramatic exit. The drawers were empty, no suitcases anywhere and the bathroom cabinet had been cleared apart from some children's cough mixture and a bottle of camomile lotion. Pebbles' bedroom was untouched, the frilly bedcover and teddies in place. I went back to Phyllis's room and leaned weakly against the door jamb, taking in the chaos: the burnt remnants of a wicker wastepaper basket under the bed, the sheets and mattress extinguishing themselves after a half-hearted blaze. Smoke had blackened the rooms leaving an acrid stench like a fire in a laundry, hardly the work of a confident fire-raiser.

I backed out, this second disaster galvanising my shredded senses to a coherent course of action at last. Phyllis had been gone for hours, in all likelihood while the party was at its height, the manic proceedings covering her own spectacular finale. Did she imagine she could raze the place to the ground? Perhaps, after this, Carey would have the sense to install smoke alarms in this tinder-box of a house of his.

But I couldn't help feeling sorry for the old girl. To do a thing like this was so desperate, some sort of hysterical retribution after years of disinterest and injustice. To be thrown out without so much as a farewell gesture. And to be replaced by an untrained chit of a girl without even a decent command of English.

Having made sure the fire in the wastepaper basket was absolutely extinguished, I removed the key from the door and locked up the nursery suite, double checking with obsessive care and pocketing the key. No need to bring the police into this. There was enough trouble without an arson charge being thrown into the ring. Carey would have to decide on this one. I'd speak to him as soon as he got over the real tragedy of Hallowe'en. Trouble was, as Inspector Hayes was at pains to point out to me later that morning, Carey Barnes had disappeared.

"Did you try Sellafield?"

"Sent a squad car to break the news. Not only was Mr Barnes never there but the accident which you said was the reason for his urgent recall to work actually occurred three days ago. The leak was contained – no news story at all let alone a scoop. You sure you got the message right, Mrs Eastwood?"

"Ask the cameraman."

"I have. I've also checked with the news editor. Mr Barnes is on leave this weekend.

He requested three days off most particularly and no associate of any kind rang here."

"Are you saying I made it up?"

"What reason would you have to provide your employer with an alibi?"

"An alibi? Why on earth would Carey need an alibi?"

"Good question. May I take it, madam, that you have no contact number for Mr Barnes?"

I hesitated, just for a moment, but recovered just in time. Jonny Lusty would be here soon. If anyone was going to blow the gaff on Carey's secret hideaway it wasn't going to be me.

"No, Inspector. I'm afraid I can't help you."

Fourteen

Inspector Hayes is in his mid-forties at a guess, nattily got up and lynx-eyed, definitely not the sort of copper to play footsie with. He had installed himself in the library sitting at Carey's desk, occasionally taking his eyes off me to stare out at the conservatory, a not unconsidered ploy I imagine to give me the impression he was a pushover with a short attention span.

I had taken a straight-backed chair as far away as possible, hoping my housekeeper's overall would deflect his interest, allowing me to cover the bits of information I was keen to keep to myself, for the time being at least.

But Hayes had already latched on to Archie's part in the accident.

"Mr Chapman will be able to give a full statement later but I gather he did mention to my sergeant that your dog had been locked in the cellar."

"Apparently. I had been looking for Archie all evening. He must have slipped in when Mr Barnes was fetching the wine."

Hayes smiled. "Ah yes. Cunning little beggars. Ratting?"

"No! There aren't any rats in the house."

"But the dog *does* hunt?"

"Well, yes, on and off. He occasionally brings stuff in from the garden. The odd rabbit."

"And rats?"

"Sometimes."

"But PC Brewster says you pointed out a dead rat in the cellar – were very distressed about it, she said."

"Yes, I was. Well, er, not so much because of the rat but the fact that Roz – Mrs Barnes – had trodden on it on the step, broken off her heel. It gave me a nasty turn."

"You thought the dog had left the rat there and this caused her fatal fall? Mr Chapman said he tripped over the dog on the stairs himself."

"Kyle did say so, yes. But Archie didn't kill the rat. It was long dead and as I said there are no vermin inside the house – I would have noticed."

"But terriers bring their quarry home, don't they? Could the dog have deposited a dead rat in the cellar previously and was merely going over an old hunting ground?"

"I don't know why you keep on about the rat, Inspector. Roz fell because she was drunk. They both were. Your police surgeon knows it and so does Kyle Chapman.

Tripping on a dead rat left on the top step was a minor factor."

"Left on the step? Are you suggesting someone deliberately left the rodent there to cause an accident?"

"It's possible. The Hallowe'en party was well over the top. Dead rats would be just the thing to frighten the girls with. You don't know these people, Inspector, practical jokes are just about par for the course for the sort who find playing strip leapfrog round the bonfire the height of adult entertainment."

That knocked him back. Hayes jotted some notes on his pad and took another tack.

"Tell me about yourself, Mrs Eastwood. You don't wear a wedding ring I see. Divorced? Widowed?"

I gulped, the word "widow" always catching me by the throat. "Yes. My husband drowned. I use my married name professionally – it gives people confidence apparently – and I *do* wear my ring sometimes. It's convenient when employers get the wrong idea. Lonely men..." I added in a whisper.

"Ah, yes, I see. Fortunately, your services are in great demand. You've been here since October fourth I understand? No problems with unwanted advances here though? From Mr Barnes, for instance?"

I bridled, but he continued swiftly before I

could get a word in. "Well recommended I'm sure. Odd gipsyish life for a pretty young woman like yourself though?" He smiled, quite nicely I thought. I clasped my hands in my lap, determined not to let slip my own little secrets: my knowledge of Carey Barnes' poison-pen letters and his little hideaway address in Chelsea; the not inconsiderable matter of Phyllis's attempt to set fire to us all under cover of that wild party; worst of all, the packet of Es I had found in Wanda's room, which were now sitting like an unexploded bomb in my studio flat. I felt myself go cold, sweat breaking out on my upper lip.

Hayes didn't miss a trick. He frowned, trying to gauge my spin on the apparently simple accident which had killed Rosalind de Taffort.

"Tell me about the staff."

"Not much to tell," I said, feeling on safer ground. "There's a live-in gardener, a cleaner called Doris White who comes in daily and an au pair, Maria."

"Not much help then? A big house like this – lots of entertaining no doubt."

"Caterers come in for parties."

"Ah, yes." He glanced at his notes. "Silver Service. They master-minded the Hallowe'en party."

I nodded, rising to curtail an interview which seemed to be wandering off the point. "If you'll excuse me, Inspector, there's a lot of clearing up to see to."

"But of course. Before you go, just one more thing, Mrs Eastwood. Kyle Chapman seemed to think someone locked them in deliberately. Some sort of jape?"

"Possibly, but I hardly think so. The cellar door is self-locking, needs propping open with a weight. Mr Barnes usually keeps the only key himself for safety's sake – the child you know. But because he was called away urgently—" I floundered, feeling myself on shifting ground here, Carey's apparent excuse to get away from the party leaving the situation horribly fluid— "er, because he had to leave so suddenly," I continued, "Mr Barnes must have forgotten to take the key. He was usually very punctilious about the wine cellar being locked."

"Just as well, wasn't it? As the door did lock behind the victims you would have been unable to let them out if he'd taken the keys with him. And your dog, too. It doesn't bear thinking about."

"It was Archie who alerted me to the cellar! Kyle and Roz could have remained undiscovered for hours if the dog hadn't been trapped too."

"What's the story on Kyle Chapman?"

"I'm new here, Inspector. You'll have to ask someone else. I know nothing about the Barnes' circle. If you'll excuse me?"

I backed out, Hayes eyeing me with a keen appraisal I found confusing. Was he just doing his job or was the man considering a possible date? He could hardly blow up a fatal fall in the course of a sexual romp into any sort of career-building case, could he? Why all the questions? I grinned to myself as I reached the kitchen, wondering how long I could sit like a broody hen on all these unconfessed facts about the Barnes' household without Inspector bloody Hayes smelling a rat. I sobered.

A rat. Somehow things always swung back to that sodding rat. If only I could question Archie about it. *He* knew who put it there.

Jonny Lusty was seated at the kitchen table gabbling away in Italian, his feet well and truly under the table, the new au pair, Maria, waiting on him like a body slave.

"Hi!"

He jumped to his feet and gave me a hug and my swift flash of – could it be jealousy? – melted away. Trouble was Maria was a stunner. In the few days she had been ensconced in the gatehouse she had hardly been allowed a look in, Phyllis Cannock insisting on working out her notice to the letter and letting the new girl have no sort of association with Pebbles.

It had all been rather petty and Miranda, having dumped Maria on us, just left her to fend for herself. I had made use of the girl in the kitchen, palming her off with odd jobs in the vegetable line and teaching her to lay the dining-room table. But her English was practically non-existent and until Phyllis departed it was impossible to gauge what Pebbles would make of her. Privately, I thought the girl was a non-starter and, just as soon as Carey got to grips with the situation, she would be given her marching orders. Diana would have the last laugh after all.

But Roz's death had plunged everything into chaos. Phyllis had gone in the night. Pebbles, it had been arranged, would be staying with the George family until after the funeral and, as Gizmo had pointed out only this morning, Mark had handed in his notice. I couldn't blame him. If I hadn't been under contract myself I would have been on my way. Kington House was metaphorically falling about our ears and the fact that the master of the house had gone AWOL was just the icing on the cake.

Maria flexed her sun-kissed biceps and yawned, tired out, it would seem, from two hours' cushion patting. Jonny sat mesmerised by the girl, rapid Italian stuttering between them like machine-gun fire.

"Didn't know you were an undercover wop, Jonny," I countered, the trauma of the night's events settling like fur on my tongue.

"Ah, well, Bri, still waters etc. How about

143

showing me round?"

"The police are still here but hang on I just want to make a couple of phone calls and then we can talk in my room. Maria, would you mind slipping down to the village? Bells Cottage, just by the post office. Give Doris this note. There's a mountain of clearing up to be done – you'll have to help. I'll try and rustle up some extra hands."

I scribbled a note for Doris and shoved it at the au pair who seemed either put out or totally confused, pouting like an old pin-up picture of Bardot. Jonny rattled off something in Italian which seemed to do the trick and she bounced off, donning a man's ex-army khaki jacket on the way out.

I phoned Patricia Barrett, the vicar's wife, and begged her to lend me Lili for the afternoon. An especially Christian gesture I wheedled. I also gave Teresa a buzz to confirm Pebbles' welcome to stay on at her house until at least Carey surfaced to make his own arrangements. Miranda was under doctor's orders, sedated presumably, and certainly in no position to take the reins. Gizmo had mysteriously disappeared, his Range Rover missing from the yard and no message. I explained to Jonny about Gizmo, underlining the invaluable support the American would be in the current chaotic state of affairs.

"Hope to God he comes back. Gizmo's the only one who can deal with Miranda."

Jonny and I repaired to my little flatlet and I made fresh coffee before coming clean about my determination to keep Phyllis Cannock's little arson attack off Inspector Hayes' agenda. Archie lay in his basket horribly subdued, hardly bothering to question Jonny's claim to Wanda's double bed.

"Why get involved, sweetheart? Why protect the old cow?" Expensive property was sacrosanct as far as Jonathan Lusty was concerned – arson a hanging offence in the estate-agents' manual.

I tried to explain, but it all sounded pretty feeble. Then I heard wheels in the yard below and flew to the window, hoping Gizmo had come back after all. But it was Carey's MG, its sporty image at variance with the sad sack in the long overcoat emerging from the snazzy little speedomobile. Jonny came up behind me and we watched the darling of the newsreels trudge towards the front door.

"Blimey, he's aged over night!" Jonny breathed. It was true, Carey Barnes' grey features were those of a middle-aged undertaker.

"Quick, get out now before he sees you," I hissed, bundling Jonny out and down the back stairs.

"I thought I was invited!"

"Sorry. I hadn't thought it out. I don't want him to connect us – for goodness' sake go, Jonny. I'll explain. Book in at the Coach and Horses in Huntsleigh, five miles down the road. I'll join you later. Ring me on my mobile when you've booked in."

Aggrieved, but reluctantly acquiescent, he slipped out of the tradesmen's entrance and I watched his car disappear from the yard and drive off. I went back upstairs and lay on the bed, breathing hard, my mind in a ferment.

Archie jumped up beside me and settled down. I stroked his ears, knowing the poor little mutt sensed the awful hole we were in.

Fifteen

After defrosting some picnic pies in the microwave and laying out a cold buffet on the sideboard in the dining room, I set Doris to work cleaning the bedrooms with Lili and Maria on bathroom duties. The two girls got on like a house on fire and I managed to deflect Doris's queries about Phyllis's locked room.

Hearing voices, I knocked on the library door. Inspector Hayes held sway, his sergeant to hand, the pair of them clearly putting Carey through some sort of third degree. I explained about the buffet in the dining room and asked about coffee.

"Nothing for me, thank you, but perhaps the Inspector—?" Carey looked terrible, his suit creased as if he had been sleeping rough, his eyes bloodshot. The policemen demurred so I left them to it, deciding to put out some whisky and water just to jolly things along. I turned to go but Carey called out as I reached the door.

"Is Gizmo back?"

"Not yet, sir."

"And Miranda?"

"Still sleeping. I've asked Doris to take up a tray. The doctor's coming back this afternoon to see how she is."

"Poor kid's in shock. And Pebbles? Is Cannock looking after her?"

"Pebbles is still staying with the Georges in the village. It seemed best. I'm afraid Miss Cannock left yesterday and the new girl's not really settled in yet. Perhaps we could have a word about that when you're through here?"

"Cannock?" Hayes barked, jumping on to this new name on his cast list. "Who's Cannock?"

"Our old nanny. She was filling in on an emergency basis after our former au pair disappeared. Wanda Ludokovic. My wife

147

was worried about the girl – went down to the station and reported her missing. Some weeks ago."

The sergeant whispered in Hayes' ear, presumably filling in the blanks.

"She still missing – the au pair?"

"I think we can safely assume she's living it up in London."

"Her friend in the village got a postcard," I chipped in. Hayes pointedly waited for me to leave before continuing his interrogation, input from the domestic staff, particularly one of the modern sort who had difficulty remembering her place, being unwelcome.

Carey politely opened the door for me but looked confused, as well he might. In his brief absence his wife had died, her playmate was in hospital, another member of staff had packed herself off overnight and the gardener had left a letter of resignation.

It was after four before I got the chance to return Jonny's call by which time the caterer's assistant had dismantled the barbeque and loaded the van with an assortment of platters and extra glasses and cutlery, and Mark had cleared the garden and started a bonfire with the rubbish. In less than three hours the house was, in all practical ways, back to normal. Even the policemen had left. Doris pedalled off on her bike and only Lili remained, perched on the kitchen table sharing the remains of the buffet lunch with Maria. I paid them in cash and noted the expenses in my account book.

"You know that stuff about the disco you were askin' me?" Lili said. "About me takin' you one night to meet Leonie?"

"Wanda's guru?"

Lili looked nonplussed and Maria frankly incomprehending.

I perked up. "Yes, sure. You're going tonight?"

"Wanna come? I'm taking Maria. Mrs Bennett's lending me the mini."

"Well, as a matter of fact, my boyfriend's here this weekend. I won't be able to make it. Is Leonie always at the same club?"

"All over." Lili smirked, her brown eyes speaking volumes. "Say I tip you off if I come across her one night and you can drive down straight off? Got your own car 'aven't you, Briony?"

"Great. You've got my mobile number on the card I gave you. I'd like to talk to her about Wanda. Leonie was a special friend of hers you said?"

"Thick as two peas," Lili replied, her command of lingua franca sometimes a little off target. I packed them off to the gatehouse with a doggy bag and gave Maria Sunday off. With the house so quiet it seemed a good time to do a swift recce of the freshly cleaned rooms and I had to agree that Doris had done a smashing job. Emerging from one of the guest rooms I saw Carey on the top landing, his ear to Miranda's door.

He straightened almost guiltily as I approached and said. "I've been knocking but she refuses to speak to me. Won't even let me in."

"It's shock. Let her be and she'll come round in her own time. Have you been down to the village to speak to Pebbles?"

"Not yet. God knows what I can say..." He raked through his hair, a man to whom the glib response was normally a professional byword.

"Just go. Hug her. You won't need words. Children are incredibly responsive. But there is one other thing, if you've a minute, Mr Barnes."

I made him follow me to the other end of the house and unlocked the nursery suite. He tagged along, still in a daze, only jerked into focus when I led him through to Phyllis's bedroom.

"Christ Almighty!"

He walked round the bed, suddenly alert.

"She did this?"

"A bit of an accident," I lied. He was not taken in.

"Last night?"

"During the party. She left without telling anyone – I found out by chance this morning and just locked it away. It hardly seemed the moment to pile on the agony."

"Whew. Thank God the inspector didn't latch on to it. Who else knows?"

"Nobody. I thought you'd better see it first. Would you like me to clear everything from Pebbles' room?"

"Would you? She can sleep in my dressing room when she comes back. Just pile everything in there and make up the single bed."

"You know the new au pair has arrived? Maria. Gizmo arranged it. Miss Cannock was terribly upset being suddenly given notice."

"My wife?"

I nodded. "Phyllis was expecting to go, of course, but things were all topsy-turvy with the party preparations, and perhaps Mrs Barnes was a little off-hand." It was the best I could do, pasting over the wretched business, but as Carey surveyed the damage his eye caught mine.

"We need not trouble anyone about this at present, Briony. As soon as things are back to normal I'll get the decorators in. Where's the new girl sleeping?"

"The gatehouse. Perhaps you should interview her yourself before Pebbles comes home. Maria is—" I paused, choosing my words with care— "not up to Mrs Winterton's standards, I'm afraid."

"Gizmo engaged her you say? She was recommended?"

I shrugged. After a moment's thought he

151

ushered me out and re-locked the nursery suite, smiling for the first time. He patted my shoulder.

"You've been very tactful, Briony. Thanks. Not a word! I'll go and see Pebbles now and speak to Gizmo as soon as he gets in. Why don't you take the rest of the weekend off? It must have been a terrific ordeal for you finding Roz. I can't thank you enough. And there's one other thing. I am *so* sorry you got caught up in that little naughtiness of mine, asking my friend to phone in with an excuse that would get me away from that ghastly party."

"Sellafield?"

"Absolutely. A really shitty trick. But, naturally, at the time I felt wouldn't be missed and a couple of fellows had invited me down to Dorset to share a bit of night fishing at the weekend. Carp are my passion." Carp? Perhaps that was the trouble with the Barnes' marriage: bloody goldfish the only thing to get the man's blood racing. He touched my arm, charm at full beam. "Thanks, Briony. You're a pal. We'll talk again later."

I left him standing on the wide landing surveying the rows of bedroom doors leading off from it in the dead-eyed manner in which I had seen Jonny Lusty regard a new property on his books. I reckon Carey Barnes had no intention of staying on in the country a moment longer than necessary. And who could blame him? With Roz gone the necessity for a quiet backwater was no longer valid. Joe Reilly would put the odds no higher than seven to four on the Barnes family disintegrating entirely now the lady of the house was dead and gone.

Getting carte blanche to slope off for the weekend was an unexpected bonus. I phoned Jonny at the Coach and Horses and told him to expect me at seven and without further ado tossed my overall in my bedroom cupboard, snatched up Archie's basket and tied the yappy beast in the scullery while I finished a few chores. The fridge was well stocked and the house set to rights. My spirits lifted. A weekend in the sack with Lusty would blow away the cobwebs and put me in fine fettle for the funeral which, at a guess, would follow tight on the heels of the inquest.

I phoned the hospital and, posing as Kyle's sister, arranged to visit him at six. If he was confused he made no bones about it and, as I stuck my head round the door of his private room, he broke into a big grin.

"Hey, Kyle, private room? Who's paying for this lot?"

"Carey Barnes. He insisted. I've just been moved in. Great, isn't it?"

Kyle's suntan had taken on a yellowish tinge, the broken leg sticking out from under the sheet like a frosted yule log. The room was rocking with heat, a pot of cyclamen on his bedside table already wilting.

"I bought you some grapes from the hothouse. Mark's given notice by the way."

"No sweat?"

I nodded, plumping down on the visitor's chair, patting his plaster cast. "You OK? Won't do your rent much good being hobbled like this."

"It's OK. I'm insured. Anyway, with my best client dead I'm on the dole anyhow. Poor Rozzie."

"Yeah. Sorry Kyle. You must feel terrible about it. But I left Archie in the car so you're quite safe. He was already in the cellar when you and Roz stumbled in, wasn't he? You unlocked the door yourself?"

"It was just a lark, Briony – we were going down to the games room for a bit of a snog. Roz's idea. I told the inspector."

"I was worried about Archie causing the fall. He didn't slip in from the kitchen behind you, did he?"

"The bloody dog was *inside*, Briony! How many times? I was pretty drunk I admit but that part's clear as daylight."

"Sorry, Kyle. I'm tiring you. Just wanted to make sure. Let's talk about something else, you must be sick of repeating all this. Hey, what about this new au pair then? The glorious Maria?"

Kyle brightened up, his libido stirring in there somewhere. Not dead just sleeping.

"Wow! God bless Gizmo I say. That Wanda was a bit of a sourpuss you know, Briony. Gizmo's done us proud with this Virgin Mary of his."

"Don't get your hopes up, boy. Her English is terrible. I don't think Carey will wear it for long. Anyway, you won't be around, will you? What will you do?"

His eyes clouded but he forced a smile, the unsinkable Kyle Chapman really a nice guy under all the floss I decided. "Queue up with Mark at the Job Centre I suppose."

"Mark's a qualified horticulturalist you know. Won't have much trouble."

Kyle toyed with the edge of the bedsheet, looking sheepish. "He was leaving anyway, I bet. Before Jennie gets back with the baby."

"The housekeeper?"

"Jennie made a dead set at him from the start but he wasn't having any. Roz told me. She wouldn't lie about a thing like that. They had a thing going themselves last year before I came on the scene and—"

"Roz and *Mark*?"

"Sure. Why not? He was absolutely crazy about Roz, a real bonzo."

"And she encouraged him?"

"You bet. It was common knowledge in the village. Why do you think he stayed on? That guy turned down a job at Kew to be near Roz. Even after I came along. Mooned about like a love-sick Romeo. Gave me the creeps, but Roz just lapped it up. Mind you, when Jennie finally caught Mark on the rebound, Roz's nose got put out. Wouldn't speak to him for ages after that."

"Why didn't she sack him?"

"Roz had a cruel streak. Liked flaunting her studs round the place. Watched him eating his heart out and revelled in it. Threw Mark the odd crust just to keep up his interest. Jennie caught them at in in his cottage in the summer."

"And Jennie took all this?"

"She thought he might come round eventually. I met her in the pub in the village one Sunday night. A one-night stand she told me. Crying in her beer she was. Smashing girl, too. Can't think why he couldn't just wallow in the inevitable."

"I wondered why he was always so surly. I thought it was me."

"A man on the rack."

"Didn't Carey notice all this going on?"

"Threatened Roz a few times. Divorce. He said he'd claim full custody of Pebbles and get it too. Because of Roz's drinking and the other thing."

"Cocaine?"

"You guessed?"

"I've seen it before."

"But Carey hadn't the balls to pull the

carpet from under her she said."

"The money?"

"That too. Carey'd got used to a plush pad, expensive wine. And in his line of work everyone's only as good as the last story. The media game's fickle. Joe Public expects the personalities to look like film stars and behave like monks. Roz had the screws on him. She liked to think she could pick up her own career whenever she wanted and being dragged through the courts by Carey Barnes just wasn't on the menu."

"Kyle, you're saying they hated each other? And Mark hated both of them?"

He nodded, pecking away at the grapes I had brought, his rugged profile stiff with apprehension.

"What will you do now?"

He brightened, tossing a grape at my head. "Thought I'd join up with you, tosh. Want a washer-up?"

Sixteen

By Monday morning Miranda had come round. She was sitting in the kitchen when I got back from collecting the eggs, all togged up to the nines, sipping a cup of milkless tea, the morning papers spread out on the table before her.

"Miranda! You're looking better," I said. "Let me get you something hot – you've hardly touched a thing all weekend." It was true. Her appetite had *really* gone since the accident and, although it was good to see her up and about again, the poor kid looked as white as a sheet and somehow held in on herself as if leaving her room had channeled her endurance into a narrow determination. She shook her head at my offer, fiercely concentrating on the newspaper reports of her mother's death. The publicity shots of Rosalind de Taffort in her prime were prominently featured, the accounts of the fatal fall described in stomach-churning detail. Fortunately, the reason why Roz and Kyle Chapman were in the cellar at all was explained away by a "friend's" description of the party games and the rivers of champagne lubricating the party for the Barneses' teenage daughter. It made perfect alternative reading for a bleak November morning.

"I wouldn't get too involved with those scandal sheets if I were you, Miranda."

She ignored this, avid for the morbid details.

"It says here Carey only heard about Mummy being killed on the radio, while he was carp fishing in Dorset! I thought he had gone off on a special job, you said, some atomic plant?"

"Well, they always get things wrong, don't they? Give it a rest, Miranda. Why don't you come down to the village with me and talk to Pebbles? She needs you."

She looked up, scowling. "Pebbles still with the Georges?"

I nodded. "Until the funeral. It's better if she's out of the house while the police are still interviewing people. Have they spoken to you yet?"

"I've arranged to talk to Inspector Hayes this morning. At the station. I want to make a statement. What's all this about Pebbles being moved into the dressing room?"

"You'll have to talk to Mr Barnes about that," I countered, determined not to get involved in any further explanations.

I busied myself making tea and toast and

tried to clear the newspapers off the table but Miranda wasn't having any and grabbed them back, pushing the bundles of newsprint into her tote bag under the table, her mood icy. Maria came through the back door at that moment, her dark hair glistening with rain, Archie snuggled to her chest.

"Thees dog. He come to my 'ouse. Mark say he lookin' for mouses?"

The two girls eyed each other like alley cats and I pushed Maria into an empty chair as Miranda rose to go.

"You're off?" I said, keeping my tone neutral, but, really, Miranda was only a teenager after all and her continued refusal to speak to Carey created a vacuum in which even poor old Phyllis Cannock would have been useful. The girl needed *someone*.

"I'm going straight to London after I've spoken to the police. I'll see Pebbles when I get back. She's safe with Teresa. I'll take the Rover now mummy doesn't need it any more," she added bitterly.

"Does your father know?"

"He's *not* my father," she retorted, glaring at Maria who, goggle-eyed, watched our exchanges as if we were actors in an incomprehensible Noh play. "I'll be at Gizmo's place."

Miranda left, grabbing a sheepskin jacket from a hook in the scullery on her way out, jiggling the car keys as if daring me to object.

"Bloody hell," I muttered, unsure whether to be glad or sorry the girl was leaving. On reflection, I thought as I eyed Maria with growing irritation, it was probably all for the best. There was the inquest to get through, then the funeral and already the press photographers were camped at the gates trying to milk the Roz de Taffort story for all it was worth.

It was a relief to see Doris breeze in, her frizzy mop clamped under a plastic pixie hood, her mac drenched. Maria stirred her coffee, vacantly stroking Archie who, as ever, was on the spot to take up any cosy lap on offer.

After a few studied opening gambits, Doris and I repaired to the dining room and I filled her in as best I could.

"Don't answer the phone, Doris. The press have been ringing since Saturday morning. Mr Barnes is fending them off and will be working in the library all day. I've left some sandwiches and a thermos of coffee on a tray for him, so when I've cleaned out Pebbles' room I'll pop down to the village if that's OK?"

"Pebbles movin' out?" she gasped.

Doris was my anchor, the only still point in this whirlpool, but I must remember to be more careful. Doris is no fool.

161

"No, of course not. Just moving over to Mr Barnes' dressing room when she comes home for the funeral. I'll make up the bed for her myself ... Miss Cannock having left so suddenly." I floundered, wishing now I had kept my big mouth shut.

"This new foreign girl ain't stayin' then?"

"Well, yes, for the time being at any rate. But she's – er – *new*. And Pebbles being so upset..."

Doris gave me a knowing look and set off to air the library before the police came back filling the place with their fug and big boots. I told Maria to give Doris a hand and went in search of Mark.

He was in the potting shed loading up a barrow with pruning shears and heavy-duty cutters. He looked as morose as ever, a weekend's growth of beard accentuating the hobo look. His eyes held mine with tired indifference, as if my sheer existence was yet another cross to bear.

"Yeah?"

"Mark, I need your help."

"I was just about to start cutting back the wild holly off the drive."

"This is urgent. And confidential. You must swear not to mention it to a soul. We've got enough trouble already—"

"I'll drink to that."

"Leave this for the moment," I said, waving vaguely at his tools. "There's a

162

problem up at the house. Miss Cannock had a bit of a fire in her room."

His eyes flickered with interest and while I had his attention I decided to let the wretched guy into the secret. I just couldn't hack it alone.

"I need you to help me move Pebbles' chest of drawers and wardrobe into another room. Not her bed. But Mr Barnes wants it done straight away, while Miranda's in London. He particularly wants to keep the fire out of the news. It has absolutely nothing to do with Mrs Barnes' accident, but you know what these journalists are when they get on to a story."

"The old lady scarpered? After this fire in her room?"

"Yes. She must have taken fright. She was going in any case, of course."

Mark shrugged, probably thinking I was trying to cover up some mismanagement of my own with all this hole in the corner stuff. Oh, well, so what?

He followed me into the house and we made short work of manhandling Pebbles' bedroom furniture into the dressing room. He shoved the narrow spare bed against the wall and between us we managed to make what was merely a box room linked to Carey's bedroom into a pretty nookery for a small girl. I repeated my insistence on his staying mum about Cannock's fire and, to be fair, I was lucky in that this unhappy soul was the last to be shooting his mouth off in the village pub. He even smiled, and to cement our new-fangled complicity I persuaded him to stay around in the kitchen while I made him a toasted cheese sandwich and a mug of coffee. Being a cook means my first instinct is to *feed* men to keep them on my side and, old fashioned as the notion is, it always works.

"I'm sorry you're leaving, Mark. You've made the grounds a real showcase. How long have you been here?"

"Three year. But there's no future in it," he muttered. "No under-gardeners and the place isn't even open to the public."

"You've got something else in view?"

"Might have."

"You must have known Wanda," I ventured.

He quickly looked away, stung by the mention of her name.

"I only ask, Mark, because the agency I work for brought her to England. The agency has responsibilites for these young girls. Most of them are pretty innocent and Wanda had never even been abroad before. I'm trying to find her so she can go home. If I don't track her down she will have outstayed her permit, be classed as an 'illegal' – not funny for her CV if she gets deported. And while she's in London on her own she has to take any work she can find. People take advantage of girls like that. The agency is anxious to help her before she gets into any real trouble. Do you know why she took off like that?"

He stirred his coffee, the circles under his eyes black as bruises, the private nature of the man's personality an inevitable barrier between us.

"I know where she's at," he admitted after a lengthy pause, "but I promised Wanda."

"She might be in danger, Mark. Did you know she was dealing?"

He nodded, making eye contact at last. "Wasn't her fault, Briony. I told her to lay off but she got into bad company. Needed the money for her sister's hospital treatment she said. How did you find out about the drug pushing?"

"She left some E's hidden in my room. I expect she intends to come back for them – or send someone. But what frightened her off so suddenly like that?"

He shrugged. "Ask Lili."

"Lili doesn't know, I'm sure of it. I'm getting desperate. All this news in the papers about the Barneses might frighten Wanda into doing something stupid, make things even worse for herself. And if the tabloids sniff out her connection with Roz – especially the drugs – well, your guess is as good as mine. You knew Roz well, didn't you,

Mark? She dabbled in coke, I know that. Do you think Roz was using Wanda as a courier? Asking the silly girl to collect supplies for her?"

He jumped up, his agitation flaring like I'd touched some hidden fuse.

"I've got to get on," he said, lurching towards the door in such a rush that Archie woke in a fright and almost got the poor devil's ankle for the second time. The door slammed and I subsided at the kitchen table, cursing myself for rushing my fences with Mark Hughes. I should have known better but events at Northchurch seemed to have a momentum of their own, one disaster following another like the fall of a house of cards.

While Doris and Maria were still busy with the living rooms I slipped upstairs to put Pebbles' clothes away in the drawers and make up the bed. In fact, the room didn't look too crowded and till Carey made up his mind about the new au pair, keeping the child under his eye seemed sensible. It was touch and go whether Miranda would ever return to live under the same roof now that Roz had gone but who knows? It was all in the lap of the gods.

I checked the main bedroom, Roz's presence already expunged, the bits and pieces on her desk tidied away, the subtle scent of the woman the only remaining evidence that she had so recently been here at all.

On impulse, I riffled through the pages of her address book but there was nothing of Miranda, not even forwarding addresses to cover the two years she was touring. Had Roz really been out of touch all that time? Would she not have moved heaven and earth to put her mind at rest about the safety of her damaged teenage daughter after that car accident? But perhaps initially Roz's own injuries had prevented any practical moves or maybe she had known all along where the girl could be contacted and had kept the information to herself. But in that case why would Roz connive in the disappearance of her daughter? And why would she pretend to everyone else that Miranda had simply vanished into thin air?

I nosed through the addresses, somewhat miffed to find my own and Phyllis Cannock's listed together with a temporary one for my predecessor, Jennie, under the bald heading "STAFF". I tore out the page, stuffing it in my pocket, determined to cut off any links with the Barnes family once my stint at Kington House was over.

The front doorbell pealed through the hall, followed up by a heavy tattoo on the knocker. I hurried across the landing and looked down into the hall, hoping Doris wasn't opening the door to a posse of newsmen. It was Inspector Hayes and his sergeant and I craned my neck to hear their exchange with Carey who had emerged from the library. It was all over very quickly, Carey bundled out into the waiting police car and driven away.

I ran down the stairs. Doris, standing open mouthed at the door, watching the vehicle disappear down the drive, turned to me. "They said he was wanted at the station. To help them with their inquiries."

"God Almighty, Doris. Do you think it was anything Miranda said in her statement? Whatever could the stupid girl have said to make Hayes take him away like that?"

Seventeen

I was reading in bed when I heard the taxi pull in. Carey Barnes had been "helping the police with their inquiries" for hours! Dragging on my housecoat, I reached the hall just as he was closing the door.

"You all right?" I blurted out.

He looked round, bleary eyed, a man in a fog. "Oh, Briony. Yes. Sure. Lousy night out there, absolutely pissing down." Funny how

168

the English still politely comment on the weather even if the world is falling about their ears.

"I'll make some sandwiches." He nodded absently, weaving unsteadily across the parquet to slump on the sofa in front of the dead ashes of the library fire. His breath smelt of whisky, presumably he'd stopped off to drown his sorrows.

When I got back with a tray of coffee and savouries he was still sitting there, the slope of his shoulders registering utter exhaustion. He half rose and smiled as I set down the tray, and reached for the decanter on the sofa table behind him.

"Join me, Briony. Please. I could do with some company."

I perched on the club fender watching his erratic handling of the glasses and, just to have something to do, poured his coffee, placing a plate and napkin on a side table. He handed me a stiff whisky and downed his own in one gulp.

"You ever had anything to do with the police, Briony?"

"Only when my bike was stolen," I muttered, clutching the folds of my tartan housecoat to my knees, pushing away my dealings with the Gardai when Charlie disappeared.

"Take my advice. Never volunteer information. One thing leads to another and, before you know it, you've tied yourself in knots."

"Why keep you so long? Was the doctor worried about Roz's injuries?"

He sighed. "No. Apparently the medical evidence is all perfectly straightforward. She died almost immediately – her skull was already fragile after that car accident three years ago. No one could have saved her even if she and Kyle had been discovered straight off."

"Then what's the inspector looking for?"

"Miranda set him up."

"How?"

"Went down to the station and made a statement off her own bat."

"About what? There were no suspicious circumstances. A straightforward accident."

"It wasn't only about her mother's death. Old stuff regurgitated from way back to support some cockeyed theory of her own – says I set out to kill Roz."

I gasped, my mind reeling.

"She's in shock – I'm sure the inspector won't be influenced by a teenager's tantrums."

"She discussed it with you?" He looked up, startled, his lean features gaunt in the half light from the single lamp on the desk.

"Of course not. But she's made no secret of bitter ill-will towards you and she announced at breakfast she intended to make a statement."

"Some statement!"

"How can she possibly blame you? You weren't even here!"

"Miranda's off her head. She told the police I knew Roz was already drunk before I left but says I told Gizmo not to let her have any more champagne, which was the only true part of the bloody statement. She says I gambled on her mother's weakness; deliberately left the cellar wide open knowing Roz wouldn't be able to resist helping herself to extra booze after Gizmo put the brakes on at the bar."

"But the cellar door wasn't wide open! I was there myself just before you were called away."

"The key was in the lock. An open invitation to a drunk. Miranda insisted to Hayes that I *never* allowed anyone else access to the cellar and kept the key with me always."

"Anyone can forget. And that urgent telephone call from your office—" My voice petered out, stumbling on the recollection of the false message I had innocently passed on.

"Ah yes. Sellafield." He smiled and poured another drink. "That didn't help either."

"But your friends in Dorset?"

"Actually, there wasn't any fishing trip and Gizmo swore to the sergeant my car did not leave the party when I said it did. That's true too. I was packing up some papers in my dressing room – it must have taken longer than I thought. You see, Briony Eastwood, what a terrible fibber I am?" He said this with a charming grin, lifting his tumbler in a mock salute before downing the dregs and refilling.

"I'm sorry, but you've lost me. Say it again. You knew the Sellafield message was a set-up between you and a friend to give you an excuse to leave the party and drive down to Dorset? OK?"

"Not Dorset. No. I just made up the malarky about the fishing trip on the spur of the moment when the news broke to cover something else. Stupid."

"Something else?" My mind doesn't run at its best on neat whisky and Carey's lies piled on lies were forming a nebulous cloud in my head.

"I drove to London. I've never been a party animal but I knew how important it was to Roz to make a bit of a splash for Miranda after she'd been abroad so long. A sort of fatted-calf welcome home to the prodigal daughter." The irony of this last remark put a flinty edge on his attempt at rationalising the mess of his own making he was in. "I thought a decent excuse would let me off the rest of the weekend and no questions asked. I had stuck around till after midnight," he complained.

"It was an *awful* party, wasn't it?"

We laughed, picturing the antics which had preceded the tragic denouement.

"Miranda guessed you had ducked out?"

"Actually, no, she didn't. If Gizmo hadn't spotted my MG leaving an hour later, everything might have been simple."

"Where did you go again?" I felt bound to ask but his reply was almost a foregone conclusion.

"I have a little place over a sort of shop. Nothing much. But private. I don't invite friends there and even Roz and my office know nothing about it. If I'm wanted, they ring me on my mobile and Roz always assumed I stayed at my club."

"Why?"

"You mean why would I need a bolthole? If you only knew the life I lead, my dear, you wouldn't ask. I'm travelling all the time. Staying in horrible hotels and always working in a team. And because some jobs are tricky, dangerous even, passions flare and tempers run short. It's bliss to know I have a couple of rooms to call my own, a quiet place where I don't have to clock in or even make myself pleasant."

I sipped my nightcap, sifting the confidences he was sharing. He was drunk, of course, and would certainly regret what had been said if he remembered any of it in the morning. Should I admit I knew the address of this hidey-hole of his?

"So you had to tell Inspector Hayes your real whereabouts that night?"

"Only because Miranda, curse her, had gone to the police with this *fantasy* that I had not only deliberately left the cellar available to Rosalind but had left a dead rat on the top step for her to fall over."

"Blimey! And the police swallowed it?"

"Wait, there's more. She says my master plan was to lie in wait, push Roz down the stairs then polish her off with the doorstop and lock the door."

"And Kyle?"

"Ah. Kyle was an unexpected blip. Miranda reckons I had banked on her mother making her drinks foray alone – Roz *was* something of a secret drinker I'm afraid. Doris regularly disposed of empty bottles hidden in her room – and, according to the Miranda scenario, when I realised Kyle was in too I just banged the door on them both and hoped the subsequent crash had been fatal."

"A very iffy murder plan for a man of your intelligence, anyhow. And Hayes grilled you all *day* over this loopy idea?"

"Well, he had to confirm my whereabouts with my London landlord. He was working Saturday morning in the downstairs premises and vouched for my presence thank the Lord. Saw me leave as he was opening up luckily or *nobody* would have been witness to my final admission that I had not been fishing in Dorset, nor was I following a lead in Sellafied but had, in fact, spent most of the night working on a story in my flat."

"And will all this come out? The press will tear you to pieces when they find out you lied *twice* about where you were that night. You must admit, Carey, it sounds awfully fishy." All this heart-to-heart stuff had finally blown away any inhibitions about using his given name, in private at least.

He shrugged. "That's small beer compared with the real nub of Miranda's freaky outpourings. Even the police consider her cockeyed notion of my plan to murder my wife by luring her into the cellar then battering her head in as the hysteria of a teenager in shock. No, the thing which really grabbed their attention is Miranda's sworn statement that I sexually abused her as a child and that Pebbles is in terrible danger."

The silence swung like a pendulum between us, the appalling indictment eclipsing any discussion of the death which had brought us to this strange meeting.

"She can't be serious."

"Absolutely determined. Miranda had some therapy in America apparently. Hayes made some phone calls and confirmed it. Roz never knew, I'd swear, though Miranda had always been a little odd since the car accident. I suppose we were all so concerned with Roz at that time that Miranda's needs were ignored, causing terrible resentment."

"And this American psychiatrist believed her story about the abuse?"

"Oh, in the States psychotherapy and counselling, especially for middle-class nuts who can pay for it, have escalated in recent years. A girl goes to her counsellor with the usual array of teenage moans and hey presto the quick fix is 'Well, dearie, it's your parents' fault.' If a parent is normally loving and outgoing the psychotherapist might suggest one's father probably abused you. If the kid says, 'No, never,' she's in denial. Freudian crap. And, naturally, once a vulnerable person is persuaded to say, 'Well, maybe he did' the game runs away and it's too late. The mother gets dragged in: collusion, you see. And the next step the bloody shrink insists upon is that the patient can only be free from her anxieties if she faces the parents with their guilt and goes public."

"You sure of all this psychobabble?"

"I did an in-depth investigation of it once but the producer got cold feet. It's called False Memory Syndrome. You can't blame the girls, they're led by these crazy therapists with their insistence on the repression which has blighted the girl's life ever since the father violated her. Before you know it, the kid 'remembers' rape, bestiality, anal abuse, weird rituals, black magic. You name it."

"And Miranda accuses *you*?"

"Says I buggered her from adolescence. Says now I've got rid of Roz I've already moved Pebbles into my bedroom and the poor baby is next on my list."

"Is Miranda making a criminal charge of all this? There's no proof is there? Just the stuff the psychiatrist put in her head. Anyway, who paid for all this expensive therapy?"

"That's the mystery. It was certainly paid for. Miranda says Roz paid for it. She says her mother was told about the molestation and did not believe her at the time. Later, phoning from the US, Miranda says she threatened to give the game away, expose me and ruin my career. So, according to Miranda, Roz paid up and pretended she didn't know where she'd gone. In fact, my dear wife was sending a monthly cheque to a bank in New York for her, Miranda took her US bank accounts to Hayes so that part of it's true. But whether it was to pay for a shrink and whether Roz was party to a cover-up is impossible to prove either way."

"Roz loved you. She would naturally do everything to protect you from her own daughter even though she didn't believe her.

Stepfathers inevitably get a bad press. Miranda just lit on a terrible weapon to wave about, and from Roz's point of view paying a psychiatrist to sort her out must have seemed a decent enough solution."

"By why didn't Roz *tell* me? I thought the wretched girl was just touring as young people do, taking time out, working her way round the world, seeing the sights before settling down to study."

"Roz had been at death's door don't forget. She was in no state to cope with a lively infant plus a bolshy teenager. The poor woman opted for a quiet life and hoped Miranda would mature away from home and get some perspective on life."

"You don't believe this incest junk, do you, Briony?"

"Of course not! But everyone in the public eye is vulnerable to innuendo. Do you think any newspaper would dare print Miranda's story? The police won't act just on Miranda's say-so."

He downed another slug of whisky and hunched forward, his head in his hands, not even bothering to lie to himself.

After several minutes I cleared the untouched coffee things and slipped out. There was nothing more I could do, the poor devil was damned either way.

Eighteen

Carey holed up at home while the police investigations continued, his melancholy presence casting a pall over the entire house. It seemed as if we were all in limbo, waiting for something to happen, each of us shut in with our private anxieties.

Miranda refused to return from London despite several conciliatory phone calls to Carey from Gizmo who even appealed to me to intervene.

"There's nothing I can do, Gizmo," I told him. "Miranda is the one who threw all the stones and only Miranda can repair the damage." As a third party it was difficult to have any sort of frank conversation with him, a good-hearted bod who clearly hated all this family discord.

"Miranda won't tell me what her quarrel with Carey was about, Briony, but you know what she's like, a temper like a virago, she doesn't mean half she says."

"Miranda's a spoilt brat, Gizmo, and we both know it. If she wants to return to the fold she'll have to bite the bullet and say sorry."

"Uh huh. You're right. But you can see my problem, can't you, Briony? I'm stuck in the middle of all this. Miranda has lost her mother and because she can't bring herself to make it up with Carey she's losing her little sister too. She *loves* Pebbles, don't you see?"

I sighed, longing to point out that my job was cook not agony aunt.

"Listen, Gizmo. Tell Miranda the first step is to put things right with Inspector Hayes – she knows what I mean – and apologise to Carey before the funeral. The poor man's tortured by all this in-fighting, he can't leave the house to get on with his job and, until the burial is over, the press are never going to give up on the story. You've no idea how famous Roz was in her heyday – fans are leaving bunches of flowers down at the gates for God's sake, people of all ages down there mooning about like groupies. It's like being under siege."

"Gee, really? Do you think there's a chance with Carey if I can get Miranda on her knees?"

"He's not a vindictive man, Gizmo. Family squabbles are inevitable when a sudden death throws everyone back on old resentments and Miranda has gone *well* over the top this time. Give me a ring in a couple of days. See what you can do at your end. I'm hardly in any position to approach Carey on this, the moves must all come from Miranda."

I put down the phone and got back to my shopping list but a squalid thought persisted. With Roz's estate at stake no wonder Miranda was having second thoughts. In their search for a fresh angle, the reporters had already commentated on the amount of money likely to move over to Carey's bank account once probate was settled, Roz having willed everything to her spouse including the care and maintenance of her two daughters. It was a will made just after Pebbles' birth when presumably everything in the garden was rosy. No wonder the prospect of divorce was unpalatable to a man whose standard of living had soared since his marriage. But being publicly cuckolded was surely a price which even Carey Barnes would have found hard to swallow for much longer.

With Pebbles in the comforting arms of the George family and Miranda off on her own personal rampage there was not a lot for me to do. However, the uselessness of Maria was balanced by her sweet disposition and at least while Pebbles was being cared for in the village by Teresa, Carey was able to shelve that particular problem. But there was no doubt about it: if ever the household got back to any sort of normality, a trained nanny or, at the very least, an experienced au pair must be substituted.

While things remained quiet, I determined to take time off to visit Phyllis Cannock. In the aftermath of her little bonfire, coming as it did the night her employer was killed, the poor woman must be frantic with worry, waiting for the police to knock on her door, terrified out of her wits. Carey seemed indifferent to my movements and in the last twenty-four hours almost philosophical about his future, busying himself sorting material for an in-depth investigation of the Eastern European mafia. Fiddling while Rome burns it strikes me, but who am I to complain? I left a message stuck on the fridge door with my home telephone number and told Doris I was taking my Wednesday off as usual.

"Best thing too, my duck. As soon as we gets the all-clear to see to the funeral you won't have a minute to yourself."

I didn't tell anyone I was going down to Rye to see Phyllis Cannock and I didn't telephone ahead. Chances were she wouldn't see me if she could avoid it. I spoke to Jonny Lusty and we arranged to meet that evening at a quiet bistro in Soho where the booths ensured private conversations remained private. I had neglected Jonny lately, my mind circling the ever-present conundrum of the Barnes' final bust-up. It would be good to be able to speak openly for a change, my tête-à-tête with Carey Barnes, after his grilling at the police station, lay unmentioned between us, the nature of Miranda's accusations too horrible even to think about let alone discuss with *anyone* under the same roof. Carey had never referred to our talk and naturally I had let the incest charge stay buried, but it was difficult to decide if he really couldn't remember the details of our midnight conversation or whether, from sheer humiliation and in the cold light of day, he hoped his hazy recollections were mistaken.

Archie leapt into the car with alacrity, his excursions beyond the immediate vicinity of the house circumscribed by the fluctuating numbers of people gawping in through the gates. I drove straight out at speed, wondering if the gorgeous Maria had established any sort of rapport with the rat pack while she was living at the gatehouse. If she was bothered by the pressmen she hadn't said so.

The house Phyllis shared with her sister, a Mrs Edna Morrison according to the page I had torn from Roz's address book, proved to be a neat semi on the outskirts of the town. A former farm cottage at a guess, basic but pretty with it, a glazed porch filled with pot plants, the net curtains crisp as starched linen.

A grey-haired lady answered my knock, her china-blue eyes alert and friendly.

"Mrs Morrison?" I said brightly.

"That's me."

"I've come from Kington House. My name's Briony Eastwood – I work there. I wonder if I might have a word with Phyllis? I didn't have a chance to say goodbye and we've been anxious about her since the tragedy."

Her smile faded but she touched my arm, drawing me inside, lowering her voice to a whisper.

"Phyllis mentioned you, Mrs Eastwood, when you first arrived that was. But I've been *so* worried about her since she came home. Come through. I'll make some tea."

"Isn't Phyllis here?"

"Oh yes. But she's rather poorly. Took to her bed as soon as she returned – fancy that, coming home in the middle of the night! *So* unlike Phyllis. I hope you can advise me, my dear. She thought you *such* a sensible in-fluence on Miranda."

Edna Morrison showed me through to the sitting room, a chintzy parlour in which every polished surfaced was crowded with framed snapshots of children.

"I've left my dog in the car, I can't stay long I'm afraid. Please don't bother with tea."

"If you're sure?" She pulled a fireside chair nearer the sofa as I sat down, and I began to wonder why on earth I had gone to all this trouble. Still, having got here, I might as well come out with it.

"Did Phyllis tell you what happened?"

"That's the awful thing. We have always been so close but my poor sister is in a terribly nervous state. I had to call the doctor and he prescribed some tablets to calm her down but it is *very* difficult. Do *you* know what occurred, Mrs Eastwood, to make her rush away in the night like that?"

"Call me Briony."

"All Phyllis will admit is that she had to leave her employment very suddenly."

"That's *all* she said?"

Edna moved closer, her mouth twitching with unspoken confidences. "Let me be honest, my dear. Phyllis is a difficult woman, we both know that, but she became very bitter after her previous period of work with little Pebbles was abruptly cut short – she arrived here at a moment's notice on that occasion too."

"She explained that?"

"Between you and me, Briony, there was some unpleasantness about missing silver. Before your time, of course. Just as if Phyllis could possibly be involved in such a thing! Rosalind de Taffort dismissed her without a hearing, but later, I assume the mystery was solved although Phyllis was never given any sort of explanation or apology. But they wouldn't have asked her back, would they, if they still thought she had been implicated? But, of course, in Phyllis's line of work, references are vital. She found it impossible to get a new situation after that episode, so accepting the Barnes' offer to return on a temporary basis until a new au pair was engaged was something she could not afford to turn down."

"The silver is all accounted for, Mrs Morrison, I've seen it myself so please don't give the matter another thought. It was very unfair of Mrs Barnes to send your sister away under a cloud but these theatrical people often act on impulse and don't realise how hurtful they are. But that's all in the past. If you think Phyllis is well enough to see me I'm sure I'll be able to put her mind at rest about the current situation at Kington House."

"Ah yes. The accident. How terrible for those two children, especially little Pebbles. Phyllis raised her from a baby, you know." Edna indicated the massed photographs of children I can only conclude were Phyllis Cannock's previous charges. "She loved that child, you know. Such a pity my sister couldn't see eye to eye with the parents. Shall I see if Phyllis is awake? I'm sure she would love to see you, especially after coming all this way. On your day off too, I expect."

She disappeared upstairs and I jumped up, twitchy as a cat, the sheer coziness of the cottage closing in on me like a smothering blanket.

Edna reappeared in a moment, smiling, the blue eyes bright as a girl's.

"Go straight up. I've left the door ajar. You would probably like a word in private what with all these terrible events happening since Phyllis came home."

The stairs were steep and narrow and the back bedroom low-ceilinged, increasing my feeling of claustrophobia. I hardly recognised Phyllis without her wig, her cheeks now flabby and mottled as if something had leaked away inside. She wore a knitted bedjacket, her white hair wispy and sparse, her hand gripping the pink ribbons at her neck as if I had come secretly armed and likely to cause her some fearful injury.

I sat in the bedside chair feeling lumpish and inarticulate, and when I eventually spoke the words were steeped in banality, sick-visiting never being my forte.

"You're not well, Phyllis. I'm so sorry. I should have brought you something, some – er – grapes...?"

Her little eyes narrowed, the fear hardening.

"What do you want?"

187

"I was worried about you. Since the accident..."

"She's dead I hear. Can't say I'm sorry."

"Roz de Taffort was unkind to you, I know. But we all have our faults, Phyllis. You mustn't let it spoil your life. Your sister is anxious to see you back on form – it's lovely here. So near the sea."

She pursed her lips impatiently and, thinking of the possible havoc Archie could induce if kept waiting too long, I decided to stop pussy-footing around.

"That fire in your room, Phyllis. It was deliberate. Technically, arson."

She stiffened, her nervousness distilled to rancour.

I plunged on. "I discovered it myself early next morning. The police were already in the house, Phyllis. It was lucky I got there first."

"And you think I *owe* you something, miss? Gratitude?"

"Probably. But never mind that. I've come with the best of intentions: to reassure you. Mr Barnes is the only one who knows about it apart from Mark who had to do some clearing out for me and Mark won't tell."

"Mark has as much cause for revenge as I," she said with all the petulance of a juvenile delinquent.

"It was a very stupid thing to do and you know it. If Carey Barnes felt so inclined he could press charges. You make a rotten arsonist. Does Edna know?"

The mention of her sister's name penetrated a chink in the bitterness and a tear trickled down her putty cheek.

I waited a moment and then continued. "No one's going to pursue the matter, Phyllis – there's too much else to be concerned about. But to make yourself so ill? Why? Edna is sick with worry about you. You owe it to her to tell her everything." I paused before aiming a final shot. "That night of the party, Phyllis. Was there something else? Something you need to share? We're all friends here you know. I don't have to ask *why* you tried to burn the house down, from what I've heard about Mrs Barnes' treatment of you over the years it's a wonder you didn't freak out before."

She reared up. "Freak out?" That flicked her on the raw.

"On your way out through the kitchen, seeing the cellar door open, you didn't put something on the cellar steps by any chance, did you? Not maliciously, I don't mean that, but as a sort of protest. Those stairs are lethal and that dead rat just inside would have given anyone a nasty turn."

"What rat?"

"Oh, just something of Archie's. You didn't notice the cellar door open then? Shut it – for safety's sake? Not knowing at the time, of course, that Roz might be behind the door?"

She looked at me blankly, her piggy eyes wide with incomprehension. It had been a long shot but I knew when I was beaten. On reflection it was a daft idea. Phyllis Cannock is terrified of rats – even to spook her nasty employer the woman could never bring herself to set a trap like that. Even *touching* the maggotty thing would have been an impossibility for her. And trying to pin the slamming of the door on the old girl was a real shot in the dark. I didn't attempt to elaborate, even talking about it turned my stomach. I got up to go.

As I turned to leave, Edna appeared in the doorway, a cup of tea in her hand for the invalid.

"Oh, you're looking better already, dear," she said, placing the cup on the bedside table. "Perhaps Briony would come again? And bring little Pebbles next time?"

I started to make my excuses but Edna rattled on, avid for news. "Tell me, how are things at the house?"

"Pebbles is staying with a family in the village and—"

Phyllis cut in. "The Georges?"

"Yes. They've been very kind. It's just until the funeral."

"Then the new au pair will take over?"

I laughed. "Maria? Hardly. Mr Barnes has

transferred Pebbles' things into his dressing room. He will look after her himself. Miranda has gone."

"Gone?"

"They had a fearful row. She made some appalling accusations about her stepfather to the police but, of course, no one takes any notice. Miranda's something of a fantasist, isn't she, Phyllis?"

The old woman seemed to shrivel, her hand trembling at her throat.

"We've tired her, I'm afraid," I said, getting to my feet.

Edna smiled. "But you will come again, won't you?"

Phyllis suddenly lunged forward, grasping my hand. "I must speak with you," she insisted, the old assertive Nanny Cannock rearing up from her pillows. I could see what Edna meant. Her sister's mind had been subtly unhinged by what had happened, periods of lucidity breezing across her concentration like breaks in a cloudy sky. But I was in no mood to be privy to any more skeletons in the Barneses' cupboard which she was anxious to share. Chances were poor old Phyllis had some bitter stories of her own about the dysfunctional family and I had already been dragged in deeper than I had ever wished to be.

I shook her off and shuffled to the door, grinning like a fool.

"Of course. Next time, Phyllis. But I'm a bit tied up just now – the funeral preparations and everything. I'll call you shall I? In a week or two?"

Getting into London again was bliss. I showered and took Archie for a sedate trot round Burton's Court which took ages as the little runt insisted on lifting his leg on *every* tree, leaving pungent messages for his doggy pals. Then I browsed the shop windows in the Kings Road and treated myself to a divine purple satin blouson.

Jonny Lusty was already seated in Elio's when I got there and his uncharacteristically effusive welcome knocked me off my perch a bit. But by the time we had got into the second bottle of Beaujolais he came clean. Funny what a guilty conscience will do.

"I couldn't get her out of my head after our weekend."

"Roz?"

"No, Maria."

"What!"

"No, not that. It was something she said. About her previous job."

"When you were rabbiting on in Italian you mean?"

"Yeah. As a matter of fact, she's not Italian. Maria's Albanian."

"So what?"

"Miranda got her the job with the Barnes

you said."

"Through a contact of Gizmo's, some office cleaning company he has connections with apparently."

"All Clear."

"Sorry?"

"All Clear. That's the name Maria told me. She did night cleaning and a few service flats. I use the firm myself. It's jolly good. Employs resting actors and models who've gone off the boil. That sort of thing."

"Jonny. Is there some point to this?"

"Don't you see? I thought no one had spare keys to Barnes' flat but me. But Freda's been handing them over once a month for cleaning. She thought it was all part of the tenancy agreement, two hours every first of the month. It was a condition of rental with the previous tenant, that filthy pop musician, Pascoe – my way of checking he wasn't breaking the place up. Freda just forgot to cancel the booking with All Clear when Pascoe left and I've only just found out."

"And Carey never noticed the place had been hoovered or anything?"

"Jesus, Briony, the bloke's been working out of hotels for years – he'd never notice a thing like that."

"And the cleaners never came when he was there?"

"Freda says not. Two hours once a

month's not exactly a rush-hour job, is it? I've cancelled it now and fortunately Barnes never twigged it so we're in the clear. But I *do* feel bad about it."

"That's big of you, Jonny," I retorted acidly.

"The cleaning company had regular access to the place and any one of those temporary guys could have sussed out who occupied the upstairs flat from his papers and things."

"You don't usually labour the point, darling. You're pissed."

"The poison-pen letters, dumbell! What really cheesed Barnes off was that some of those letters were posted to his *flat* as well as to the TV centre. God knows what this mail inferred, but for all we know he's been getting death threats and the whole bloody cleaning crew know where he's holed up. Should I warn him, Briony?"

"No way! Jonny, just keep this under your hat, will you? It's a chance in a million anyone else has had a cosy *conversazione* with Maria, certainly no one at the house. And *she* never cleaned his flat, did she? She would have told you, she's too brainless to be devious. Let's sit on it. I'll have to think this through. Albanian you say?"

Nineteen

The inquest rattled through like an express train although the pathology report gave the press a few tacky morsels to sign off a story which by mid-November was already stale. Carey fixed the funeral for the twentieth with no announcement in the quality papers as one might expect, although he had conceded to Ray Levy, Roz's agent's insistence, that a well-publicised memorial service in London just before Christmas would be the very least the fans would expect. Levy was worried about his late client's reputation since the post mortem revealed that at the time of death Roz de Taffort had, in addition to the booze, taken a quantity of cocaine and suffered from "drug abuser's lung", a build-up of fluid likely to cause heart failure. But Christmas being a sentimental season forgiveness is all. A nicely timed turnout by public figures both from the media and politics would erase any adverse commentary.

The funeral was to be a very private interment conducted by the Reverend David

Barrett in Northchurch for family members only. Pebbles had settled remarkably well with the Georges and showed all the stoic resilience of a well-balanced six-year-old, enormously helped by the wholesome atmosphere of the vet's family in their cosy cottage and, at a guess, Teresa's all-embracing affection, not only towards the two little girls, but also towards the procession of sick animals which got their share of cuddles, especially the ones hospitalised overnight in the surgery. Pebbles had been lucky: she had always known a loving home and when suddenly whisked away from the tragedy, the George household was as good a resting place as she could have possibly found.

Teresa had purposely brought her back to the house with Katie for tea on several occasions to ease her into the changed circumstances and we were all keeping our fingers crossed that by the time Pebbles moved back permanently the new arrangement would hold no terrors.

Big sister Miranda on the other hand was still in orbit, though it seemed she would be returning to attend the burial service and, Gizmo assured me, would make her peace with her stepfather and settle in for good.

Gizmo has taken to phoning me at regular intervals, usually late at night when I can pick up the extension in my room. We have developed a certain rapport, our relative positions in the Barnes' set-up being similarly periphery but, because of our involvement, impossible to escape. I suspect the guy uses me to check out the current state of play, having quickly given up on any suggestion that I would act as go-between with Carey. But Gizmo's easy going and I must admit our private conversations in the quiet hours are something I'm beginning to look forward to.

"Miranda wants to look after Pebbles herself," he confided. "Christ knows why. Tying herself down to care for the kid is some sort of penance I guess."

"Penance?"

"She's riddled with guilt about her family. Personally I think more counselling is way overdue."

"A shrink?"

He gauged my incredulity with good humour and his southern drawl slid over my reservations like a limousine over cobbles. "You Brits are *so* cheesy about psychiatrists, Briony. That poor kid needs help."

"She's been to a therapist before?" I asked, keen to hear another side of the story.

"Sure. Why not? In the States we don't take such a stuffy view of professional advice. Miranda's had a whole lot of shit to deal with over the years. Believe me, the woman she saw in New York was the tops, I wouldn't let my best girl get hooked up with a faker."

I had no intention of sharing my own information on the consequences of Miranda's doubtful therapy gleaned from Carey's inebriated confidences and presumed she fought shy of confessing to her boyfriend that her deflowering had allegedly been at the hands of her stepfather. The whole story was patently absurd. Gizmo was right. Miranda needed a nice sensible British psychotherapist to unravel these terrible false memories. Blowing hot and cold with her accusations could only destroy the tattered remnants of any family unit.

Carey gave me a list of those he thought likely to return to the house for lunch after the funeral. It was a *very* select band. Kyle had diplomatically taken himself off to Scotland and the only house guests would be Sonia and George Parry, Roz's cousin and her husband, who were motoring down from Wales and would be staying the one night. Roz's agent was included, together with her solicitor, a Gerald Firmstone from Lincoln's Inn, plus a smattering of relatives, mostly women, who had probably only agreed to attend out of curiosity. And, of course, Teresa and Bill George were bringing Pebbles.

Miranda appeared unannounced on Sunday

morning, Gizmo at her elbow, her expression as she strode up to the house one of stony determination. Humble pie is a bitter dish. I opened the door and without a word she made for the library, her trainers soundless on the oak boards. Gizmo tagged along behind and, as the library door slammed in our faces, followed me to the kitchen.

"Coffee?"

"Sure. I saw that gardener – Mark? – working in the hothouse as we drove in. How do you get these guys working *Sundays*?" His tone was light, spaniel eyes crinkling with bonhomie. The man has a grace which is appealingly old-fashioned, something I had ceased to associate with men of my age who, since feminism had taken its toll, either resorted to slick defensive banter or a macho stance, both attitudes comparing badly with the natural courtesy of such as Hilton Raphael III.

"Mark's leaving at Christmas. He's got a job at Kew. I expect he's trying to put his tender plants to bed."

"Kew? Wow. I went there with my aunt last summer. She was dying to see some real English herbaceous borders while she was over." He produced a couple of Smarties for Archie, who had evidently been bribed before, and sat drooling at his knee.

I poured coffee for us both and blurted out,

"Miranda's accepted the inevitable then? On her knees like you promised?"

He laughed. "Near enough. She withdrew her statement to the police, the alleged abuse stuff. I reckon she and Carey'll do a deal. Suits them both to sign a truce. Miranda wants to come home, she regards Pebbles as 'blood and bone', apologising to Carey is something she just has to swallow."

"But she still blames him for Roz's problems?"

He shrugged. "These stepparent relationships are a minefield. Miranda likes to dramatise herself – she's only nineteen after all. Hey, d'ya mind if I take the little tyke for a run round the lake? Carey once told me it's stiff with Japanese koi."

"Well, I've never seen any, but you may be right."

"Too cold maybe."

That was true enough. The weather in the past few days had taken a nosedive, the skies clear and frosty with a foretaste of winter. The edges of the lake crackled with ice which lasted until midday. Perhaps that was the reason Mark was beavering away in the greenhouses.

I clipped on Archie's leash and pushed them outside, watching Gizmo trot off down the drive and aim like an arrow for the gatehouse. If he was lucky the guy would catch the delectable Maria in her nightie, never a girl to be up with the lark. After all, he was the one who found her for us.

The day of the funeral dawned misty, the black branches of the ash trees stark against leaden skies. I was up early, galvanising Maria into action before seven. The breakfast table was laid formally in the dining room all ready for Carey and the house guests, Cousin Sonia and her husband.
Miranda and Gizmo had moved back three days before and had settled in her familiar set of rooms without a blush. The arrangement suited us all. The family thus presented a united front, and Gizmo's emollient effect on the strained relations which persisted between Miranda and Carey paid off. Luckily the truce held, the terms agreed remaining a secret between them and, at a guess, with Pebbles the chief bargaining factor. Miranda was insisting on giving Maria notice, claiming she herself would be taking sole responsibility for her little sister. Carey was clearly anxious to keep matters on an even keel at least until after the funeral and was putting up no objection to Miranda's notion of cancelling the appointment of an experienced child minder. Frankly, I think Pebbles is merely a pawn in all this mawkish haggling and once Miranda appreciates the sheer boredom of being at the beck and call of a little girl, her

own natural inclinations will resurface.

But at present all was sweetness and light. Even the diamond lip stud has been temporarily ditched, perhaps to avoid any unpleasantness with Sonia, who I met briefly before dinner last evening and who struck me as a match not only for the Barnes tribe but for the whole county. A formidable lady, tall and with the same fine bone structure as her late cousin but cast in a sturdier psychological mould, her trim figure honed by years with the local hunt, her complexion tanned by country living.

Sonia buttonholed me after breakfast, clearly used to running a more prestigious outfit than Kington House, and quizzed me on the lack of staff.

"My dear girl, you can't possibly run this place single-handed," she said, eyeing the lunch preparations laid out on the kitchen table ready for us to tackle as soon as Maria finished clearing the dining room.

"It's all organised," I retorted stiffly, tapping the menu sheet in front of me. "Salade Niçoise. Filet de Boeuf Prince Albert – that's stuffed with foie gras and truffles – cheese, followed by pears and blackcurrant coulis."

"Ah, you serve cheese *before* pudding, *à la français*?"

"Mrs Barnes preferred it."

"And you are temporary staff?"

I nodded.

"And that Italian girl?"

"Maria is leaving at the end of the month."

Sonia Parry pursed her lips, the thought clearly forming in her mind that Carey's household needed some practical input. "Have you been here long?"

"October." I hated all this third-degree stuff and anyhow what business was it of hers? "If you'll excuse me, madam, there's a lot to do."

"My point exactly! This really *won't* do. Later this afternoon we must have a little talk. Miranda is far too young to take control of this house and Carey is obviously distracted by grief."

I rather doubted that. Carey's distraction, it seemed to me, was entirely due to his anxiety to get back to work.

It was a relief when they all drove off to church and Doris arrived, the only sane person in this crazy set-up. She skidded off to tidy the rooms and light the fire in the library. Maria, for all her deficiencies, is now an expert in the dining room and also a dab hand with the flowers. She's a quick learner and decorative to have about the place. The fact that her English is still appalling is really a bonus: it saves a lot of useless chit chat and Maria's dumb smile charms the pants off every male who crosses the threshold.

But Sonia Parry did have a point. Unless Jennie, the former cook, returned after her maternity leave, the Barnes household would be seriously understaffed.

An hour and a half later the family returned, their faces rigid with the freezing fog which had descended to block out the day, their feet leaden as they trudged through to the library for lifesaving shots of whisky and vodka. Pebbles clung to Teresa's hand, her eyes wide with incomprehension, and, after a brief circuit of the guests, Teresa sensibly whisked her upstairs to Carey's dressing room which Maria had done her best to make child friendly. Teresa rejoined the pre-lunch drinks party after a few minutes, mouthing assurances to me over her shoulder that Doris had taken Pebbles in hand together with Archie who, convinced that one little girl spelt more fun and games than a roomful of mourners, had joined them upstairs.

Maria and I served lunch and after a decent interval the mood in the dining room lightened, subdued laughter seeping under the oak door like a warming breath. Gizmo sloped into the hall as I was wheeling the trolley into the drawing room where Carey insisted on serving coffee. He followed me back to the kitchen, lighting up as I slumped at the table. It had been a long day. I felt bushed. He poured two glasses of wine and, ignoring my well publicised ban on smoking in the kitchen, offered his pack. We both relaxed in a haze of tobacco fumes.

"Well, that's that, honey."

"Everything went smoothly?"

"Like silk."

"Will you stay on with Miranda?"

He shook his head, frowning.

"Can she cope alone, do you think?" I wondered.

"Miranda's a big girl now. I've got stuff to catch up on myself. But I'll be around…"

He blew a smoke ring, then another and another, their perfect symmetry proof of an indolent youth. I took a close look at Gizmo for probably the first time, his regular good looks enhanced by the formal suit and black tie, his narrow fingers tanned by summers at the beach and, at a guess, winters on the ski slopes. Miranda was a lucky girl finding a rock like Gizmo in the shifting sands of her life.

"Where did you two meet?"

"Miranda and me? Oh, Vegas. About a year ago. I'd no idea how young she was or I would have run a mile."

"I'd forgotten she'd been in Las Vegas. Working?"

"Sort of. She'd tagged on to a French couple and was minding their kid while they did the shows."

"Babysitting?"

"Yeah. She wasn't short of money though. I suggested we move on to Aspen. My folks have a place there, an hotel. I said I could arrange for Miranda to have a room and save her money for seeing the sights."

"Right. Lucky girl. Then what?"

"Gee, you should be in the CIA, Briony – questions, questions, questions!" He grinned, dissolving the implied rebuff and I sipped my wine, waiting for him to continue. He shrugged and, loosening his tie, lit another cigarette, eyeballing me like a combatant in an arm wrestling contest.

"We fell in love," he said, the simplicity of his response taking me aback. He rambled on a bit about their life in New York, then Miranda's sudden determination to go home.

"And she never talked about her family?"

"I'd heard of Roz de Taffort, of course, but Carey's work was an eye-opener. He's some guy, isn't he? All that investigative stuff. I've become quite a fan."

"He's writing a book about the mafia in Eastern Europe."

"You don't say?" He whistled. "Dangerous stuff."

Gizmo's transparent admiration was hard to dislike, the lack of any irony or hint of sarcasm a basic structure of his personality which I suspected even middle-age would never diminish. Perhaps this had been the attraction for Miranda whose parents lived a life of patent insincerity, in which truth came a poor second to dramatic interpretation.

The reverie induced by wine and cigarettes after a hard day was rudely broken by the backfiring of a car screeching to a halt in the yard. I ran to the window convinced I had cause to remember that coughing motor engine. Sure enough. It was poor demented Phyllis Cannock come all too late to share the funeral meats.

"Shit!"

Gizmo joined me and then, quicker off the mark than I, ran out to the stable yard and caught Phyllis's arm as she turned towards the front entrance. Gripping Archie's collar I watched them from the back door, the dog's barking drowning any hope of making sense of Cannock's hysterical outpouring. Gizmo steered her into the kitchen, the woman now trembling with anger and frustration, her wig askew, her tweed jacket hanging loosely over the shrunken bosom.

"She says she wants to speak with Miranda," Gizmo gasped, sensibly holding on while I attempted to quieten her down.

"Not now, Phyllis. Does Edna know where you are?"

Her eyes caught mine in frenzied determination.

"I've got to talk to Miranda, I tell you. It's a matter of life or death."

"Yes, well, that's OK, Phyllis, but Miranda's busy right now." Gizmo patted her shoulder, nudging me to pour some wine for the old bat while we thought up our next move. The door burst open and Sonia marched in, taking in the scene with the instant recognition of a potential family fracas.

"Ah, Cannock," she said, her grey eyes flinty. "How lovely to see you again after all this time. Now, you and I will have a nice little chat about old times while Briony here telephones your people." She seated herself beside Phyllis and motioned Gizmo to clear out. He left, looking decidedly baffled, while I rang Edna and promised to drive Phyllis back to Rye within the hour. Maria joined us, wide-eyed, and without benefit of explanation quickly assimilated the problem.

I tried to explain the situation to Sonia without mentioning the fire in the nursery wing but I could see she was fighting an inner battle, hearing Phyllis's anguished pleas, trying in her oh so British way to be fair.

"We must allow Cannock to speak to Miranda. She's driven all this way in the fog..." Abruptly making up her mind, she said, "We owe her a hearing. It will probably calm her down," she lamely concluded.

Leaving Phyllis slumped at the table she hurried out, coming back a few moments later with Miranda in tow. Miranda's image had had a makeover. Out of her teen togs and stripped of the lip stud, she stood in the doorway with her bright hair smooth as a halo, a replica of Roz, uncannily mature in her black designer dress and gold earstuds. It had never struck me before but, no doubt about it, the kid in the blue jeans had metamorphosed into her glamorous mother.

Phyllis darted forward, grasping the girl's arm, bleating a torrent of alternate pleading and apology.

"Miranda darling. I was so wrong. So cruel to you. Please, please forgive an old woman. Let me speak out – I beg you!"

Miranda shook her off, ugly in her repudiation, and pointed at me.

"Get her out of here!" she screamed. And, turning to the old woman, "You're too late. Years and years too late. Bugger off, you fucking fraud."

Turning away, she left me to struggle with the limp bundle that was all that remained of Phyllis Cannock. She smelt bad. I became aware that Phyllis was standing in a spreading pool of urine, the wetness staining her lisle stockings, puddling her sensible shoes. She wept, loud sobs of utter despair. It was as if a death rattle echoed round the safe, normal surroundings of this country

209

kitchen. Sonia drew back.

"Get her *right* away. Immediately," she snapped.

Between us Maria and I bundled Phyllis into the back seat of my car. The girl sat beside her holding her hand, crooning some sort of incomprehensible mantra. Bloody hell, what a day!

I smiled at Maria, reversing in the foggy November dusk and tacking down the curving drive with all the speed of a limping tortoise.

Poor Phyllis. She may be barking mad but she had been cunning enough to get dressed, sidestep Edna and drive that God-awful jalopy of hers all this way in the fog. Whatever was on her mind – and I rather felt arriving in the throes of Roz's wake was no part of it – Miranda's erstwhile nanny was convinced she had something vital to beg the girl to forgive her for.

Twenty

It was less than three weeks after the funeral that I got a call from Lili.

Things at the house had settled into some sort of order with Miranda tense, but formally approachable, and Carey back at work, recently returned from a quick trip to Moscow to gather research for his TV programme.

Pebbles was understandably subdued, her responses guarded as if coming back had finally brought the tragedy home to her. Teresa George tried her best but Miranda has taken against her, jealousy no doubt, and insisted on monopolising the child's playtime herself, refusing to allow her to stay with the Georges overnight or even to visit them after school which, before Roz's death, had been a regular feature.

Teresa was worried. We bumped into each other outside the chemist's in the village.

"Miranda's attitude doesn't help, of course. Before the funeral Pebbles was coping so well," she wailed. "I can understand Miranda clinging to Pebbles like this, after all she's really her only blood relation, but it's unhealthy. Pebbles needs her own little friends. Can't you talk Miranda round?"

"She barely speaks to me, God knows why. Probably thinks I encouraged Phyllis Cannock to make her ghastly appearance at the house."

"Well, in a way, you did, didn't you? Visiting her at home and all."

"I felt sorry for the old bird," I protested. "Honestly, Teresa, there's more to it, but I promised not to tell and anyway the whole thing's history now. Phyllis is temporarily in some sort of home, Edna thinks she'll be all right but it must have been a desperate responsibility watching her sister day and night."

"Alzheimers?"

"No, nothing like that. Just old-fashioned remorse, I'd say. Phyllis is guilty of *something* but whether it's to do with the family silver or some long-past cruelty to Miranda she blames herself for, your guess is as good as mine. Frankly, I'm more concerned about Pebbles. I'd hate to see her turn into a potential headcase like her sister. Pebbles was such a solid little person before all this – a miracle with a mother like Roz!"

Teresa got back in her car and then, as a cheering thought, threw out, "Oh, by the way, the school's been hit by another embarrassing hygiene problem."

"Not more nits?"

She laughed. "Worse! Threadworms. Can you believe it? Tell Miranda to keep her eyes open, will you? Though whether a teenager barely past coping with her own pimples is capable of spotting such a thing is a moot point."

But, as I was saying: Lili. It was about midnight on Tuesday night when she rang. I was already hunkered down under the duvet with Archie and a new Danielle Steel which, believe me, was doing nothing for my anxieties about my love life. But I had arranged to meet Jonny on my day off and the prospect of a bit of a lie-in next morning before bombing off back to London was rosy enough to warm my cold lonely bed.

I picked up the phone.

"Briony?"

"Yes. Who's that?"

"Lili. The vicar's au pair."

"Speak up. There a terrible racket in the background. I can hardly hear you."

"I'm at Bootleggers, the disco place on the Brighton Road."

"I know it."

"Leonie's here. You said ring you – you still interested?"

"Leonie? Oh yes, I remember. Wanda's friend."

The payphone started burbling and Lili's money ran out.

I lay back on the pillows, idly pulling Archie's ears. Did I really want to turn out on a freezing night to screech above the jungle beat for news of Wanda? A girl I'd never met and who, frankly, didn't appeal what with her drug peddling and all. I sighed. Well, I had promised Diana, hadn't I? If I could trace the missing Croat I could shove the problem straight back through Diana's letterbox and let her deal with it. It was a long shot, but tracking down an "illegal", which was Wanda's current status since her contract expired, was less likely to end in tears if Diana handled it rather than the police. It occurred to me that preferring to snuggle up with a paperback instead of dancing the night away was a bad sign. Was I getting old?

Galvanised by this terrifying conjecture, I leapt out of bed and threw open all the drawers. Jiving gear had not been included in my country-style wardrobe but if I was to infiltrate Bootleggers some funky get-up was first call.

After a frantic dress-up session, which even Archie grew bored with, I reluctantly concluded the only possible combination likely to pass muster with the ape on the door at Bootleggers was a lime-green leotard and mauve tights topped by my new purple satin blouson – unworn, dammit! I'd kill the guy who slopped his can of

Diamond White down this little number – and the Emma Hope boots. A raid on Miranda's miniskirts would fit the bill but in extremis the only solution was to lop eighteen inches off a suede skirt which admittedly I'd tired of. Actually, the skirt looked a whole lot better, the ragged hem authentic rave material. I left Archie with Danielle Steel and crept out to the car, reversing out of the yard as smoothly as a cat burglar.

The bouncer at Bootleggers cast a leery eye over my ensemble but the Ray-Bans clinched it even on this freezing winter night and he let me through, my heart thumping fit to bust. I was all fired up, the throbbing disco beat drowning any reservations about busting a club unescorted, the place jammed and smelly like rush hour on the Northern Line, the kids barely distinguishable in the sweaty haze. The strobe lights were blinking like Belisha beacons and the clientele were shiny with exertion but, all else considered, Bootleggers wasn't the bog-trotters' ball I'd imagined in my snotty Chelsea way.

I sidled to the bar careful not to nudge myself into any bother, the troubleshooters stationed on the edge of the floor easily distinguishable with their shaven heads and big muscles. Jesus, finding Lili in this heaving mass of bodies was going to be near impossible. I shuffled round peering at the boppers through my shades, hoping no oafish feet would trample my lovely boots. Someone tapped my shoulder and I spun round, all "attitude". A black girl in a spangly jumpsuit grinned, her teeth fluorescent in the lights.

"New here, babe?"

I nodded, wondering what basic instinct had singled me out and why, in a matter of minutes, this grafter was on my trail, sensing an easy number.

"Let me buy you a drink," she said.

"I'm waiting for a friend. Thanks all the same." The track changed and "Sessions Nine" belted out, familiar from the Ministry of Sound, the sheer relief of recognising something at last giving me back my street cred. I felt a touch on my elbow and I stiffened, taut as an alley cat.

"Hey, you found 'er then? Leonie."

It was Lili. Lili looking distinctly un-vicarage-like in a luminous bikini top, cut-off pants and stilettos.

"This is Briony," she shouted over the din. "The one I told you about. Wanda's friend."

It was impossible to talk and after a few garbled attempts Lili disappeared into the melée leaving me to be drawn to a side exit by my new pal, Leonie, and thence down a narrow passageway which led to the toilets. We braced ourselves against a wall and between the intermittent passing traffic in their day-glo items managed to hold a reasonable exchange.

"Let's begin again," I said. "My name's Briony Eastwood. I work in the kitchen at Wanda's old place – I expect Lili explained. I'm worried about her – her visa's expired and she's in danger."

"You know her?"

"No. But I work for the woman who brought her over from Croatia. She's concerned that Wanda will get into trouble. Diana wants to send her home before anything bad happens. Lili says Wanda confided in you. Do you know where I can reach her? I swear I mean her no harm."

There was only a single bulb lighting the passageway and the whites of Leonie's eyes gleamed in the murk, her curving lashes thick as brushes. As she listened I could picture flashes of a penetrating intuition informing her assessment of me.

"Do you know why I come here?" she asked.

I hesitated, wondering if the Es were included in Wanda's heart to heart. "Presumably to dance," I said.

"Not entirely. I'm actually employed by a pentecostal church, one of the very few caring institutions to recognise the needs of these lost children of God."

"Oh my."

Her gaze was unwavering and I felt as if I was being skewered to the wall like a bug on a collector's pin. I decided to go for broke.

"You think I'm chasing after Wanda's Es, don't you, Leonie?"

She remained unfazed. "I knew all about Wanda's little sideline. Warned her what would happen if she got caught."

"But you never threatened to shop her to the authorities?"

"Never! Whatever these kids tell me is as confidential as the confessional. It's taken nearly two years to gain their confidence. How long do you think I would last if I was an informer?"

"And you're paid to counsel these boys and girls?"

"A nominal sum. Call it missionary work," she added with a grin. "Who else would come to places like this, be available all night? Some of these children have never known a real home. The love of God is at first a joke, then a problem and, if I'm lucky, eventually a solace."

"And you keep their secrets? Even about drugs? Is that wise? Or even ethical? Ecstacy kills."

"Sin kills. I offer nothing but a listening ear."

"Tell me about Wanda."

Leonie offered me a cigarette but I declined, urging her on, far from certain how long this unexpected contact would indulge my curiosity.

"Wanda comes from a good home. In that way she differs from many of the lost sheep here. England was a cultural shock to her and to many of the foreign girls who arrive at clubs like this. They are dazzled by it all, vulnerable to the vultures who prey on young boys and girls greedy for all the good and the bad things in life. I would be happy to see Wanda deported if that is the only way of release."

"Diana, my employer, will pay her airfare, get her out of the UK without too much fuss. Will you trust us?"

Leonie shook her head, the myriad beaded braids clashing like brightly coloured plastic counters. "I don't know where she is. If I did, my church would have helped her to go home. I tried to persuade her. I failed poor Wanda."

"Can't you tell me anything? I already have a bundle of her tabs which are burning a hole in my room. What else could you possibly tell me which is more confidential than that? I've kept her secret so far but, believe me, Leonie, I'll turn the drugs over to the police and the dragnet for her will be out in earnest. Is that what you want? Deportation would be a soft option. Peddling drugs in venues like this will put Wanda in prison!"

Leonie stubbed out her cigarette and edged towards me to let a couple of lads go by. One slapped her bum and shouted amiable insults as he passed. Leonie, the Jesus freak, a familiar stoker in this Hell's kitchen, answered back, cheerfully giving as good as she got. She waited till they'd gone.

"OK, I'll level with you. It's worse than you think. Wanda's pregnant."

"What?"

"That was why she skipped. She wants to stay here in England to be with her boyfriend. He promised to marry her and she knows once she leaves she can't come back. This is her one chance. If he comes through, she won't be sent back. But he'll never marry her, of course."

"You know this bloke?"

Leonie sighed. "I know dozens like him. She talked to me about the creep. Smitten. Never been in love before, you know, the usual spiel."

"His name?"

"No name. But he wasn't local."

"She said that?"

"That was the attraction, I guess. A sophisticated guy just passing through I'd say, using her for money and sex. That silly girl had no sense at all. It was the boyfriend who supplied the Es. I caught her trading at Planet one night and slapped her down. Cried her heart out, said she needed the cash. At first it was to send home."

"To Croatia? You believed her?"

"Sure. You don't know this babe. She's not like these other girls, not streetwise at all. But later, when I guessed she was still doing the rounds she admitted she might have to pay for an abortion. She can't go to any NHS doctor – she's an illegal, forced to go underground."

"The man isn't sticking around then?"

"No way. But he offered her a place to stay in London and a job till she got herself fixed up. He promised to look after her."

"Didn't you know she was reported missing?"

"She phoned me two days after she left. I knew she was safe, there was no point in getting involved with the police. Nothing's secret in this town. If the kids here suspected I was a nark my work would be finished. They *need* me. I'm on neutral ground here, they know they can come to me with their troubles and I won't damn them. They can tell me anything. Sometimes I help them get away."

"From the law?"

"From themselves. Get jobs away from here, start fresh. We have brothers and sisters in Christ all over the country."

It all sounded perfectly possible. "But you won't tell me where I can find her?"

"Wanda's in a squat. A converted railway

arch. Brixton or maybe King's Cross, I forget. She's got work."

"What sort of work?"

"Domestic."

"And the boyfriend?"

"Still on the scene but nudging her off I'd say. She won't admit that, of course."

"You realise there must be thousands of converted railway arches in London? Hardly pinpoints her, does it?" I muttered bitterly as I passed her one of Diana's agency cards. "You'll speak to Diana if Wanda rings you again? You could go with Diana and persuade the stupid girl to grab the air ticket and fly away."

Leonie shrugged, finally accepting that my motives were roughly in line with her own.

"I'll give you till Christmas," I said. "If you can't come up with anything by then, the offer's off. Wanda will just have to go to jail like every other shitty little pusher."

I pushed past, sick of the ammonia stink seeping from the loos, and left Leonie to her frisky parishioners. A slob in a grubby singlet grabbed me on my way out in a bid to get me on the seething, heaving dancefloor. I shoved him off and stormed out, feeling I had wasted my time in this cesspit. Bloody Wanda was a loser and nothing Leonie or her band of tambourine shakers could do would save her grimy soul.

Twenty-One

Initially, my pursuit of the wretched Croat had been a gesture to Diana who, since Charlie's disappearance, had provided me with a decent living and a growing self-confidence which had never featured in my life before. But since my spat with Leonie my interest in the missing au pair had sharpened. It was a challenge. Not that I was bowled over by all that stuff about "this poor naive girl ruined by a pimp who is not only using her for casual sex but to distribute his drugs". No girl was *that* naive and getting herself pregnant may have been Wanda's lever to force the guy to marry her and so share his British passport. And peddling dope in order to send money home sounded more like a saccharin Hollywood weepie to me. But there again, maybe my suspicious nature, developed since living with Charlie, was getting in the way. After all, Diana, who was never a pushover for the hard luck stories her employees pulled, was convinced of Wanda's innocence.

Jonny Lusty is, I admit, a distraction. A

decent enough bloke with all the right motives. But was I ready to take the plunge again even if Charlie was proved dead and gone? Deep down, I dare not let go, that's the problem. I had adored that chiselling crook and convincing myself I am back on my own is still a frightening prospect. If I could finally shut the door on Charlie Eastwood he would stop haunting my dreams, I'm sure of it. In fact, I got back so late after my stint at Bootleggers and was so wired up that what little hours which remained found me wakeful as a nervous polecat so one problem was solved: Charlie's infiltration of the small hours was out of the question that night at least.

I sighed, dragging myself out of bed to brew some coffee, Archie watching from his basket with all the scepticism of my old pal Joe Reilly.

As I sipped my coffee the thought of Joe assumed the brightness of a gleam at the end of the tunnel. If Wanda was holed up in a squat and possibly working nights as a washer-up or cleaner, winkling her out was a needle in a haystack job. But if there was some way of doing it, Joe would have the answer. Perhaps he could put in a word for me with Fancy McGill who was, in a sense, already on the Barnes' payroll and to whom the whereabouts of Carey's missing au pair might have a bearing on his case? We might even be able to swap a bit of information – every little helps as they say.

By the time I had given Archie a sniff of the bushes behind the lakeside teahouse and checked that Maria and Doris were on their toes for my regular Wednesday off, an Arctic-looking sun was reddening the sky. December had blown in on a bitterly cold wind straight off the Russian steppes, the lake now frozen clear across, apart from a ribbon of sluggish water where the current pushed between the reeds. A few wild duck skidded on the ice like flat-footed skaters, their coot neighbours complaining as usual. Knowing my car heater to be on the blink, I bundled up in a ski jacket and Archie and I headed back to the smoke.

My Chelsea flat was warm as toast and in no time at all I had showered and changed into fresh jeans and a classy cashmere sweater even my mother would have approved of.

Joe Reilly was at Aintree but my disappointment melted the heart of his manager at the betting shop and he gave up Joe's mobile phone number after a bit of haggling. I stopped for a coffee in Fulham Road and got through to him straight away, explaining my urgent need to speak to Fancy McGill about the Barnes case.

"Sommat up?" he barked.

"A lead I think. Intuition you'd call it."

Joe wasn't the sort to scoff at such whimsical notions and rattled out McGill's number. I promised to get back to Joe on my next Wednesday off and then put a call through to McGill leaving a message on his answerphone and suggesting, if he were free, linking up in the Queen at one o'clock, hinting at more solid information about the Barnes' case than I actually had.

In fact, it wasn't my day at all. Jonny Lusty was also out, off on a developers' promotional junket in Chelsea Harbour and not expected back at the office till three. Freda confirmed from his diary that he'd booked a table for us at Daphne's at eight which took my breath away. Perhaps I shouldn't treat Jonathan Lusty so casually, Daphne's being a seriously chic eatery.

I bought a bunch of freezias to freshen up the stuffy atmosphere of the flat and fed Archie his favourite nosh of rabbit and chewy bits before making a beeline for the Queen.

This excursion to meet Joe Reilly's "enforcer" was not one I am particularly proud of. But my night out at Bootleggers had flicked me on the raw: flushing out the Abominable Maiden had become a fixation and if outsiders didn't occasionally romp in first past the post, where was the fun in risking long odds? I settled for a corner table screened from the customers by a rootbound rubber plant with a layer of dust like dandruff.

Fancy McGill recognised me straight away, presumably filed away with his ex-copper's mental mug shots. I fetched him a double Bell's and we got straight down to business, the pub already raucous with a pre-Christmas office party on its way upstairs to the private room.

"Can we keep this between ourselves, Mr McGill?" I said. "I'm currently employed by Mr Barnes and he doesn't know of my connection with his landlord, Jonny Lusty. And I want to keep Jonny out of this too, if you don't mind."

He nodded, the grey folds of his cheeks stubbled with more than one night's growth. "What's your spin on this, girly?"

"There have been accusations, temporarily withdrawn at present, about Mr B's criminal tendencies with regard to underage girls. Are you with me?"

His reptilian eyes never blinked. I banged on, my voice croaky with nerves. "It could be a conspiracy," I ventured, a ludicrous idea bearing in mind Miranda's involvement but it was one way of getting the detective interested. She apparently hated her step-father enough to spin these malicious yarns in the first place, it was only one more step to imagine the poison-pen letters emanating from the same crazy imagination. But how could she possibly know about Carey's secret pied-à-terre over the estate agency? Even Roz had been unaware of it. That was where I hoped McGill came in.

"My immediate concern is for another employee of the family, a girl called Wanda Ludokovic, twenty years old and well educated. She disappeared nearly three months ago and it is important I get in touch with her straight away." I handed him a snapshot taken from an album I'd found in Roz's room and outlined the story.

"The police know about this?"

"Yes, but she's no longer an urgent case because Wanda's been in contact with a girlfriend in the village and also spoken to a counsellor, a church representative called Leonie who befriends kids at discos and acid-house parties."

"Not dead then, this foreign girl?"

"I'm sure not. Latest news is she's pregnant and holed up in a squat, a converted railway arch, most likely in Brixton as her two best girlfriends both live south of London, this Leonie and another au pair called Lili."

"And they don't know where she's at?"

"No, I'm sure of that. Her visa's expired but she's rumoured to be working as a domestic. With all your contacts, could you suss out any dodgy firms suspected of hiring 'illegals'? And while you're hobnobbing with the *Big Issue* lads, could you please check out the likelihood of any railway arch being used by squatters?"

"These converted railway sites are normally in demand, useful for smalltime car dealers and such like. I've never heard of squatters being able to muscle in, not on any long-term basis any road. It shouldn't be too difficult to flush out any squats by the railway, I've got a mate in Head Office. The other way of tackling it, trawling the thousands of places taking on cheap immigrant labour, would take months. You don't know what you're asking, love."

"Whatever you think best, Mr McGill. Actually there is one other thing." I scribbled a name on the back of an envelope and passed it over. "This outfit. Could you find out anything about it? Names of the people running it, any complaints from clients, say?"

He squinted at the envelope, sighing deeply.

"I could pay you for your time, Mr McGill. Joe Reilly will vouch for me. A deposit?"

He shook his head, mouthing something about owing Joe a packet already. "You and me might be dancing from both ends of the same greasy pole, lady, but I reckon we'll swing it better without being blindfolded an' all."

"The only thing is, Mr McGill, I have to be very careful. My job is at stake. If Mr B found out I knew about your investigation into the letters and that Jonathan Lusty is a sort of collaborator of mine, I'd find myself out on the street. I can't tell you more about these awful allegations – little girls and all that – because I was told in confidence and the matter may still be on police files. But it is a coincidence, isn't it? The letters *and* this other young girl's independent accusations?"

"There's a little six-year-old in the family you say. For her sake, we should keep an open mind. There's no proof, of course, but I take it you are worried about this kiddie's welfare, working in the house like you do?"

"The missing au pair was very fond of Pebbles. I can't believe she would walk out on her if she thought she was in any danger."

"That's the charitable view, miss. Believe me, human nature being what it is, and seeing as this lot ain't exactly down to their last penny, money's a factor we can't afford to ignore. If I find this Wanda for you, will she talk d'ya think? Give evidence?"

"She's on the run for a start, no valid visa, that's a lever and a half. Also she's pregnant which makes her doubly vulnerable. There's a gardener working at the house who may know more about Wanda than he admits, but so far he's staying mum. But *if* you find out where she lives I could get my agency boss to lean on her. She's willing to foot the bill to get her back home before any scandal attaches itself to her staff. Bad publicity about a domestic agency can be a death blow to the business especially if a girl like Wanda ends up in court." I shrugged. "We'll have to cross that bridge if we come to it but between you and me, Mr McGill, this girl's been peddling Ecstacy tablets at clubs over a period of months and it's only a matter of time before she gets caught. I'm quite sure the domestic agency would cough up a nice bonus for you if you could track her down so that Mrs Winterton could ship her out without any police involvement."

McGill swigged his dram like a veteran, the light gleaming in those lizard eyes, the smell of a lead in his nostrils. We parted on good terms and for myself getting some help of a more professional nature than the amateur sleuthing of Jonny Lusty to some degree nullified the sour aftertaste of my abysmal performance at Bootleggers.

In less than three days Fancy McGill had traced Wanda to her squat and followed her at night, clocking her shifts, and on Sunday morning he phoned to tell me the whereabouts of the rathole Wanda worked from. He was following it up to find out who had given her the variety of jobs she seemed to be involved with, and a right old hotchpotch they sounded. Still, at least she wasn't into the call-girl game as yet. I told Fancy to keep his distance, when the time was right I would approach the girl myself. It would be a disaster to scare her off and have to start looking from scratch. He promised to get back to me as soon as there was anything definite, but my mind had already skipped a step in this hunt the thimble lark, a combination clicking into place like the tumblers on the locks of a bank vault. Now all I had to do was square it with Jonny.

Twenty-Two

The news from Fancy McGill was a giant step forward. It would only be a matter of days before the trap would close on Wanda the Wanderer.

My Wednesday evening with Jonny had been something of an ordeal, a bit of a disappointment for the poor guy who had come back from his promotional bash at the Harbour in a great mood, my distraction with my own thoughts putting a damper on our night out.

As it happened he had more news to tickle my fancy: Carey Barnes had signed the rental contract for a small house in Pimlico starting on January the first. "I reckon we'll be seeing his Sussex place featured in *Country Life* any day now," he said.

"Won't Roz's death put buyers off?"

He laughed. "They'll be queuing up to make bids. Houses linked with personalities like Roz de Taffort are hugely attractive to a certain type of client, especially if there's a bit of rumpty-tumpty in the background. They only wish they could put up a blue plaque."

"Will you be handling it?"

"Well out of my league, worst luck, but renting out this London house has dividends. How else do you think I can afford to bring you to this place?" he added petulantly.

I patted his hand. "Don't sulk, lover boy. I can be grateful." I bit my lip. "Miranda doesn't know about this move, I'm sure of it."

"He said nothing to me about needing space for two children. It's quite a small set-up: three beds, two reception rooms and a kitchen in the basement. He particularly wanted a place close to that day school on the green, Hoskins Prep or Lady Hopkins House, something like that. Expensive area."

"Doesn't let the grass grow, does he?" I murmured. "Miranda's firmly dug herself in as far as Pebbles is concerned. She's going to hit the roof when she finds out. New Year's Day, you say?"

"Naturally he doesn't have to move in then but it's a smart little number and Barnes clearly wants to up sticks as soon as possible. There's no other woman in the background, is there? He's not been keeping a Roz mark two on the back burner by any chance?"

"Not that I've heard. Has he given notice on the tenancy over your office?"

"Definitely not. With a kid bouncing round in a small house, he probably needs my place as a work station. It's not exactly homey, is it?"

Having put down the phone on Fancy McGill this morning, there was no time for idle speculation. Carey had invited some people over for Sunday lunch, the first since the funeral. Some sort of turning point perhaps? I mulled over the reasons why Carey Barnes had organised this lunch party at all. Maybe he just wanted to entertain his own friends for a change instead of Roz's hangers-on. Sundays had been a favourite when she was alive and frankly I enjoy cooking for a crowd at weekends, but with his wife hardly settled under the turf, it seemed a bit tactless.

I had argued strongly for retaining Maria on the payroll and, reluctantly, after a bit of argy-bargy, Miranda agreed on the strict understanding that Maria was *my* responsibility and did not interfere with her exclusive care of Pebbles. Explaining all this to Maria took a bit of time, her English having made a little progress though, since she took up with the postman, some surprising vernacular phrases occasionally erupted.

I glanced at my watch and ticked off the things to be dealt with in the half hour before the guests were due at twelve. It struck me as an odd bunch of people and in the light of Jonny's disclosure about Carey's secret relocation plans it might be the last party I'd be catering for. A sort of leaving party.

We were expecting Tom Symmonds, a presenter from the regional TV news programme with his wife Philippa and their two daughters, presumably invited as company for Pebbles, plus a rather twee interior designer called Anthony Hagan, a regular in the glossy home magazines. Strangest of all, the Barretts from Northchurch vicarage had been asked. Carey had never to my knowledge been a supporter of the local church and had probably attended only once, on the occasion of Roz's funeral. Perhaps it was a sort of "hail and farewell" gesture or even a bid for respectability after all the indecent exposure following the inquest.

I buzzed into the library to collect Carey's coffee tray and make sure the fire was still providing the right ambiance. Carey stood in the conservatory staring out at the garden, the leafless trees still spangled with frost, the frozen lake smooth as a painted backdrop. A heron stalked the reeds looking for prey, its grey plumage sombre as the leaden sky. It was not a cheerful prospect and Carey turned, his expression lifeless. The accident had afflicted him, the shadows of depression burying his natural spontaneity.

"Ah, Briony. All set?"

"It was good of you to back me up over the business of keeping Maria on. Miranda can be obstinate."

He nodded, steering me towards his desk. "Here, look at this." Lifting a folded sheet of brown paper, he disclosed a tiny picture of the Virgin and child imprisoned in a dull metal casing. It glowed with gold leaf and lapis lazuli, the sheer beauty of it robbing me of speech.

"It's genuine. A Russian friend of mine is a dealer. I brought it back with me."

"Do they allow icons to be exported just like that?"

He smiled, pinching my cheek, and slipped it back in its wrapper. "Ivan acts as my interpreter, a fixer with a delicate ear for trouble. Did you know that according to intelligence sources two-thirds of the Russian economy is said to be under the influence of mafia groups and these Ruski mobsters are moving west, gaining control even in Britain? Extortion, fraud and every imaginable sort of racketeering."

"You're building up evidence for your book?"

"And a TV exposé once I've got my stuff sorted."

"Isn't all this a bit dangerous? Working alone, I mean."

Before he could answer the door burst open, Miranda, ashen faced, gripping Pebbles like a captive, the child dressed only in her vest and knickers, weeping and struggling to get away. Maria appeared from the dining room, drawn by the racket.

Carey pushed me aside and reached out to his little daughter who flinched, leaping back to cannonball into Maria, clinging to her and sobbing.

He gestured roughly to Maria to clear out.

"Get Pebbles dressed, Maria," I said, nodding in an encouraging way, hoping the stupid girl had the nous to pick up the vibes.

"No, wait!" Miranda shouted, lunging at the child, pitching her forward between herself and her father like a weapon.

Carey slapped Miranda's face, the hard blow ringing in the air like gunshot. He tried to wrest Pebbles from her but Miranda stood her ground, the impression of his hand flaring like a birthmark on her cheek. She clung on to the child's wrist as if her life depended on it.

"I knew you'd go for the poor baby. Why else move her into your dressing room? You're a fucking pervert, Carey Barnes, and this time I'm *not* backing off. Anal abuse it's called. And don't I know it!"

"What the hell are you on about?" Carey said, his voice controlled, a miracle of forbearance. Presumably slapping Miranda was as far as he dared to go with two witnesses in the room. Pebbles' cries had diminished to a pitiful hiccoughing shudder, for all the world like the keening I'd heard at night from my room.

Miranda wildly gazed at us each in turn. "Just look at her, all of you. That's what happens to a kid at the mercy of a man like this."

"Miranda, what's going on?" I burst out, wondering how this terrible confrontation had suddenly erupted on just another ordinary Sunday morning. Completely out of the blue.

"I was changing her, ready for lunch," she spat out. "Her poor little bottom's red raw, chafed to sandpaper. I'm taking her straight off to see the police surgeon. Right now!" She spun round. "I *knew* you would revert to type, your sort just can't leave it alone, can you? Not even with your own flesh and blood. At least I was just Roz's by-blow, a non-event in this family."

Maria quietly closed in, stroking Pebbles' hair and gently loosening Miranda's grip.

Carey spoke. "Take her upstairs, Maria, and get her dressed. Our guests will be arriving any minute. Miranda and I will talk about all this later this evening." He turned on the girl, his expression cold as death. "The evidence won't disappear in a few hours, Miranda. There's no point in punishing the child with your own spiteful hysteria. If you still want a medical opinion when you have had time to consider the consequences I will ring Doctor Forman tonight."

Carey's sang-froid was astonishing.

After having gone through the humiliation of admitting to the police that her statement had been a total fabrication, why would Miranda grab this moment to reopen the paedophile angle? And to use Carey's adored little girl as a battering ram with which to attack her stepfather? Were we misreading Miranda's motives? Was jealousy a cover for greed? Was the prospect of contesting Carey's claim to his dead wife's considerable estate the real reason for such a nutty reversal? And if so, was a teenager capable of running a hate campaign without someone in the background plotting her moves? How did Pebbles fit into all this? Had she been brainwashed to back up this vindictive attack? Or was it perhaps true, after all?

A car went past on the drive and parked by the front windows. Almost immediately the doorbell started ringing. The bloody vicar and Patricia were on the doorstep. Before Maria could whisk Pebbles away Miranda made one last desperate throw. She knelt down to her level and, shaking with emotion, said, "Listen, sweetheart. Stop crying. Nobody's cross with *you*. Just tell Daddy what you told me in the bathroom. When I changed your panties. Then when you're dressed you can play with your little friends who are coming to lunch."

Pebbles knuckled her eyes, her lips trembling.

"My botty hurt," she whispered.

"Louder, darling. Daddy didn't quite hear you."

"I said my botty hurt."

Carey remained stoney faced as if considering the possibility that Miranda had coached Pebbles in this, had brainwashed her in the weeks since her mother's death. The silence lengthened and Miranda rose, eyeing the man coldly with all the appraisal of a hanging judge. Pebbles sucked her thumb, hiding her head in Maria's skirt.

I hurried forward, gathering Pebbles and Maria and pushing them into the hall.

"You go and get dressed for the party, poppet, and Maria will find you some bread for the ducks. Those poor ducks can't get any food while the lake's frozen. You could take Tammy and Gemma on to the little bridge and throw crusts to them."

She brightened and trotted off with Maria, eager to escape.

"I'll show the Barretts into the drawing room, shall I? Offer them some sherry...?" I lamely added, closing the door on the two of them, hoping there'd be no blood in the ring before I sounded the gong for the luncheon guests.

As it happened Roz's daughter put on a professional performance, entering the room just as Carey was mixing the drinks for his guests, the TV producer and his wife, Philippa. Miranda's was a class act, embellished by concern when Carey, clearly confused slopped the drinks on the tray, the girl mopping up with a sweet smile and relieving him of the salver. Anthony Hagan was playing joker, prancing about the room directing Patricia's awestruck attention to the painting of Roz over the chimneypiece.

Outside, the three little girls jigged on the Chinese bridge, the wildfowl alternately whirling round their heads or slithering about under the planking, scrabbling for the chunks of bread thrown out on to the ice and trying to evade Archie who had somehow managed to join the children on the bridge, his manic barking lending a raw accompaniment to the kids' laughter.

Maria was offering the drinks tray as I announced luncheon. In mid-sentence my voice dried, pierced by screams from the bridge. We all rushed to the windows. The three girls were howling in terror, Archie having leapt on to the ice after the ducks, the sheer proximity of the quarry clearly too much for the little runt to resist.

As I apologetically offered to save the situation and call him off, the children's cries shrilled across the lake.

"The dog's fallen through the ice," someone gasped.

"Christ! She's climbed down – she's trying to hook him out," Anthony stuttered.

Miranda screamed. "Pebbles is out on the ice!"

I flew outside just in time to see the little girl disappear, the red sleeves of her anorak vanishing amid chunks of splintered ice, the dark surface audibly cracking like a mirror.

The cold air caught my throat in a stranglehold as I ran on to the lawn shouting at the other little girls to get back. There was no sign of either Archie or Pebbles. Even the ducks had flown off, circling the oriental teahouse like black arrows in the sky. Mark appeared at the door of the greenhouses and I yelled at him to fetch a ladder.

But as I turned back, Miranda ran on to the unbroken circumference of ice, closely followed by Carey. Miranda lurched as the ice broke under her feet and disappeared into the water, then struck out, diving and resurfacing in a frenzied search. Carey struggled to remove his jacket and shoes and plunged in after her, the water seething with their efforts.

Carey swam in circles, his stroke slower and less confident, affected by the sub-zero temperature and clearly much less fit than the girl. The rest of us huddled on the shore, gutless with fear.

Just as Miranda surfaced with the lifeless child in her arms Mark raced to the edge with his ladder and tackle. We formed a rescue party, balancing his contraption as he scrambled out to reach for them, pulling the two girls to safety with a lifeline, holding Pebbles in his arms as Miranda dragged herself exhausted from the shards of ice.

The Barretts crowded in and as Mark laid the little girl on the grass, Patricia launched into an expert resuscitation routine. After agonising moments Pebbles retched and a stream of filthy water shot out. She opened her eyes and Miranda fell upon her, embracing the sodden bundle, wildly covering

243

her face with kisses.

No one in those harrowing moments had given a thought to Carey and it was left to Mark to make a second sortie and drag him out. The man was practically a goner, collapsing on the grass like a castaway. A shout went up as Archie was seen to scramble out on the far side, lolling on the steps of the teahouse, panting his wicked heart out. Carey struggled to his feet and stood leaning weakly against a tree, coughing fit to bust, his soaking garments daubed with mud and duckweed, tendrils of torn water lilies roped about his ankles like leg irons.

Philippa had had the sense to ring for an ambulance and it arrived almost immediately. Mark gently lifted Pebbles on to the stretcher and Miranda, draped in Patricia's loden jacket, leapt in behind her, crooning over the half-conscious small body under the blankets. The ambulance drove off at speed leaving the rest silent, standing at the edge of the frozen lake like refugees in a Swedish movie. Carey, stiff with cold and looking more dead than alive, stumbled back to the house behind the others supported by the two men.

Anthony insisted Carey got changed immediately and made a hearty attempt to pull things round, pushing the shivering group into the library, propelling Carey upstairs and barking at me to make some fresh coffee for the guests and bring some up straight away.

By the time I got back to the library the men had helped themselves from the decanter, the women shivering round the library fire. The shock of the near fatality visibly thawed into painful actuality in their minds as the heat of the coffee and brandy touched their nerve ends. For myself, I couldn't stop trembling, the thought flashing into my head that Archie, following the mystery of the dead rat, had almost caused the death of a second member of Barnes family. Anthony bustled in, looking important and murmured to me as he passed, "I've left Carey in the master bedroom – get moving, girl!"

I trailed upstairs to knock at Roz's door but getting no answer pushed it open anyway, setting a tray of coffee on Roz's sofa table at the foot of the bed.

Carey had showered and changed, the steam still filtering from the ensuite bathroom. The man sat crouched on the bed, his head in his hands, making no sound. I waited, working myself up to ask. Finally I blurted out, "Would you like me to drive you? To the hospital?"

He looked up, his eyes bloodshot, frowning as if trying to remember who I was.

"Mr Hagan is looking after everyone

downstairs. Would you like me to tell them to go home? Let me take you to see the girls – you must be frantic."

"Ah, Briony!" he said, as if everything had suddenly clicked into focus, and smiled, jumping up to grasp my hand.

"You're an angel. But no need. I phoned. Pebbles is going to be just fine. Miranda seems to be the one in trauma. Hysterics."

"You're not going then?" I said open-mouthed.

"Better let Miranda cool off first. I imagine she's bawling out the doctors to acknowledge my perverted attacks on her and her sister. Me being there will only queer her pitch. She's insisting they keep Pebbles in, make certain tests ... But in Miranda's present state of mind even a half-baked medico can see she's off her trolley. The ward sister said best let Miranda get it off her chest without my presence firing her up even further. She thinks it's the shock, but we know better, don't we, Briony? Can't say I relish the thought of defending myself in a fracas in a public ward."

He looked pale as death, the bravado sitting uneasily on his bleak conjecture of the situation at the hospital. "Tell everyone I'll be down in a jiffy. We'll just go ahead with lunch. I'll sort out Miranda tomorrow... " he lamely concluded, dismissing me with a grimace and a peck on the cheek. I left.

So he hadn't forgotten our little conversation after all? The drunken maunderings when he confided Miranda's false recollections of her sexual interference at his hands were a secret bond between us and it occurred to me, not for the first time, that perhaps I had been naive, taking his story at face value against Miranda's emotional outbursts. I ran downstairs, admitting, nevertheless, an agreeable frisson of excitement at the dramatic turn of events.

After checking the oven, I hurried to the library to tell Anthony Hagan the luncheon party was to go ahead. I had hardly got inside the door when Carey strode into the room, flushed and smiling, extending his arms affectionately to his friends.

"She's going to be all right. Miranda's staying with her overnight while they do some tests but the doctor assures me she will be discharged in the morning with no ill effects."

"And *you'll* be all right? You're sure?" Philippa murmured, reaching to squeeze his arm.

"I phoned Roz's cousin, Sonia. She's coming down from Wales to take charge here while I sort a few things out. You've all been terribly kind. But are your kids OK?" he asked with the sudden realization that no one had mentioned the other children caught up in the disaster.

"Your au pair's giving them lunch in the kitchen. Best thing. Take their minds off things. They're busy towelling down the dog." Everyone laughed, a nervous twitter, each eager to break the tension.

Carey rubbed his hands, accepting a stiff whisky and water from Anthony with a grin.

"Then let's waste no more time. Come on, folks. Let's eat!"

Twenty-Three

The lunch party dispersed at three leaving only Anthony Hagan to share the evening with Carey. I laid a light supper in the library at eight and they fell on it like schoolboys. The two of them were in unnaturally high spirits and I couldn't help wondering how Carey managed to compartmentalise his life so effectively: his child almost drowned; his wife recently killed in a dubious accident; his stepdaughter already laying her accusations before the medics in the hospital. The man was either incredibly courageous or, for years having escaped bullets and threats as part of his job, felt himself to be immortal, untouchable in effect.

Hagan drove off about midnight and judging from the light streaming through the windows on to the garden into the small hours, Carey, like me, had trouble sleeping.

Next morning after Doris had made her first rounds, we sat at the kitchen table with our mugs of tea mulling over the accident on the lake.

"I'm not surprised Miranda was the one to save the poor little mite," she said. "As I told you, it was Miranda dragged her mother out of the river when they had their car accident three years ago. In all the papers it was: 'Girl saves Mother despite own grave injuries.' And people say lightning never strikes twice!"

"She's a marvellous swimmer. And the water was absolutely Arctic."

"My Trevor says that's what saved little Pebbles. The cold-water shock. Slows down the functions, he sez. Like that toddler in the paper last winter, fell into a garden pond she did and was under ever so long and survived."

I take a lot of Doris's words of wisdom with a pinch of salt and Trevor's input sounded no less fanciful. But Doris had worked here for years and kitchen gossip was all I was likely to dig up in my line of business. I had no intention of disclosing the accusations Miranda had thrown at our employer just before we were all embroiled in the lake disaster, but one thing still bugged me.

"Tell me, Doris, did you ever get the slightest impression that Pebbles was upset by something going on here? I mean before Roz died?"

"Old Cannock could be a bit of a tartar sometimes – old fashioned, strict, if you know what I mean. But spanking the child you mean? Never laid a hand on her."

"And her father? Mr Barnes can be a bit short-tempered at times."

"Soft as butter with little Pebbles. Spoilt at times and no mistake but it never did her no harm. What you on about, Briony?" she added, her eyes narrowing with suspicion.

I sighed. "It's just I've been hearing a child crying at night. Woke me up a couple of times. It's been on my conscience – I should have taken steps—"

Doris laughed, her big belly shaking like a jelly. An unsympathetic response I thought.

"You should have nabbed that gatehouse while you had the chance, my gel. Shoved Miss World up in that room of yours."

"There's something wrong with my room?"

"All milarky my Trevor sez but you just ask in the village. Wanda got quite upset about it when she was 'ere. It's the Kington House ghostie. The kid in the apple store."

"What apple store?"

"Your room used to be an apple store before the Barneses got it made over for the staff. No one told them it was haunted."

"Haunted?"

"The story goes that a boot boy was shut up in there one time for stealing. Years and years ago o' course. There was a case against the butler. He was hanged."

"The boy hanged himself?"

"No! The boy died of a beating – the butler was hanged. But your room has this funny crying in the night – so it goes. Not everyone hears it, oh no. Just them with an ear for it, you know."

"Well, I haven't got an ear for it. You're pulling my leg, aren't you, Doris?" I chivvied her, half convinced that the mysterious weeping had all been in my imagination and half afraid that I was what Joe Reilly would seriously regard as "one of them". But I couldn't really swallow all this ghostie nonsense, stuff like that hangs about an old house like ivy, growing more tendrils with every nightmare like my own. I wish now I had never mentioned it. I smirked, wordlessly rubbishing this old wives' tale.

"Don't take *my* word for it," Doris retorted. "Ask Mrs Fisher down the post office. Her mum used to work 'ere before the war. She 'eard that poor boy an' all, wouldn't stay in the house another night after that, give her the willies it did."

Pensive, I rose to clear away the mugs, trying to fit a rational explanation to my own conviction of the weeping I had heard. Later, knocking on the library door I got a muffled reply and went in to find Carey at his computer. He swivelled round, looking tired as death.

"You've had no breakfast. Can I bring you some coffee? Some croissants, maybe? Won't take a jiffy to defrost some I put in the freezer at the weekend."

"Coffee. Please. But nothing more. Sonia will be here by lunchtime. She's at the hospital now. I'm hoping Pebbles will be coming back with her. And Miranda, of course," he quickly added.

"Will Mrs Parry be staying on?"

"Until the weekend possibly. It all depends..."

"Any news of the girls?" I ventured.

"They're both fine. You must excuse Miranda's little outburst yesterday. She's like her mother: highly strung."

"Little outburst" was a funny way of putting it but I could understand his desire to downplay her criminal accusations. Even so, Carey Barnes was playing a cool hand in all this.

I put on my warm jacket and took Archie for a stroll, calling in on Mark working in the hothouses to ask for some fresh vegetables and herbs for lunch.

"Mrs Parry is bringing Pebbles back with her. It was very gallant of you coming to the rescue with your ladder and ropes yesterday. You and Miranda saved her life between you."

He stared, the taciturn manner warming a fraction.

"Miranda was lucky not to top herself. People have drowned diving straight in to save kids in stupid accidents like that. It's important to have the proper gear and, anyhow, if anyone saved the little girl it was the vicar's wife with her mouth to mouth. Never had much time for Mrs Barrett before but, fair do's, the woman knew what she was at."

I nodded, mulling over all the interlocking pieces which made up the rescue, each interdependent, the only hero entirely disregarded being Carey whose bravery had been not only foolhardy, but entirely useless. I changed tack as Mark stripped the last of the autumn raspberries from the coolhouse canes.

"Since we last spoke about Wanda I've heard some news. I've found out where she's living. Would you like to come with me and try and persuade her to go home? She was a friend of yours, wasn't she? A special friend?"

He paused, staring at the winter fruit in the bowl in his hand.

"What makes you think I could make her see sense?"

"She's pregnant. You knew that."

He laughed, the first time I'd actually seen the man laugh, his tanned face breaking into lines of amusement.

"Is there something about my lunch box that gives all you women the same idea?"

"Wanda's baby's not yours?"

"No! I admit to fathering Jennie's and I reckon it's going to cost me a packet but that was *her* secret agenda, nothing I was in on whatever the old crows in the village got to say. I was attracted to Wanda, make no mistake, but once a certain bloke appeared on the scene, a rich bugger throwing his money about, Wanda wasn't looking at the bloody gardener no more. Stands to reason." He viciously tugged at more fruit, filling the bowl with any old berries, ripe or not.

"Oh, sorry, Mark. My mistake. Still, she's not living it up in any penthouse now I assure you. And she *does* need a friend. Think about it. I'm going to London on Wednesday, come along if you like."

"Why should I? As you're so nosy I'll tell you something to really make you laugh. Roz was the love of my life if you must know. Messing about with these other girls was just airing my socks. I'll be glad to get away from this rotten hole."

"But Wanda's been dumped in a squat. She needs help, Mark."

His only response was to go outside to fetch some sprouts and broccoli from the kitchen garden.

As Archie and I walked back to the house with my box of veggies, I noticed an estate car neatly parked in the yard. I hurried back, tying up Archie in the scullery, wanting no row with Sonia Parry over the untrained terrier which had nearly caused the possible demise of the last three twigs on the Barnes' family tree.

Neither Pebbles nor Miranda were back home. I served lunch in the dining room, Sonia and Carey closeted like conspirators, insisting I leave everything on the sideboard so they could help themselves. I climbed up to my room, cuddling Archie, shutting the door on the whole wretched crew. Maybe it was time I gave up this job, took a secretarial course or something, worked nine to five like normal people. But there was Archie. This gypsy lifestyle of mine suited us both, at least until I'd laid my own particular ghost to rest: Charlie Eastwood, God rot his sinning soul.

I spread out on the bed and put through a call to Jonny, laying my pent-up miseries on his doorstep. I was nervous of saying too much on the phone now Sonia had moved in, never entirely sure my conversations would not be overheard on the kitchen extension which is on the same line as my own, the Barnes having their own number and, for all I know, Carey using his mobile for privacy. What a suspicious old world we live in.

By the time I took up my station at the tea trolley at four o'clock, Carey had gone out, his MG revving up like a turbo jet.

Sonia was settled in the drawing room, her short hair expertly cut, the sage-coloured suit accentuating the green lights in her eyes.

"Won't you join me, Briony? Fetch another cup. I'd like to discuss a few household matters with you, if I may? Mr Barnes has gone back to town, an urgent call."

I did as I was told with some ill grace I'll admit. Diana had warned me that the boss element of this job would be fluid: Roz hardly the domestic type and Carey off on his own course, but a third party barging in was something else.

I poured myself a cup of weak Earl Grey, the slightly perfumed aroma recalling other uncomfortable interviews over the tea table, my mother's careful barbs overlapping Sonia Parry's polite enquiries.

"Pebbles will be staying at the Clinic in Tunbridge Wells for a day or two. Treatment for a childish complaint. I persuaded the doctor to transfer her to a private place."

I nodded, sipping my tea, all agog.

"And Miranda?"

"Miranda has moved in with her boyfriend I gather. Flounced out as teenagers are prone to do," she added with a nervous laugh. "I'm hoping to persuade them both to join us all in Wales for Christmas. Pebbles will be spending the school holidays with me there and after that she will be attending a new school. A fresh start. And we shall drop that childish nickname of hers and start treating her more sensibly. Portia. It's a delightful name – I can't think why 'Pebbles' was allowed to become so established." She sipped her tea, eyeing me frankly. "You know this American quite well, don't you, Briony? What is your impression?"

I gabbled some rigmarole, meaningless phrases clearly showing I hardly knew Gizmo at all in fact.

Sonia sat erect, her feet firmly placed together on the Chinese rug. After a moment's hesitation she moved closer to me on the sofa and scrunched up her sleeve displaying a silver bracelet, a substantial art nouveau setting of an enormous chunk of polished amber.

"Look, Briony. There's a fly caught in it. Millions of years ago this unfortunate insect drowned in resin and what you see is perfectly preserved, every feeler, each delicate wing caught for eternity."

I politely admired the thing, wondering if this was Sonia's idea of being matey.

"I always think of Miranda when I examine this poor trapped creature, a beautiful thing to me but a tragedy for the fly. It never had a chance, doomed to be in the wrong place at the wrong time."

Then she took the plunge and said what was really on her mind. "I understand you were a reluctant listener to Miranda's outburst yesterday afternoon, witness to her ludicrous suggestion that the child had been tampered with."

"Yes. Maria was there too."

"Forget Maria," she snapped, impatiently consigning our live-in-lovely to the rubbish heap. "Maria is stupid to start with and her comprehension of a row like that is nil."

I had to agree.

"So. May I be assured of your total discretion in this? Miranda has been a problem for some time."

"Of course," I replied stiffly, getting to my feet. "If that is all, madam?"

"Oh, just sit down for heaven's sake!" She sighed. "I must apologise. It was unnecessary to question your loyalty. Will you forgive me?" She urged me back to my place and I flopped down, wondering what else was bugging the woman.

"As I say, Miranda has problems. She needs our special consideration. Carey seems to think this man Gizmo is a good influence on her, though for my part I find his casual attitude difficult to understand. After all, the girl's only nineteen and at an emotional stage in life to be allowed to live under the protection of a comparative stranger."

"Gizmo seems very sensible," I admitted, thinking Miranda a sight more fortunate in her choice of lover than I had been at her age.

Her hands opened in a gesture of defeat and this self-controlled creature began to fray at the edges, a fleeting likeness to Roz surfacing like a blush, then disappearing as quickly as it had come.

"Miranda needs help, psychiatric help. We have discovered that my cousin was secretly sending money to her daughter in the States, paying enormous bills to a therapist who may have planted wicked lies in the girl's head. She was so vulnerable, you see. That terrible accident when Roz's car went into the river left Miranda with mental and physical scars and that therapist person played on her jealousy. Once Pebbles was born Miranda felt discarded. It is a classic family situation these days: a second marriage, an attractive stepfather, a silly girl imagining herself sexually involved with him, taking her mother's place in his affections as she thought, revenging herself on a mother who, it must be admitted, was a very self-regarding person, unimaginative of others' needs."

"You've lost me, I'm afraid. I'm not sure teenage tantrums are really that complicated. If you'll excuse me saying so, you were not there, Mrs Parry. Naturally, you believe Mr Barnes' version of all this but he lied to the police about important factors. He's a very convincing man, but can we really believe everything he says? Why would Miranda make such a serious accusation about her stepfather unless she had reason to think Pebbles had been sexually abused?"

"That's what worries me about this American boyfriend of hers. He's very worldly wise and may have turned the girl's head. To put it bluntly, my late cousin was a very rich woman. Disputes about inheritance may be at the bottom of all this, especially now that it has been proved that Miranda's accusations are pure fabrication, a result of a mental problem fostered by too much counselling of the wrong sort," she said with finality. "Pebbles has been subjected to close examination by two separate physicians and is currently undergoing some very sympathetic questioning by a child-guidance expert. I can assure you, Briony, Pebbles is absolutely fine, a little upset by all the fuss but a sensible little girl you must agree. She insists her father never hurt her in any way at all – these sexual fantasies are all in Miranda's head."

"But the chafing?"

Sonia laughed, throwing back her head in merriment.

"Only a teenager obsessed with this awful incest claptrap would have jumped to such a bizarre conclusion. The child has *worms*, a common parasitical infection which will be cleared up in no time at all. The ghastly irritation drove the poor little scrap to tear at herself and, since Cannock left, no one has thought to cut Pebbles' fingernails. Entirely self-inflicted. I've seen it before in my own children. Worming isn't only for dogs and cats, my dear."

I was poleaxed, the simple explanation exposing Miranda's interpretation to farce. No wonder Carey Barnes had been unmoved by Miranda's threats. The poor devil had been innocent all along and now he had two hospital doctors and a children's therapist to prove it.

Talk about storm in a teacup!

Twenty-Four

Carey did not return and Miranda also stayed away, humiliated no doubt by the medical findings with regard to Pebbles.

Sonia was making herself unpopular by interfering with the household routine though, in fairness, she did put a rocket under the decorators to move in pretty damn quick and start repairing Phyllis's damage to the nursery suite. Maria has become increasingly sulky under this new regime and pretends to understand even less, turning blank eyes on Sonia as she attempts in halting Italian to get the wind behind our Girl Friday. Doris alone relishes the ructions, and, mindful of my own limited employment here, I've managed to take a philosophical view, agreeing with the bossy cow, then going on as before.

Archie is the real problem, congenitally volatile, and short of actually sinking his teeth into Sonia's elegant calf makes himself impossible, doubling his ratting exploits and once adding a very pretty weasel to the dead bodies secreted about the scullery and washhouse.

Pebbles came home at teatime a few days later, bouncing in bright as a button, greeting Maria with wet kisses and almost strangling Archie with affection.

"We shall be off in the morning," Sonia announced. "I've packed her warm things, perhaps Maria could parcel up her old school uniform and take it down to the vicarage for the jumble sale? You like Auntie Sonia's farm, don't you, sweetheart? We must find a nice kitten for you, something of your very own, much better than smelly old Archie."

I swiftly butted in before Pebbles could protest, seeing the light of battle in her eye, Archie being the next best thing to Father Christmas in her mind.

But we did have a jolly farmhouse tea all together round the kitchen table, Maria's sunny disposition overriding her reservations about the new madam, and it occurred to me that this might be the last teatime special for Pebbles in this house. But wasn't it all for the best? It was an unlucky house; the horrible recollection of Roz lying in a mess of blood at the bottom of the cellar steps still vivid in my mind.

Sonia packed the car overnight ready for an early start on Wednesday, and buckling Pebbles into a rear seat straight after breakfast left little time for sad farewells though Maria burst into tears, spoiling her mascara. Poor Phyllis had finally lost her last charge: it was unlikely Pebbles would ever see her again.

I made my escape shortly after, slowing down on the drive to make a final appeal to Mark to join me in seeing Wanda. He shook his head and continued filling the trailer with what broken branches remained after the hurricane the weekend I arrived at this benighted place.

Back at my flat I made a long phone call to Diana outlining my plan and then rang Jonny to make sure Carey Barnes was not in situ.

"He's not been here for a couple of weeks at least," he assured me. "Why?"

I sketched a résumé of the latest brouhaha at Northchurch and he whistled, continually impressed by all the drama I managed to find battened down "in the sticks" as he put it.

"Can't talk now, Bri, I'm just off to Cambridge for the day. An important client has a site he wants me to survey for him. A possible new hall of residence on the Granchester road. Big lunch, big bucks. See you tonight. If things pan out I'll make you an offer you can't refuse. Might even open a second branch, what about that?"

I made all the appropriate noises and rang off, my nasty little brain forming a plan which, with luck, would collar Wanda and salve my conscience over Archie's undeniable part in not only the frozen lake business but the dumping of the rat on the cellar steps.

The next move was the dodgy one. I called All Clear and introduced myself as Mrs French the new manager of Lusty's estate agency in Chelsea.

"We've done business before, Mr-er—"

"Brownlees. Michael Brownlees. Yes, indeed, clients' flats as a rule I seem to remember."

"We have a problem at this end, Mr Brownlees. A tenant has left one of our places in a fearful mess and the new people are due to move in tomorrow. I know it's short notice but could you send a team over straight away, say this afternoon? There's one particular girl I've been very impressed with in the past. Wanda Ludokovic. Is she still on your books?"

"Oh yes. An excellent worker, one of our very best. Generally works with Owen. One moment there, madam, while I check our staff rota."

I tapped my pencil, the seconds dragging by, refusing even to imagine Jonny's reaction to all this. Mr Brownlees came back on line, his tone apologetic.

"I'm very sorry, Mrs French, but the girl you requested is on night shift, not due on duty till nine o'clock. We have other excellent teams I could send over straight away who are—"

"No. It's an important letting. I must have someone I'm happy with. Is it possible she could come here at nine?"

"I could switch her on to your rush job I suppose," he reluctantly agreed. "What's the address?"

"Just tell your team I'll meet them outside the agency – it will be easier if I show them round myself."

"It's *that* bad?"

"Some people live like pigs, Mr Brownlees. You'd be appalled at the state even expensive properties are left in."

"And don't I know it, Mrs French."

We finalised our arrangements, agreeing to settle the rate on a one-off basis depending on the hours All Clear found it necessary to spend on the job.

I put down the phone, wide-eyed with my own audacity.

"Crikey!"

But before I lost my nerve I phoned Fancy McGill and explained my idea. Not normally a man for showing emotion, McGill was bowled over by my short-circuiting him on All Clear.

"How did you get on to it? I've only just

tagged your bloody runaway with them my-self. You got information you're not sharing, miss? I thought we had a deal," he said, clearly narked.

"I'll explain later. But listen, Mr McGill, are you in or out? Nine o'clock outside Lusty's and if you're not there I'll go in alone."

He wasn't impressed but reluctantly agreed providing he took charge of the keys and we met in the Queen at eight thirty for a run through.

I called at the bank to cash an astronomi-cal chunk of my hard-earned savings, took Archie for a run giving Jonny an hour to leave the office then sauntered down there, surprising Freda in a tête-à-tête with her express-delivery driver, gormless Terry.

They leapt apart as I strolled in and Terry made a quick exit. Freda's one good eye winked at me and we chewed the fat for five minutes, Freda explaining that I'd missed Jonny by a whisker.

"Yes, I know, he told me he'd be out all day. I just popped in for a peek at his diary, Freda. I'm hoping to arrange a surprise holiday for us for his birthday so don't tell him I was in, will you? I'll catch him later." She nodded, all smiles, her sentimental heart going pitter patter.

The phone rang and while Freda dealt with it I buzzed into Jonny's office and, quick as a flash, removed the spare keys to Barnes' flat from the hole in the wall behind the Canaletto lookalike, emerging with his diary under my arm just as Freda came back on line.

"I'll bring it back in an hour, I promise."

"Suppose someone wants to book a viewing while it's gone?"

I grinned. "Just say he's out and you can't promise anything till he gets back. No problem."

I felt a bit of a heel dragging poor Freda in on my little scam but it was the only way. I drove over the river to a keycutting service in Battersea, a "while-u-wait" joint I'd used before as a kid when I'd lost my mother's keys and wanted no questions asked. Dead set on security my mama. It only took ten minutes and I emerged like a marathon winner, punching the air in triumph. This cloak and dagger lark is growing on me, the excitement revving up my pulse rate no end.

Dumping the diary back in Jonny's office and replacing the keys in his safe while Freda was checking her horoscope was a piece of cake. I prayed that the rest of Plan A would go as smoothly.

I perched on the edge of her desk looking doleful, moaning away like mad about my lousy job.

"The only day off all week and they ring through and say I've got to get back straight away. Complete U-turn."

"Not more accidents?" Freda gasped, goggle-eyed with all the goings-on at Northchurch.

"My stand-in's gone sick. You'd think those people could go out for a takeaway like everyone else, wouldn't you?"

"You're driving back *now*?"

"Fraid so. Could you tell Jonny I've been recalled to duty? Tell you what, he could drive down to Sussex tonight, straight from Cambridge. I'll be finished by nine and he could stay the night. His diary's empty tomorrow, I've checked. They've promised me tomorrow off instead – we could make a decent break of it and slip through the tunnel for lunch in Paris."

"Sounds great. He usually checks in with me before I go off at five. You'll ring him yourself though, on his mobile, just in case he misses me?"

"Absolutely." I jumped up, grinning like a fool, keeping my fingers crossed that Fancy McGill and I didn't have to resort to Plan B. "I'll do it now," I said, and using Freda's extension caught Jonny at lunch which left him little room to manoeuvre. He agreed to drive straight back to Northchurch afterwards but would be arriving very late, probably after two. "I've been invited to dine with the Burser and we have some designs to discuss," he said, going on to enthuse about the prospect of Christmas shopping at Fauchon, no doubt to impress the client listening in, bless him. With luck I'd be tucked up in Kington House before he left Cambridge.

It was lucky Jonny was such a trusting chap, Charlie would never have swallowed a load of old rubbish like that.

I left Freda misty-eyed with the sheer romance of the notion of seeing the Christmas lights in Paris and as I left she flipped back to her horoscope in the paper just to check that the stars didn't forecast something almost as good in the Libra slot.

Twenty-Five

I walked over to the Queen at eight thirty and found Fancy McGill already sitting up at the bar deep in conversation with the landlord, getting the lowdown on some poor debtor on his wanted list no doubt. He bought me a drink which was a good omen – though it may have been Fancy's idea of establishing who was boss – and dragged me through to the snug, a horrible little room at the back frequented by secret lovers hoping for some quiet nookie.

"Before we get stuck in on this set-up of yours, missy, hand over the keys. And the money to pay off the cleaning crew gaffer. If anyone's going to get caught out at least I'm *employed* by Barnes to nail this poison-pen woman and can talk my way out of being on the premises."

I did as I was told, passing the newly cut keys under the table together with a plastic envelope containing my twenties. He scribbled his mobile-phone number on a business card, an impressive affair with his fax number and everything, and handed it over. "For emergencies," he said.

"You brought the letters?"

He patted his raincoat pocket, the garment perfect for a private eye in one of those fifties detective movies.

"Now tell me how you got on to this cleaning firm?"

I cleared my throat. "As you know, Mr McGill, my boyfriend—"

"Lusty?"

I nodded. "Jonny Lusty. Well, he's had trouble with Mr Barnes over security and has had to change the locks on more than one occasion."

"Break-ins?"

"No, just a feeling he was being followed. Mr Barnes is paranoid about his flat – wanted a place that no one knew about, not even his wife. He's been investigating some

Russian mafia connections in London – didn't he tell you this?"

"Just get back to the point, love. Lusty kept changing the locks you said."

"Yes, well, Jonny thought Barnes was just being difficult but, in fact, someone *had* been in the flat and so the hidey-hole *was* known after all. You see, Jonny discovered that owing to a misunderstanding with his secretary All Clear had access. He cancelled the booking straight away but it was too late, the letters had started to arrive on Mr Barnes' doormat and some at his office too."

"Barnes found out about the cleaning crew nosing round?"

"No, definitely not. Jonny was going to explain to Mr Barnes but I told him to let sleeping dogs lie."

"Quite right too. The fat was already in the fire," Fancy agreed, his lumbering responses reminding me of a tank moving inexorably on, flattening everything. "Now what made you think the Polak was working for this cleaning outfit?"

"Wanda's Croatian, not Polish."

"Same difference. Just get on with it, we 'aven't got all night."

"Jonny knew All Clear had been in the flat and I found out another girl, an Albanian, who is working in the Barnes' country house *also* came from the same firm – she'd been a cleaner too. It crossed my mind that Maria, the Albanian girl, might be an illegal immigrant and as Wanda's visa has expired it stands to reason she *must* be working without a permit. Q.E.D."

Fancy looked askance at this piece of feminine logic, having none of Joe Reilly's trust in intuition. "You saying Barnes makes a habit of hiring illegals?"

"Absolutely not! His stepdaughter Miranda introduced the Albanian au pair through a friend who had contacts with All Clear. For all I know Maria's not 'illegal' at all, but personally I think the cleaning firm's on to a lucrative racket, probably pays these people peanuts and in jobs like office cleaning nobody asks too many questions, do they? Can I see the letters?"

He fanned out the letters on the smeary table, over a dozen of them, all short and all vicious. The allegations were clear, the vague threats less so. I peered closely at them, wishing I knew more about handwriting analysis. "There's no demand for money, is there?" I said.

"Funny that. Can't see the point really unless it was just to give Barnes the shits."

"He's not an easy man to scare off."

"Not with bombs and bullets maybe, but scandal's another thing. Why do you think he passed the letters to me instead of turning them in to the police? Remember that

TV bloke whose wife told the divorce court he was forever dressing up in ladies' underwear? Never worked again after that. And child abuse is *criminal*. Just a whiff of it, right or wrong, would finish him."

"But Mr Barnes isn't that sort of man. It's his stepdaughter – she's spreading lies about him and it's all in her mind. She said he was abusing his little girl and it's been medically proved to be untrue." I explained the business of Pebbles' hospital stay and the doctors' pronouncements.

"Don't prove he ain't fishing another pond though, do it?" he sneered.

"Whose side are you *on*? I thought we were both out to nail the poor guy's persecutors once and for all? Here, look at these envelopes, Mr McGill. See the address? Number seven. It's written with a slash across it – a continental seven. And I've brought this notebook Wanda used for her English classes I found in her room. Look! The writing's the same, I'd swear to it. Those letters must have been written by Wanda." He looked sceptical, putting on his glasses to get a better look at my flimsy so-called evidence.

I gathered up the notebook and stashed it in my bag.

"Why? Why would a half-baked Slav, who's already on the run, go to all that trouble? Tell me that Miss Cleverclogs."

I couldn't answer and, glancing at his watch, Fancy lumbered to his feet, dragging me out to his wreck of a car, an old Vauxhall smelling of longdead cigarette butts and littered with rancid takeaway cartons.

We parked outside the estate agency and McGill left me sitting in there while he trooped round the back to knock at Barnes' flat. There were no lights showing upstairs but he persisted, banging away loud enough to wake the dead.

After five minutes, he reappeared, giving the thumbs-up and said he was going on up and would let me in when the cleaners arrived. I insisted he called me "Mrs French" in front of the All Clear crew just to keep my connection with Jonny Lusty out of the picture.

The cleaning gang was late, the guy driving saying he'd had trouble starting the van. The dark outline of a girl in the passenger seat remained immobile. The vehicle was a smart enough advertisement for All Clear, the paintwork gleaming, and when Owen, as he introduced himself, slid open the side door the array of vacuum machines, scrubbers, polishers, mops and buckets was very impressive.

I touched his arm. "Leave that for the moment, Owen. My colleague upstairs needs you to help empty the lock-up garage at the back. Wait here, will you? I'll go on ahead with your partner and show her what's what."

"The place is *here*?" he said.

"Over the shop. That's the trouble." I added with a grin. He shouted to the girl.

"Hey, Wanda, get a move on, kid, there's work to do."

My first sight of Wanda was a surprise, not at all the type I'd imagined. She was all bundled up in a fraying donkey jacket much too big for her, denims and dirty trainers, her eyes red-rimmed and blinking as if she had been working in the dark far too long. I tried not to stare and while Owen was shutting up the van, McGill joined us at the kerb and pulled him to one side, out of earshot. I don't know what McGill said but eventually I saw most of my hard-won savings slide into Owen's pocket before he sauntered back to brief Wanda. He told her to go on ahead with me, get started on the clean-up while he went with McGill and sorted out some rubbish in the lock-up.

Wanda nodded, fetching a bucket of cleaning materials from the van. I urged her on ahead. Wanda had certainly been there before and bounded on ahead, swinging her bucket. The access was tricky, you had to go round the back of the agency and along a passage between two houses to reach the front door, a dim entrance beside Jonny's private office. McGill had left the place wide open, the feeble light on the uncarpeted stairs creating long shadows on the wall.

The living room was brighter, neat as a pin, the plain furnishings anonymous as those of a safe house. McGill had pulled the curtains and put on all the lights. Wanda's apathetic gaze sharpened as she looked round, and she frowned.

"Owen said this was a big clean-up," she said, confused. I mumbled some nonsense and filled in while we were waiting for McGill by showing her the rooms which she admitted with a degree of exasperation she was already familiar with. After ten minutes Fancy came back and stood leaning against the wall, saying nothing. The van started up in the street below and I quickly crossed the room and peeped through the curtains, seeing it disappear towards Royal Hospital Road. McGill nodded to me and sat down at Carey's desk watching the girl who stood in the middle of the room still clutching her bucket.

"Sit down, Wanda," I said. "I've something to ask you."

Without warning she made a dash for the stairs but McGill got there first, forcing her on to the sofa. I sat next to her and laid out the poison-pen letters on the coffee table like a game of patience.

"You wrote these, didn't you, Wanda?"

She remained silent, stiffly alert, her eyes

darting between me and McGill.

"OK, I'll tell you what I think and you say if I'm wrong. You wanted to come to England to improve your qualifications, get a language certificate and experience living in another country. You worked hard and Diana Winterton who gave you the job through her domestic agency – the same agency which employs me as it happens – was very pleased with you. I know the Barnes family and I know Pebbles. Pebbles loved you, didn't she, Wanda? And at first you were happy at Northchurch."

The girl nodded, fearful of what was coming, clearly terrified of McGill sitting across the room like a chief inspector, eyes like gimlets.

"Then things started to go wrong. Lili introduced you to clubbing, didn't she? You got a taste for fun and probably for the first time in your life had a chance to enjoy your-self. Do you understand all this?"

She nodded and from the intelligence in her gaze I knew I was dealing with someone of a different intellectual calibre than Maria.

"I found all those Ecstacy tablets in my room. The ones you left behind in your rush to get away. I've still got them."

"You took my place as au pair?"

"Near enough. I'm not important. The thing is Mrs Winterton at the agency has been terribly worried about you. Your visa has expired and now we find out you're pregnant. Was that why you left North-church so suddenly – had someone *raped* you?"

She gasped, clutching her belly as if to defend herself.

"Oh no! I was in love."

"Falling in love's not a crime, Wanda. Why run? Was anyone at Kington House threatening you? Mark knew about your drug dealing and I expect Lili did too. Your friend Leonie told me you were sending money home but that wasn't true, was it?"

"At first it was," she retorted, flushing in anger. McGill smiled, glad the interrogation was hotting up at last, wishing he could butt in, I bet. I threw him a warning glance and pushed on.

"Was someone blackmailing you? Taking your money away," I added, not altogether sure how fluent her English really was. I needn't have worried, Wanda suddenly let go, the tears trickling down her cheeks, her words bursting out like a geyser in the desert.

"I did it for *him* at first. To buy pretty clothes, make-up … sexy panties. I only had a little money from Mrs Barnes, not enough to send home to my family *and* look nice. My boyfriend suggested it – he knew a chemist he said and it was no worse than alcohol, everyone took Es he said, just for fun. He was very kind to me and promised we would get married but it must be a secret from Mrs Barnes. He did not want her to know we loved each other."

"She would be jealous?"

"Jealous? Of me?" Wanda smiled, scrabbling at her wet face in a clumsy gesture, her fingernails chipped and broken. "My boyfriend is in a difficult position. There is another girl," she admitted, her eyes nevertheless misting over at the mere thought of the two-timing bastard.

"But why run?" I persisted. "You've outstayed your visa, you're working like a slave and there's the baby to consider. And having taken this crummy cleaning job you add to your troubles and start writing bad things about Mr Barnes who as far as I know never did you any harm. Mr Barnes isn't the father, is he?"

"No, of course not!" The tears started up again and McGill, satisfied that he had the poison-pen writer in the box, grew bored with all the whys and wherefors and signalled he was off to buy some fags.

When he had gone, Wanda relaxed, recognising me as some sort of ally, and poured out her all too common tale of seduction.

"My boyfriend wanted to *frighten* Mr Barnes. He said he was 'treading on important people's toes' but I was not sure what he meant. My boyfriend has friends in the mafia he says and—"

"The mafia? You sure?"

"Yes. I didn't believe him either. I think he was just trying to persuade me to write those letters for him. There's no mafia in England, is there? He thinks I am just a stupid foreigner."

"You quarrelled?"

"He said if I told anyone about the baby he would tell the police about the stuff I sold at discos. He had heard I was already under suspicion and it would be safer to go away immediately, not to tell the Barnes or any of my friends because the manager at Disco Beat had been asking about me. He said he would look after me, promised to get me a new job in London right away from the clubs where I could be identified and when things had cooled down we would run away together and get married."

"What about this other woman? His wife?"

"Oh, no. He is not married. But he has important business to deal with. But since I ran away he has been avoiding me. I think he will marry this other girl."

The tears began to flow in earnest and keen to get her off the premises I explained that Diana was willing to buy her an air ticket home and to accompany her as far as Amsterdam just to make sure Wanda had no trouble leaving the country.

"It's a wonderful chance for you, Wanda. Do you have your passport?"

She stared, wide-eyed, patting the pocket of her jeans. "You can leave *nothing* in the place I live. They would steal the teeth from your head," she added bitterly.

"Well then, what do you say? I'll take you to Diana's flat straight away, she's expecting you. In the morning you can leave London with her, leave all this mess behind."

"And the letters?"

"They will be destroyed. It was stupid of you copying out all that stuff for your boyfriend just to scare a man like Mr Barnes. Did you really think he would take any notice of silly accusations like that?"

"Gizmo said it might drive him to kill himself. He deserved it, he said. I hate men like that. Mr Barnes is a nasty man, he does things to little girls. It's *true*."

"Gizmo?" I gasped.

"It's not his real name. His name's Oscar Vassermann, I saw it in his passport."

"*Gizmo*'s your boyfriend? The man who got you into this mess in the first place? The father of your child?"

She smiled, nodding like a proud parent, unaware of the electric shock coursing through my nerve ends, not realising I was all too familiar with her American.

I gave up. "Let's go. We can talk about this in the taxi."

"What about Owen?"

"Don't worry about Owen. My friend Mr McGill has fixed things with Owen."

As if on cue Fancy burst in, his face a picture.

"Quick, get out of here."

He ran round the room dousing lights, checking everything out, finally snatching up the letters and stuffing them in his pocket.

"Someone's coming?"

"Just leave, damn you! I've got a cab waiting."

He pushed us downstairs and slammed the door. Out in the street, a taxi was ticking over at the kerbside. "Get in," he said, shoving Wanda inside. He grabbed my arm before I could join her, his fetid breath in my face as he hissed, "Dump this tart at your mate Diana's like we said and drive back to that country-house place straight away. I've just seen a newsflash on the telly in the newsagents. Barnes has been found dead in his car."

"Suicide?"

"No, murder! Garrotted. Sounds like a contract job. Take my advice. Say nothing, know nothing and shake off this bloody Wanda woman before we're all in the shit. We're not dealing with amateurs here, missy. Get her to sign a witnessed statement when you get there admitting she wrote the letters but without bringing Barnes' name into it. Privileged information, see? And make her set out in detail her terms of employment at All Clear. Get it? Send me a fax tonight and first thing in the morning I'll be on the doorstep at All Clear and shove the girl's statement straight up Brownlees' arse. I'll put the frighteners on that shyster till he scrubs tonight's booking off his computer while I watch him do it. I've already squared Owen so *he'll* cause no aggro, forget his own mother's name he would for a couple of quid."

"Brownlees didn't know we were going to Barnes' flat, Mr McGill. And Owen only knew it was somewhere above the agency, he may never have been there before. Only Wanda knew who the tenant was and she wouldn't dare admit it and link herself with those letters. For all she knows the letters are under police investigation."

"That's true. Still, I'll tell Brownlees Wanda's off his books and no questions asked. But if he or Owen so much as squeaks I've got your posh friend Winterton to back us up that she employed me to track down this missing au pair of hers so she could pack her off home. The anonymous letters need never come into it." He lit a cigarette, peering at the girl crouched in the back of the taxi. "Can't see us getting any trouble from the cleaning firm angle, they've got too much to hide. But what about her boyfriend? Won't he be asking questions?"

"He's dumped her."

"Ain't her day, is it? Still, we can't stand here faffing. Take her to Winterton's, send me the fax tonight and ring me in the morning when you're back at Northchurch, just to let me know it went off all right at the airport."

But I couldn't leave London, could I? Someone had to tell Miranda, the poor kid was holed up with that two-timing Gizmo and the police wouldn't know where to go to break the news about Carey's murder. Sonia and Pebbles, her only family, were tucked up in Wales, both Roz and Carey dead and no one to turn to.

And then I remembered Jonny. After I had dropped off Wanda at Diana's and we had followed McGill's instructions to get the statement faxed over to him, I took a cab on to my place and rang the poor guy. He didn't deserve to drive to Northchurch and fall straight in it up to his neck. Luckily he was still dining, his vulgar mobile doubtless causing acute embarrassment at the Bursar's lodging.

"Don't go to Northchurch tonight, Jonny. I'm staying in London after all. I'll ring you in the morning."

Twenty-Six

I sat in my flat hunched over a mug of coffee, feeling like someone who had narrowly escaped a road accident. Just couldn't stop shaking. Delayed reaction, I suppose. Archie, sensing my nervousness, wouldn't settle and kept whining at the door wanting to go out. The poor mutt had been stuck inside for hours, probably needed a leak.

Facing Gizmo in his lair gave me the squits and I tried to drum up an ethical excuse to let Miranda stew. But I kept coming up against the same old brick wall: the girl was only nineteen years old. Someone ought to break the news if she had not already picked up on it through the telly like Fancy McGill. But somehow I couldn't picture Miranda tuning in for the news programmes – she was not even a TV fan, her addiction being a particularly funky brand of high-octane pop.

It was past midnight. I could give Archie a mooch round and take just a peek at Gizmo's house, it was only ten minutes' away. If there were no lights I'd have a reasonable excuse for thinking they'd gone, back to Northchurch even. Can you believe it? You can see what a heroine I am. Reluctantly, I put on my coat, clipped on Archie's lead and we set off out into the deserted streets. It had started sleeting, the slushy drops flopping in my face like wet feathers.

Gizmo's house was part of a smart terrace, situated on a back street I'd used until recently to avoid the Kings Road but now hobbled by speeding ramps to cut out the boy racers in their black BMWs. It was an expensive address, fitting for so-called Hilton Raphael III, I thought maliciously. No wonder poor bloody Wanda considered him such a catch, not to mention that airhead, Miranda. Number seventeen was not only all lit up, but all but vibrating with a rock beat which even permeated the windows shut against the lousy weather. I took a deep breath. There were no more excuses. Nothing for it but to knock up Miranda and try out my ministering angel kit. I rang the bell, hoping they wouldn't hear above the racket and I could slope off. But an upstairs window flew up and Miranda stuck her head out.

"Just piss off!" she bawled.

I stepped back under the lamplight and Archie started to bark. "Oh, it's you, Briony. Sorry. I thought it was that cow next door, she's always coming round to complain about the noise. Wait, I'll come down."

Miranda sounded perfectly composed, not a girl who had just learned that her stepfather had been eliminated in some sort of gang killing.

She opened the door, the light streaming down the narrow stairs picking up the sparkly flecks of her leotard and the matching gold trainers, her top half sensibly bundled up in a black mohair sweater. The gold get-up gave me a nasty turn. It was the one she had worn at the Hallowe'en party, déjà vu indeed.

The ground floor was taken up with a kitchen and dining room and she led me upstairs to a spacious living area probably constructed from two poky Victorian rooms now combined. Archie bounced in and settled at my feet. Miranda turned down the decibels to a bearable background hum and we perched on the sofa like first arrivals at a hen party. In the strong light Miranda looked distinctly bombed out, the pupils dilated, her eyes dark and glittering. Gizmo had definitely been back to his chemist friend for her.

"What brings you here?"

"I live round the corner. It's my day off. I saw it on the news and thought you might need a friend. Or haven't you heard?"

"About Carey you mean?" She stared, her

face rigid, daring me to start patting her hand. "Yeah. The police came round. Sonia gave them my address. But I already knew. Gizmo phoned me from the airport."

"And he left you here alone?"

"He's not a kept man, Briony. Gizmo's got important business to see to."

"What sort of business? Processing immigrants?"

She drew back. "Of course not. International business – hotels, I think. Tourism anyway."

"Where's he gone?"

"Zurich. Then back to the States. I'm going to join him there later when he's found a place for us to live."

"Listen, Miranda, it would be much better for you to get right out of London. The press will hound you here like they camped out at Northchurch when Roz died. You're 'human interest' – Carey's only photogenic relative. They'll pester you for all sorts of background shit. What did the police say?"

"Told me to go to Sonia's," she muttered sulkily.

"You must. Would you like me to put you on a train in the morning? Pack now and come back with me right away. To my place."

"Gizmo wants me here."

"Gizmo is a double-crossing prick. You don't know the man, Miranda. I bet you've never met this non-existent family of his. His name's not even Hilton Raphael, let alone the III."

She laughed. "Course it isn't. That was just a joke on my mother. She was such a snob, Briony. Gizmo invented that stupid name and she fell for it hook line and sinker. So we let it ride."

"That's not all. He's been having an affair since he got here."

That shook her. She flushed.

"With Wanda," I persisted. "He told Wanda he would marry her."

"Wanda threw herself at him, anybody could tell you."

I grabbed her arm. "Wanda's expecting his baby."

She leapt up, stung, and, surprised, Archie immediately sank his teeth into her ankle. She kicked out, furious, venting her rage on the little beast and on me trying to prize him off. A truly ludicrous situation. I was losing it, no contest.

"That animal should be put down!" she screamed, her arms flailing. I snatched him away and tied him to the radiator.

"It's your trainers," I gasped, winded by the tussle.

"He's bitten me before. It's rabid!"

"When?"

"When what?"

"*When* did Archie bite you before? You

never said."

"He was after the rat. When I was putting the rat on the cellar steps. I tried to stop him running in but he bit my hand. Got between my legs and disappeared down the stairs and into the games room. I couldn't go after him *there*. That's where Carey used to force me to go with him for sex," she shrilled. I gave her a little push.

"Oh, shut up, Miranda! We've heard all that rubbish about Carey before. It's False Memory Syndrome, a perfectly common delusion girls get in therapy when they're sedated or being hypnotised. The sooner you wash all that out of your mind the better. You should never have got mixed up with Gizmo's nutty shrink."

Miranda shrugged. "Doesn't matter now he's dead. Good riddance. Why couldn't those killers catch up with him before mummy died?"

"Why did you hate him so much, Miranda? He tried his best for all of you, and Roz wasn't the easiest wife in the world."

She leapt up. "How dare you criticise my mother? Gizmo saw through my stepfather from the start. The problems only started after the baby came."

"Pebbles? I thought you loved Pebbles."

"I do!" she shrieked, setting Archie off again. I threw him a handful of chocolate truffles from the box on the coffee table and turned on the girl in sheer exasperation.

"For God's sake! Get real, Miranda."

She suddenly crumpled on to the sofa and started to cry, ugly tears, her sobs retching like a child's. I shoved a tissue in her hand and forced myself not to cave in. I let her ramble on.

"That business about Carey having sex with me. It was the only thing I could think of – I was young, for heaven's sake! But even I knew it was the one thing to make my mother sit up and listen to me for a change. I wanted Carey out of her life. Like it was before..." she sniffled. "And later, when I told Gizmo about it he laughed, said it was a brilliant idea. Why didn't we spin it out a bit more? After all, Carey was only after mummy's money he said. Better off dead."

She stretched out for a cigarette from the table, the tears drying on her cheeks, a glint in her eye which unnerved me. One minute Miranda was just another fucked-up teenager and the next as cunning as a vixen. I gave up. It would need someone with a lot more time and a lot more expertise to sort out this poor kid's mind. Still, I wasn't going to let her off the hook completely and insisted we went over that admission about the rat.

"Are you saying *you* placed that dead thing on the stairs and caused Roz's fall?"

Her anger dissolved, her voice barely a

whisper. "I'd found it that afternoon, half buried in the shrubbery. I was going to put it in Cannock's bed to give her the frights. Then, while the party was jamming I went to the kitchen for some beer and saw he'd left his key in the lock."

"Carey? The cellar key?"

She nodded. "I thought he would be back for more bottles so I changed my plan and decided to drop the rat on the top step instead. I hoped he'd fall and break his neck. Gizmo laughed when I told him, said it was a stupid idea, would never work. But he was wrong, wasn't he?" She started to cry in earnest. Archie, in the hope of more chocolates, eyed us both with interest.

"But it was Roz who fell," I muttered.

"Sure. But how was I to know she'd be there? Nobody told me Carey had gone off to Sellafield on a news story. He must have rushed off and left the key there by mistake. He never allowed *anyone* else to use the cellar, not even family."

"You poor thing. Don't cry. It wasn't your fault, Miranda. It was an accident, nothing to do with you." I put my arms around her, her bones under the thin flesh fragile as a bird's.

"They said that other thing was an accident but that was my fault too," she sobbed.

"What do you mean?"

"The car accident when I drove my mother into the river." She blew her nose, extracting herself from my embrace.

"*You* were driving?"

"Mother suggested it. She was drunk, God knows how she managed to drive to the party to pick me up in the first place."

"But you were only sixteen, unlicensed, uninsured. What happened?"

She shrugged. "We swopped places at the gates of the house, unfortunately I forgot to put on my seatbelt and she *never* did if she could get away with it, said it marked her neck. I'd been driving in the grounds for simply yonks. It was very late. Dark. The roads were deserted. Considering the state she was in it seemed a good idea."

"Then you ran out of road?"

She grabbed my arm, appealing for my reassurance. "But I *saved* her, didn't I? Everyone said so. Even Cannock who hated my guts."

"Why do you loath that poor old woman? That rat business, Miranda. Crazy. I would have had a fit myself finding a magotty rodent in my bed. Was your hatred of her the reason you stole the silver, to get her dismissed?"

"What silver? Oh, that. Gosh, I'd almost forgotten. Heaven knows how she got blamed for it – they just jumped to conclusions I suppose, knew it was an inside job and picked on the lowest form of life. No, I simply needed the money to get away. No one would tip up the cash, they said I was too unstable to travel abroad alone, but don't you see, it was being trapped at home that was driving me nuts? Once I'd gone, I made Ma send me an allowance. She didn't tell Carey. Said I was making my own way, lost to the wide wide world ... glad to see the back of me, I bet. She could cuddle up with Pebbles and that creepy sod with no awkward teenager causing embarrassment." Envy flickered in her eyes like pale fire.

"But you came back, Miranda. And things were all right between you and your mother? Did she have any recollection of the accident, know you were driving when it happened?"

"We never spoke of it. But she knew. I'm sure she knew. But my mother was the sort who never found it necessary to dwell on nasty things or to blame herself for what happened to *me*. Imagine the ructions if *she* had smashed her face in?"

She touched her mouth with trembling fingers, forcing herself to relive the terrible sequence of events. "Coming home was Gizmo's idea. That guy put me together again. I could never have confronted all of them if he hadn't made me. He had business in Europe anyway so I agreed to tag along, just for a visit. After my mother died, it was Gizmo who made me stay on, 'see it through' he said. I set a trap for Carey and my mother died because of it. It was only after that that Gizmo began to make plans. He asked me to marry him, you know."

"Really?" I couldn't quite keep the edge off my reply and she looked up sharply.

"Yes, *really*. He said Pebbles and I could live like princesses once Carey was gone. Why wait? I'd get all that money to spend just as I liked. Oodles of it."

"Not necessarily. Not if the estate is in trust until you come of age. It depends. Gizmo won't hang around for ever. Ask Wanda."

The girl paced the room, plucking at her fuzzy jumper, the effect of Gizmo's mind-benders probably wearing off, doubts clouding her horizon. I went for the jugular.

"Did Gizmo have anything to do with Carey's murder?" Such a wild idea, off the top of my head, but the effect was electric.

She spun round, white-faced, and leapt at me, pushing me to the door. Archie snarled, bucking against his leash.

"You just get out of here, Briony East-wood! Clear out, do you hear? And don't ever dare come near me again."

I untied the dog but turned back before leaving.

"Don't say I never warned you, Miranda."

Twenty-Seven

When I got back to my flat I dropped my coat inside the door and lay on the bed, pulling up the duvet to shut out the world. Archie jumped up and licked my face, smelling powerfully of wet dog.

Everything had got way out of hand. If things had been simpler, just the Miranda problem for instance, I could have gone to Jonny and lain in his arms, pooling my problems. But I dared not tell him about Wanda's entrapment and thus make the poor guy some sort of accessory to the break-in at Barnes' flat, especially since the horrific murder. Garrotting. Wasn't that something like strangling someone with piano wire? My only clue to such an arcane method of killing being vague recollections of a gangster movie.

There was so much I could never share with Jonny, he was too decent to shoulder such a burden. Charlie now, *he* would have taken my fears, screwed them into a ball and chucked them out of the window. Withstanding police enquiries, withholding information about the existence of the poison-pen letters, denying any knowledge of Barnes' private life was not something Jonny could handle. No way. I could hardly cope with it myself and I had been Charlie Eastwood's apprentice in deceit.

The relationship must end. I would just have to work with McGill on my own and keep my secrets to myself. At least in a few hours Wanda would be finally out of the frame, but after the conversation with Miranda my confusion about Gizmo's motives was frightening. Did Gizmo kill her step-father to gain control of the girl? It was all guesswork but his motives for deceiving the Barnes family were highly suspicious. Unable to close my eyes I eventually got off the bed, donned my coat and dragged Archie down to the car. I would drive back to Northchurch now and at least be on hand should the police came knocking on the door at first light.

Next morning I roused Maria early and explained that Carey had been murdered. It took several attempts, the girl's eyes widening with horror as the facts eventually sunk in. She begged to leave and I stumbled into a flurry of explanations why flight would be the very worst thing for her to do. I said Gizmo had left the country and Wanda, who was still officially missing, had been traced to All Clear which might involve her in questioning if the police found out she had previously been employed by the same cleaning firm. I eventually shook some sense into the silly creature and without actually expressing the disquiet which might be raised about her own working documents, inferred she would be well advised to sit tight and play dumb. In exasperation, I privately concluded that should be right up her street. She started to cry.

"Just carry on as usual, Maria, nobody's going to take any interest in you while there's an important murder inquiry on the go. As soon as it's safe I'll tell Sonia you want to go home for Christmas and what you do after that's your affair."

"Will Miranda come back for me?"

"Miranda has her own troubles. I don't think you can rely on any help from that quarter. Just do as I say, Maria, and cheer up. No one's going to hurt you if you stick to routine and keep a low profile. Believe me. But don't discuss this with anyone."

Then Doris arrived, fairly bursting with excitement, and close on her heels an unmarked police car disgorged plain-clothes men with a search warrant. They practically cleared the library, emptying Carey's files and research papers into boxes, carrying off his computer and turning the place inside out. I kept well out of range and Maria fled back to the gatehouse. Only the decorators kept up a bold front, banging on with clearing out the debris from Phyllis's room and dumping the charred furniture in a skip. I sent Doris up with mugs of tea and closeted myself in my room with Archie, absenting myself from any kitchen gossip.

When I emerged the detective in charge of the search cornered me in the dining room to ask about Carey's movements since the weekend. How would I know? In fact it later transpired he had been staying with Anthony Hagan who presented himself at the Chelsea nick to volunteer a statement. Not that he could vouch for anything, Carey having never confided any details of his latest dangerous investigation, the so-called Mafia Connection. Interpol were in on the act my gabby police sergeant let slip but no one asked anything about my employer's alleged paedophile tendencies so I kept my mouth shut as McGill had recommended.

It was almost lunchtime before I managed to slip away to call Fancy from a pay phone in the village. "Take no chances," he had insisted, determined to bury our intrusion of Carey's pied-à-terre.

"Diana got Wanda out on the first flight, no questions asked," I assured him. "The police are at the house now clearing out the files but they haven't asked about his flat."

"Remember you know nothing about that," he said.

"That's not practical, Mr McGill. It would have been perfectly reasonable for Lusty to mention to me about my new boss renting rooms above the agency and I don't want to involve Jonny or his secretary in lying about it. But beyond that I admit nothing. I've never seen Mr Barnes or any of his associates there and obviously I stay mum about Wanda."

He reluctantly agreed, seeing my point at last but only on the understanding that I said nothing about knowing about Barnes' flat unless the police asked me directly.

"OK. But what about the keys?"

"Down the drain."

"Good. And you saw Brownlees at All Clear first thing?"

"Went like silk. Just like we agreed. Put the fear of God in the bastard, we'll have no trouble from that direction."

"Well, I'm having trouble keeping the lid on the Albanian girl. Scared shitless, poor thing, especially since the police arrived."

"Christ! The police tracing a connection back to All Clear's the last thing we need! Can't you get her to disappear?"

"I'd rather have her here where I can keep an eye on her. It's safer. Anyway the police are not concentrating the investigation here – it's being centralised, probably being dealt with by some special team in London." I went on to give McGill a run-down on my abortive efforts to get Miranda to join Sonia in Wales.

"She's the loose cannon in all this," he said savagely.

"Don't worry. I've met Sonia, she's a resourceful woman, used to getting her own way. I'm sure she will have no trouble dragging Miranda back to the farm once the press start hassling the girl. She's only a kid, Mr McGill. Acts all grown up but she's living on the edge and her boyfriend's topping her up with marching powder."

"Coke?"

"Probably."

"Where's he?"

"Gone with the wind." I laughed, the first happy thought for twenty-four hours.

The investigation dragged on but nobody seemed interested in the Barnes' empty country house. Roz's memorial service was delayed so it could be staged as a double bill and briefly renewed the media's interest. Headlines screamed stuff like, "The Barnes Curse" and what with the Hallowe'en party which had ended with Roz falling into the cellar, closely followed by Carey's blood-curdling murder, there was plenty for them to get their teeth into. Miranda appeared at the church taking centre stage and, from the photographs in the newspaper, looked abnormally thin and tragically bereft.

The intervening weeks must have been a tremendous ordeal for her alone in Gizmo's flat. I had been wrong about Sonia's ability to whisk Miranda back to Wales out of harm's way and held a sneaking admiration for the girl in sticking it out in London until after the joint memorial service. Straight afterwards, Sonia confided, Miranda had flown to New York, a blessed relief to all of us including Fancy McGill who feared what an hysterical outburst from Miranda might provoke in the way of a fresh angle on the investigation.

In fact not a breath about incest surfaced. Miranda had presumably been instructed by Gizmo that any uncorroborated accusations would only provide ammunition for Sonia to pitch her into a drug clinic or, worse, a private psychiatric hospital. Whoever was advising her, Miranda was making no waves.

I had broken off with Jonathan Lusty, initially excusing myself by pressures at Northchurch now that I alone was resident, Maria having quietly slipped off to Paris as soon as the dust had settled and Mark gone to his new job. Sonia has arranged for a garden-maintenance firm to take over until Kington House is sold. "No point in employing new staff while everything's so uncertain," she said. "And Jennie won't be coming back."

Having little with which to occupy myself now the house was deserted apart from the decorators still working on the nursery suite, I phoned Cannock's sister and suggested I called in to see them both.

"Phyllis is home, isn't she?"

"We are taking things slowly but she's here now, convalescing you could say."

"Well enough for visitors? You see, Edna, Phyllis's car is still parked in the yard since she came that last time."

"Heavens, of course it is! I don't drive myself so with all my other anxieties I hadn't given it much thought. Getting the garage people to bring it over would be expensive I suppose?"

"I've started the ignition once a week just to keep it ticking over but I shall be leaving in a fortnight. Will Phyllis be well enough to drive again do you think? I could bring it over to Rye myself tomorrow if you like and come back by train."

"How very kind of you, Briony dear. But we couldn't impose on you like that."

"No trouble. I'd enjoy the change of scene to be honest. It's very quiet here."

"Well, if you're *really* sure?"

Offering to drive Phyllis's motor was a saintly gesture, the gears slipping in and out like nobody's business. I left Archie tied to Edna's gate, intending to hand over the car keys and buzz off without any socialising.

Edna opened the door wearing a pinny, her hands all floury.

"Breadmaking," she explained. "Nicer than that supermarket stuff and cheaper too." She led me into the living room and dashed back to her baking which was apparently at a critical stage.

Phyllis half rose from her chair, a shadow of her former self, thinner and looking distinctly aged without her wig. She beamed, holding out both hands in welcome.

"Did Miranda send you? I saw her picture in the paper. Looking rather peaky I thought."

"Ah, well, perhaps you're right. She's had a lot on her plate, of course." I sat on one of the low chairs, feeling her eyes boring into me, requiring some sort of response which I didn't quite understand.

"Phyllis, why did you think Miranda sent me?"

"Forgiveness. To say she accepted my utter contrition. I have suffered, Briony, since that last time I drove over to Northchurch in the fog. It's a terrible thing to know yourself to be the object of such hatred. To have deserved such contempt."

"I'm sure you're wrong, Phyllis. Miranda's young – says things she doesn't mean. Why would she hate you? You were like a mother to her when Roz was absorbed in her career."

"She loved me once, you know. She did, really."

"Of course she did. Please stop worrying about it, Phyllis, you'll only make yourself ill again."

"I will never be well until Miranda forgives me."

I grew impatient. "Look here, you're the one who deserves an apology. Miranda stole her mother's silver and left you to take the rap. You have *no* reason to appeal for her forgiveness I promise you."

"That's not true, Briony. Until I can absolve my sin there will be no salvation." Her rheumy eyes burned with the pain of this imagined transgression.

I rose to go, wondering if this nameless sin of hers had been fermented by over-zealous religious fervour. She grasped my arm, her hold vice-like.

"Please, you must appeal to Miranda for me, Briony. *Beg* her to come. I cannot share my guilt with Edna, she's too good, too trusting. Edna believes only the best in people."

This plea echoed my own misgivings about involving Jonathan Lusty in my nasty manoeuvres with McGill and I fell back in the seat, knowing that I must hear her out at least.

"When Rosalind married that man, Miranda was only eight or so. It was years before Pebbles arrived on the scene. That was before the days of au pairs," she muttered crossly. "Miranda had always been a wiful child but not really naughty if you understand me. But she changed, changed dramatically and I assumed her bad behaviour was caused by jealousy. Miranda had been the diamond in her mother's crown until she remarried and the new baby only made things worse. Miranda's school-work suffered, she started biting her nails, sleepwalking, the classic symptoms of dis-tress, but I was unsympathetic and Rosalind utterly absorbed in her own affairs. One day Miranda came to me, a beautiful child she was, tall for her age and very fair. She wept, telling me appalling tales about Mr Barnes forcing her into the basement games room for sex. Naturally, I was dreadfully shocked that a young girl should even know about such things, but TV has a lot to answer for I say. I slapped her face for being a filthy minded little fibber. She said she had told Rosalind but her mother didn't believe her either and, in fairness to myself, the man was all charm, devoted to his wife and Pebbles. A well-respected public figure, nothing like the men one associates with such deviancy. I did not go to her mother to report Miranda's outburst – such a dreadful thing to accuse the man of and nothing but childish wickedness born out of envy."

"You insisted she was lying? Refused to accept her word?"

Phyllis started to weep, very quietly, scrubbing at her cheeks with a lawn handkerchief, her large hands incongruous in that pitiful gesture.

She nodded, her podgy features suffused with emotion, and said, "Miranda turned against me that day and has hated me ever since. Now do you understand? Because Miranda had become such an unlikeable girl I denied her, sent her away in disgrace, ignoring her cry for help. I had never had any experience of such shocking accusations and put it down to all this modern nastiness one reads about in the newspapers which even schoolgirls get to hear about. Later, I regretted giving Miranda no chance to back up her story but it was too late, she was openly hostile to me and would barely speak to me on any subject let alone that painful one. If her mother had also refused to listen where would I be repeating such awfulness to her? I may have been dismissed for even suspecting such depravity of her husband. So I devoted myself to Pebbles and tried to bury my guilt. But as time went by I knew myself to be a failure and may, by my cowardice, have ruined a young life."

I patted her hand, a feeble gesture but all I could think of at the time. I wasn't sure if she had been told that Carey was now dead.

"Phyllis. Listen to me. Miranda lied about all that abuse stuff. She has withdrawn her statement to the police and admitted to me that she made it all up about Carey molesting her as a schoolkid. She said it was just to get her mother's attention. She wanted, in her adolescent way, to wreak havoc on their relationship. Jealousy is a terrible thing, Phyllis. It must have festered in her mind. I'm not sure that she didn't begin to believe it herself in the end and Miranda's psychiatric treatment in America encouraged bad imaginings. Under hypnosis, I suppose." I tried to explain about the girl's therapy but Phyllis merely looked stunned. Disbelieving. Unconvinced by what she probably took to be misplaced kindness on my part, a silly notion that the word of a stranger could expunge the guilt now deep in her soul.

"I don't believe you. I must hear Miranda admit her lies to *me*," she insisted, her mouth set.

"I'm afraid it's too late, Phyllis. Nothing either you or Miranda can say will help now. She's gone abroad. It's best I think. Give you both a chance to put all this behind you and make a fresh start. Carey Barnes is dead. He died horribly and if he was unknowingly the cause of Miranda's mental breakdown no one could have suffered greater retribution. The guilt was not *all* yours. Roz refused to listen too. No wonder the girl grew up with so many problems. Your first reaction was right, you know. Miranda was making it all up out of spite and envy. Children do terrible things to get back at their parents."

It was the only sop I could offer and Phyllis turned aside in despair, feeling herself now the object of pity.

Edna came in with a tea tray, taking in her sister's distress with a knowing look. It would be a long, perhaps endless, via Dolorosa for Phyllis Cannock. After a decent interval I left, taking Archie for a last splash in the sea before catching the train. I thrust Phyllis's tearful appeal into a Pandora's box of things I couldn't bear to think about and counted off the days to my release from my contract with the house of the dead.

Twenty-Eight

A week later I got a call from the Irish police. Would I come over and identify some items attached to a body discovered in a cave on the beach a few miles from Pipers' Point?

I was mooning about in the library at Northchurch when the message came through, gazing out at the lake sparkling under a marble sky, wondering what to do with my aimless existence.

The shock of the police request to examine what they presumably thought to be Charlie's remains left me numb. Disbelieving. What would Charlie be doing in a cave for God's sake? I swiftly arranged for Doris to move in to the gatehouse with Trevor for a few days to act as joint caretakers while I was away. Sonia was agreeable, no doubt finding the continuing worry of Kington House a burden. In fact she suggested I called it a day seeing as I was so near the end of my contract, probably thinking there was little mileage left in a sad sack like me.

A Philippino couple had been engaged to start work on the first of February and Doris was happy to fill in till then.

I drove to London on auto-pilot, dumped my stuff at the flat and phoned Joe Reilly.

"Joe, there's been some developments. I've got to fly to Cork this afternoon."

"They've found the boy?"

"I think so. There are some personal articles they want me to see and—"

I broke down, my sobs choking my resolve to be strong. Gradually I pulled myself together and mumbled, "It's Archie. Could you keep him for a while? Till I get back?"

"Brenda'll take him home with her. I'm coming with you, Bridey love. Hold on, bonny girl, I'll meet you at the airport. Cork, you say? Which flight?"

The policeman who escorted us to the morgue was a kindly soul, all too familiar with the routine of identification. Joe never let go of my arm, breathing shallow breaths as if his heart pulsed in concert with my own palpitations.

An attendant raised the sheet. The face of the corpse was that of a mummy, desiccated, not that of a young man at all. But there was something about the shape of his brow, the beaky nose ... I turned away and Joe let me go. He lingered, talking quietly with the police officer, nodding sagely like a mandarin, inscrutable, giving nothing away.

312

Later, when I felt better, the nice police-man offered to show me some things: a watch, a bunch of keys clipped to a Gucci belt and a round tobacco tin containing fish hooks.

The tears coursed down, my defences stripped away like rags. I signed some papers and Joe took me back to the hotel where a log fire burned in my room. I crouched on the sofa before it, unable to stop shaking, chilled to the marrow. Joe held me close.

"It is Charlie, my girl. We both know it. And if the keys fit ... The instructor bloke who went down after the boys raised the alarm reckons he was washed up on an exceptional high tide soon after he drowned. Tossed up into that hole in the cliffs. Inaccessable except by water. Only the fact that them lads was scrambling down the rocks meant poor Charlie was found at all. They was on an abseiling course, some sort of youth group. Halfway down two of them spotted this cave and went in to have a dekko, kidding themselves they was SAS or sommat I expect. Gave them the fright of their life finding Charlie up in the corner."

He left me alone after that and eventually, when the sorrow had settled into a lump of ice in my chest, I joined him for a drink in the bar, my mind cauterised.

"One thing, Joe. I've been having these nightmares about Charlie being tossed about in the water all this time, banging about on the seabed, attacked by eels and jellyfish, gnawed to bits. Knowing he's been in that cave all these months laughing up his sleeve at us is a tremendous relief. I can't say I recognised that body, all dried out like a piece of shoeleather but there was something, wasn't there?"

"They'll do tests, just to make sure. But it was Charlie all right. Don't you go holding on to any hopes he's going to walk back into your life, girl. Charlie knew how to go out in style."

"He died trying to win a bet, Joe! He wasn't even a half-decent angler let alone a deep sea fisherman. I've been furious with him all this time, Joe. Bloody angry. Him leaving me like that, having to go it alone, not knowing if he was dead or just playing another stupid game on everyone. And all because of a crazy bet with strangers in a bar."

"But you did yourself a bit of good, didn't you? Proved you could shift for yourself? Don't blame Charlie, Briney girl. He enjoyed every minute of his life and would have no truck with moaners. Time you stopped dreaming about the boyo and got on with tomorrow."

Over dinner Joe touched on a subject I

314

had thought I'd heard the last of.

"Fancy McGill was in to see me last week. Had that packet of poison-pen letters."

"What for? Is he selling them to a newspaper?" I waspishly retorted.

"Wanted to stash them in my safe. An insurance policy."

"He's in trouble?" My mind lurched, picturing some indomitable Inspector Plod on our trail.

"He never got paid for that Barnes' job."

I laughed, caught up in the sheer lunacy of dealing with people like McGill. "But Barnes *died*. It wasn't his fault. I suppose Mr McGill could always submit an account to Sonia 'for services rendered' but she'd never pay up without putting him through the mill first. Dunning a dead man for a bad debt is taking it too far in anyone's book."

"It rankles. Call it professional pride. Anyway, old Fancy tells me that the night Barnes copped it he happened to be sorting stuff in the man's lock-up." Joe looked at me a bit sideways but I said nothing and let him run on.

"McGill's got a nose for evidence and apparently he pulls out this old car battery at the back of Barnes' lock-up and lo and behold, wrapped in a waterproof bag stuffed under a pile of rags, he finds this packet."

"Drugs?"

"An address book and a stack of computer

discs and tapes."

"So?"

"Poor old Fancy's in a fix. He was nosing about on the quiet when he found the stuff in the garridge, see?"

"He broke in."

"No, he'd got a set of spare keys from somewhere. He took this package home and ran the stuff through his machine."

My heart sank. "Paedophile clips?"

"Worse. Bloody Russian thugs."

I relaxed. "In Russian?" I laughed, picturing Fancy toiling through with no subtitles.

Joe snarled, unamused, and the lurid headlines flashed across my mind. The papers had had a field day on poor Carey Barnes.

Popular TV Journalist Murdered. The police are issuing no statement about his current undercover investigation but the bizarre killing in an East London backstreet suggests drug gangs eliminating their pursuer. Chinese triad mobs are likely to be under scrutiny.

How wrong could they get?

"You don't think that bloke got his neck sliced up for nothing, do you? Fancy dragged me round to his place and, believe me, Barnes' stuff's red hot. Names, faces, videos, the lot. Bleeding nutter to get hooked up with mafia stuff just for some TV film.

316

Some big names in the government don't come out of it smelling of roses neither."

Fear trickled down my spine like a dead man's finger.

"Arms deals," I murmured.

Joe nodded. "Bloody McGill's in a spot. He don't want to take it to the fuzz in case he gets tied in with it. At best he would have to explain why he'd been searching the lock-up in the first place and they'd want to know how he came by Barnes' keys. He didn't dare go back to the lock-up next day and try to make it look as if he'd broken in because the murder investigation was hot on the go and anyway breaking and entering's not exactly neighbourhood watch routine. Also, with word out on the street that real professionals was behind the hit, you can picture Fancy's problem – there was no way he wanted his name to feature even for a cash bonus for being such a helpful citizen."

"And the address book? Funny place to keep your telephone numbers, tucked up in a corner of your garage under a pile of oily rags."

"Yes, well, Fancy – already narked that Barnes had led him up the garden over them poison-pen letters saying it was a scam to extort a payoff just to keep his name off the headlines – he really gets the hump. Hates shirt-lifters let alone pigs what rape little girls."

"But the letters existed. The au pair wrote them and sent them to Barnes' secret address."

"Well, she's some sort of Russian, ain't she? Part of the scam."

I sighed. "No. Croatian. Wanda was just being used. Someone made her write those letters to warn Carey Barnes to lay off, to underline the fact that his cover was blown. Wrapping up the warning as a possible paedophile exposure kept Wanda off the scent and ultimately got Fancy hooked into Barnes' investigation without giving him the real reason why Carey needed to find out who was on his heels."

Joe looked doubtful. I plunged on, squeezing the lemon dry.

"Did he give you this package to put in the safe with the letters?"

"No. He wiped off all the fingerprints and sent it through the post. A sort of parcel bomb you could call it."

I blenched. "To Sonia? To back up his invoice?"

Joe sighed. "No, silly girl. To the police. An anonymous tip-off." A wicked grin flickered at the corner of his mouth. "Give them bobbies a fresh angle and the chance to shove it off on to the intelligence people."

"Oh, hell," I muttered, sick to my stomach at the black pit of international criminality we might all be dragged into.

"What d'ye say?"

"Oh, nothing." I laughed unsteadily, and tried to get the conversation back on dry ground. "Blimey, Joe, that debt-collector friend of yours certainly bears grudges when it comes to unpaid bills, doesn't he? Lucky Charlie never got in his way. I think I'll hang on here for a bit – could you put Archie in kennels till I get back? Here's the address of his usual place."

The mood lifted and we managed to get through the evening on a tide of Irish whiskey and Joe's blarney. I told him I would be staying on till the formalities were complete. "I'll bury him in Ireland, Joe. It's Charlie's sort of place."

He nodded. "You're right, girl. I'll fly back for the funeral. Then we'll have a proper wake for Charlie at my place when you get back. A real knees-up – invite all Charlie's pals, all the old crowd, do him proud."

"He would have loved it, Joe. Thanks."

"And when it's all over you take that holiday you've been talking about – get some fresh air in your lungs after all this lot."

I smiled. Joe was right. I'd take my skiing trip as I'd planned, then I would treat myself to a huge dose of amnesia and get back with Jonny Lusty again without lugging that old guilty conscience about with me. No more nightmares.

I booked in at a small guest house up the

coast, watching the wild waves break on the rocks by day, sleeping like a log by night. At peace.

In the plane going home four weeks later after my holiday, the sun was rising over the sea like a golden apple, a prize from the gods. Joe was right. Time I started life afresh.

Twenty-Nine

When I got back to London I just had time to dump my bags before collecting Archie from the kennels. I arrived as the converted ambulance was pulling into the kerb, the racket from the dogs inside sounding like all the hounds of heaven about to be set loose.

The pick-up point is useful for us city pooch lovers, the kennels, situated in Kent, collecting and delivering from town twice a week. Before first consigning Archie to this arrangement my mother had insisted I drive down and inspect the place, for all the world like an anxious parent sounding out a boarding school. It was quite a surprise to find those pampered pets who had passed their sociability tests romping together in a muddy paddock behind a circumference of high tennis-court wire fencing. No wonder they were all showered and brushed before being bussed back to Chelsea.

I didn't tell Mother about the Pekes and Afghans all up to their bellies in mud in the exercise area and I swear none of the Burton Court ladies guessed why their lapdogs returned all sparkling from their country holidays.

I paid the bill and Archie leapt across the zebra crossing like a rocket, sniffing the exhaust fumes like a chain smoker getting his first gasper after a stint in a health farm. He was probably the only dog who remained unimpressed by all that communal living or maybe – I never enquired – he never passed his sociability test and remained locked up for the duration.

Finding a policeman on the doorstep when I got home was a shock. Archie snarled and I snatched him up. It was a French policeman too. The man filled the entrance like a sentry, his bulky presence impossible to mistake for anything but Continental fuzz. I examined his warrant card, glancing from the severe photograph to the battered features of the Depardieu look-alike who had been put on my tail.

I led him up to my tiny apartment, airless after my long absence, shoved Archie in my bedroom and shut the door. The policeman smelt of Gauloise, of course he did, but I didn't offer to let him light up: he might have thought I had something to hide being as there were no ashtrays to hand. But smiling, Inspector Caux was transformed. Really a very attractive flatfoot.

"Coffee, Inspector?"

He shrugged with that Gallic gesture which speaks volumes.

"Oh, you're quite safe. I don't have instant."

He followed me into the kitchen making small talk while I fished out the beans I'd brought back from Geneva only that morning. His English was excellent.

"You're from Lyon?"

He nodded.

"All that way just to see me?"

"Not entirely, madame."

"Lyon," I murmured. "Interpol?"

He grinned, sipping the coffee with all the attention of a professional tea taster. We sat at the kitchen table, the informality taking the sting out of this unforseen interview. My mind skittered over the possible reasons for this call and a small tic in my eyelid started up. He lurched sideways on my mismatched kitchen chair to extract a snapshot from his pocket, placing it on the table like a bribe.

"You know this man?"

I looked at the swarthy face in the photograph. Over-ripe lips and a broken nose, the brow entirely obscured by a forties'-style fedora. Not nice at all. I shook my head.

"Sure?"

"Of course. It's not a face anyone would forget. Why me, Inspector?"

"His name was Ivan Levin."

"Was?"

"He was found in a car in a back street in Kiev. Garrotted."

I choked on my coffee.

"Like Carey Barnes," I spluttered.

He nodded, the bulk of him occupying far too much of my kitchenette. "There were other links, some correspondence..." he grudgingly volunteered. "I was sent out to extract lost material from Barnes' computers. They had been interfered with. It's my speciality," he added, a hint of pride seeping in. "When you were working for Mr Barnes did you see any printouts? Private video material?"

Wide-eyed, I countered, "You're investigating an international paedophile ring?"

He laughed, waving aside my remark as if a fly was about to drop in his coffee.

"And you've never seen this man Levin at the house? He worked as an interpreter, he appears with Barnes in several old newsreels I've been viewing at the centre."

"Oh *that* Ivan!"

Caux raised an eyebrow.

"Carey mentioned him to me once but only in connection with an icon this bloke

Ivan had acquired for him. Carey said he was a dealer, a fixer of some sort."

Caux suddenly veered off on a fresh tack. "You travel abroad a good deal, Mrs Eastwood. Just back from Switzerland today. And before that staying with people in the Caymans."

"Holidays! Look here, Inspector Caux, what's all this about? I told you I've never seen this guy in the photograph, Ivan Whatsit. And I've no idea how Carey handled his computer files. Have you searched his flat?"

There seemed no longer any point in holding out on this man who was no Clouseau for sure.

"The British police took it apart two weeks ago."

I gulped. Poor Jonathan, he'd think twice before re-letting that upstairs apartment.

"And the lock-up?"

"The what?" Caux frowned, juggling with this little technicality.

"Lock-up. Garage."

"Ah yes." He sighed. "Cleared out. But are you sure, madame, you have no information about Barnes' notes? He was compiling a detailed investigation, planning a TV programme. On the Russian mafia. The London connection? You were a confidante of his I am informed."

"Who says so?"

My mind churned with the knowledge of

Fancy McGill's haul currently being sifted by M15 or 6 or whatever. Did they not share their information? Was Fancy's explosive package mouldering on some plod's desk waiting for a link up with the murder inquiry? Was there to be some sort of official cover-up, Joe had hinted that there was a government scandal in there, some big-wig in the Foreign Office shielding his backside perhaps. I felt my knee begin to tremble and I grasped it under the table, my fingers icy.

He refilled his coffee cup, his ham-like fist scarred like a prizefighter's. His silence gripped me, suddenly making everything menacing.

"Well OK. Carey did share a few things with me. But only when he was drunk. There were problems ... You sure this has nothing to do with any child pornography stuff?"

He lit a cigarette, tired of playing games, the smoke drifting in the dull winter light filtering through the curtains making my tiny flat seem claustrophobic.

"There is no pornographic angle, Mrs Eastwood," he coldly insisted. "Why is it the English are obsessed with sex? Barnes was milking Ivan Levin for names. They were making dangerous enquiries in Prague. We have information indicating that an assassin dealt with Barnes and Levin took fright. Was hunted down, of course, by another contract killer but not before he had named Barnes' killer, a man called Vassermann. Apart from the necessity to protect their organisation the assassin harboured a personal grudge it would seem. Levin knew too much and spoke too freely under heat."

"Assassin?" The word bounced off the walls like a ricochet, the sheer force of such a term freezing my blood. Vassermann? A common enough name abroad I'm sure. Gizmo a hit man? I felt myself hyper-ventilating but Caux, absorbed in his own problems, rattled on though I seemed to have lost a whole raft of his monologue.

"...all this does not help us, of course. We seem to have lost the trail." He drained his coffee cup, eyeing me more kindly. "We hoped you would have a lead. Truthfully, we have been following you for weeks, hoping you would make contact."

"Me?" I squeaked, jumping up.

He rose, offering his hand. "Forgive me, madame. We, as you English say, 'clutch at straws'. Correct?"

I was in no mood to help him with collo-quial terms and lost my temper. "You mean I feature in some computer file in Lyon?"

"It is of no moment, I assure you."

"Well, you can bloody well cut me out. I *worked* for Barnes, I wasn't any sort of courier for him and the friends I stayed with in the Caymans were former clients of my

husbands. Respectable business people."
Archie started to bark, excited by my outburst.

That last bit was a flyer, I admit. Charlie's friends would probably never bear too close scrutiny, especially by a computer expert like Caux said he was. Still with steam up, I pushed him to the door, snatching the card he proferred and tossing it on the hall table with my unopened mail.

When I saw his car drive away I phoned Diana at the agency. She shut me up damn quick and told me to drive over straight away.

I flung on my ski jacket, glancing at my face in the mirror as I rushed past. My nice winter tan looked like yellow varnish over features which I knew to be white with shock. Bloody hell. Interpol?

Thirty

Diana's office is situated over a designer's boutique and I guess she gets a hefty discount as she always looks a million dollars.

I thumped up the stairs bursting into the outer office like Hurricane Hetty, giving Alicia, Diana's secretary a nasty turn. Diana's door swung open and she crossed the reception area to pass Alicia a bundle of filing before switching on the "engaged" light outside her room and pulling me inside. She snatched my jacket and poured two stiff whiskies from her "first-aid box" in the adjoining cloakroom while I gathered my wits, idly regarding the remorseless progress of a ladder in my black tights inching its way up my shin.

Diana looked worried, seriously worried, the garbled message I'd hit her with sounding notes of doom with isolated phrases like "Interpol", "garrotting" and the appalling disclosure that I had been shadowed from piste to piste like some sort of Mata Hari. I filled her in over drinks.

"But you're really off the hook now? This

Frenchman knows you're innocent? He didn't connect us with Wanda, did he?" Diana's normally smooth delivery was shrill with panic.

"Wanda? The Croatian au pair? No, Diana, of course not. He's a computer wizard I think. Brought in to unscramble data in Carey's files, trying to trace some research material Carey was putting together for a book. The man who was killed in Kiev was Carey's Russian interpreter. Wanda didn't even get a mention, I swear." I laughed. "Goes to show what a guilty conscience can do. That flight to Amsterdam with Wanda must have given you the vapours."

Diana took a swig of her liquid lunch and tried to compose herself. "Never again, Briony Eastwood. Never again. You don't think this Interpol agent was trying to tie in Wanda with this Barnes killing, do you? Part of some Eastern European assassination? And what about Gizmo? Sounds very fishy to me, flying out of the country immediately he hears Carey Barnes has been murdered, leaving that poor Miranda to face the music on her own."

"No," I lied, "Gizmo's name never came up either." There were some things I dared not share even with Diana – no point in worrying her unduly. Anyhow, chances were, Caux had just tossed in Vassermann to test my reaction. How was Interpol to know I knew Gizmo's real name? You see I'm even good at lying to myself these days.

"And Miranda? Any news?"

"Gone abroad. Presumably the States. I had a nice letter from Sonia, Roz de Taffort's cousin. After Charlie's funeral she sent her condolences, which I thought was kind, all things considered. She mentioned that Pebbles was staying on with her and that Miranda had disappeared again. I think the family have a conscience about that 'fly in amber' as Sonia's dubbed her. Miranda was lying all along about Carey being a paedophile. If he had lived she would never have got away with it, but the murder put an end to any threat of scandal being worthwhile – she was the joint heiress, of course. If hints of her crazy hallucinations ever surfaced the family could easily explain it: teenage angst run riot, aided by Gizmo feeding her coke, of course. Sonia got back to the shrink Miranda had attended in the States, traced her through Roz's bank accounts she told me. Wanted to make sure there was no doubt in my mind about Miranda's fairytales I imagine."

Diana sighed. "What a ghastly business. But what did you make of the rest of Miranda's story, Briony? That business of stealing the silver to finance her escape? Bit far-fetched I thought. I bet the Barnes lot paid to get shot of her."

"In hindsight I take Miranda's word on that. She wasn't believed when she first spouted all that sex stuff to her mother or Phyllis Cannock. Years later, under Gizmo's influence, she consulted a psycho-therapist in the States – Sonia checked it out – but it was definitely a case of False Memory Syndrome, and she retracted her statement once the police got to hear of the poor kid's delusions to the psychotherapist. Miranda admitted to me it was all a 'con' but being such a fantasist I bet she almost believed it herself in the end. That's why she jumped to the wrong conclusion about Pebbles' embarrassing itch. What started as a nasty brick to throw at her stepfather was later fostered by Gizmo as a weapon in case Carey got too close to the mafia connection."

"Who paid her bills in New York?"

"Miranda forced her mother to make secret financial arrangements for a regular allowance to be paid into a US bank."

"And Carey knew nothing about this allowance?"

"Maybe Roz chose not to admit that the girl was toting all this bullshit about sexual abuse. Didn't want to spoil the romantic bit once things had quietened down without Miranda spoiling the nuptial bliss. She probably found it easier to pay up especially

331

once Miranda started phoning from America making threats to expose the man, even if she had no back-up to prove it. Mud sticks and people in Roz's line of business know the damage that bad publicity can bring. She hoped Miranda would stay away."

"But the nanny didn't believe Miranda either, did she?"

"Actually, she did in the end but couldn't face up to it until it was too late. By then nobody took poor old Phyllis seriously, not even me. I should have heard her out myself. But life's never that simple, is it? And when it came to whistleblowing first time round Phyllis lost her nerve and now she's suffering the fires of the damned for it."

"Mad?"

"No. But damaged beyond repair, I'd say. She believes Miranda was telling the truth all those years ago and can't forgive herself for disbelieving her. And the girl will never reassure the old woman herself, admit it was all lies after all. The whole trouble with the Miranda scenario is that everyone involved, Phyllis Cannock, Carey, Roz, was each broadcasting their own version of the girl's behaviour. Even the dealer who recovered the family silver didn't realize Roz's daughter had stolen it. She steals to pay for an exit and once safely abroad phones her mother with threats of Carey's exposure if no money is forthcoming. Miranda's hysterical fears about her little sister's embarrassing itch created a situation which underlined her instability, thus arguing against anyone believing a word she said."

"Meeting this bloke in America was a wicked turn of fate."

"And how! Hooking up with Gizmo really ruined her life. Once he realised she came from a wealthy family he battened on like a limpet. Later, Barnes' importance as a top investigative journalist building a case against his own criminal associates made Miranda a key player if he needed to control Barnes' exposure of the mafia connection."

"Miranda knew he was a mobster?"

"No. She's not that bright. But she was eager, backed up by the shrink, to go along with his scheme to go public on her accusations in order to ruin Carey's career, smash up his public credibility and hopefully drive him out of her mother's life. Believe me, Diana, that Gizmo guy is seriously plausible."

"Was Barnes working alone on this story?"

"Too dangerous to share, I guess. Apart from his interpreter, of course. Ivan Levin. And he got eliminated too!"

"Gizmo proved a death sentence to all of them, even Roz died because he played on Miranda's crazy plan to kill her stepfather. Do you think Miranda will join the murdering swine? She and Pebbles are heiresses worth considering I would have thought."

"I doubt it. Any money Miranda might claim would be nickels and dimes to a player like Gizmo. He's probably vanished into thin air. Still, with Interpol piecing together the Russian mafia connections in London, Gizmo will be on the move for the rest of his life. If the international investigation ever pieces together the whole story of course," I bitterly added.

Diana's phone rang and she listened for a bit before ringing through to Alicia to cancel an appointment at two. "Let's go out for lunch, darling. All this cloak and dagger stuff has given me an appetite. But you are really sure your French detective isn't investigating my small part in all this?"

"Wanda's escape you mean? No, I promise you, you're in the clear, Diana."

"And what about that horrible debt-collector man? Will he keep quiet?"

"McGill's the one who reactivated the international dragnet by anonymously handing the police the discs and stuff he had found hidden in Carey Barnes' garage. Getting his name on the files is the last thing he wants, even for a cash buyout. Anyway, my bookmaker friend would set the heavy mob on Fancy McGill if he tried to sell the story. Fancy's got too much to lose, too much dust would be raised to make causing trouble remotely viable."

Diana shivered, buttoning her jacket, visibly shaken by the convoluted saga surrounding her innocent placement of a nice Croatian girl in an apparently ordinary household. She took her handbag from her desk drawer and rose, handing me my jacket as we hurried downstairs and out into the weak grey sunshine of an English afternoon.

"Actually, I've worked up an appetite too." I chuckled. "Tell you what though, Diana. Next job you offer me has to come with guarantees. No media types. And no crazy teenagers."